Death

Pantomime

A Clara Fitzgerald Mystery

Book 17

by

Evelyn James

Red Raven Publications

2021

First published 2019
Red Raven Publications
Paperback Edition 2021

Death at the Pantomime is the seventeenth book in the Clara Fitzgerald series

Other titles in the Series:

Memories of the Dead
Flight of Fancy
Murder in Mink
Carnival of Criminals
Mistletoe and Murder
The Poisoned Pen
Grave Suspicions of Murder
The Woman Died Thrice
Murder and Mascara
The Green Jade Dragon
The Monster at the Window
Murder on the Mary Jane
The Missing Wife
The Traitor's Bones
The Fossil Murder
Mr Lynch's Prophecy

Chapter One

Clara peered out of the window of her office, fingers twined around a warm cup of tea. It was mid-November and a sharp frost had decorated her window ledges with icy crystals and made the pavements sparkle. Clara had been working on her accounts in the peace and quiet of her office but had paused when her hands became too cold. She had a fire burning in the grate of the small fireplace, but it was not providing enough heat to warm the stark room, which seemed to leak heat like a sieve.

Being Brighton's first female private detective, and proving herself to be rather adept at solving mysteries, Clara now had enough money to move to a more luxurious office, one where the walls weren't paper thin and the windows stayed open in the summer without having to be wedged up by whatever came to hand – usually some tatty but sturdy book that could be shoved into the space. Yes, Clara could have a smart, modern office in a newer building, if she chose. Yet Clara, who was rarely sentimental over things, found the thought of leaving her humble, creaky, cold office – where it had all begun – simply unbearable. There was something about this set of two rooms, up a staircase over a haberdasher's shop, that symbolised every step of her journey to this point.

It was her starting place and she did not want to forget that.

Clara flicked her eyes from the window and looked at the large portrait of her father hanging on the wall. It had been painted a few years before his death, and she liked it because there seemed to be a slight smile on Professor Fitzgerald's lips the whole time. She liked to imagine he was looking down upon her with that smile.

"Nearly another year gone," she said to the painting. It felt less odd talking to the image of her father than just talking to herself, and sometimes she liked to air her thoughts aloud. Though not religious, Clara sometimes felt as if her father heard her when she did that. "I don't know where time goes. Seems to slip through your fingers like sand."

Clara sipped her tea.

"And now Tommy and Annie are engaged, things move on. They are talking about a spring wedding, but they don't seem able to make any exact decisions about anything concerning it, so I suspect spring will come and go with them still debating which church to hold the thing in. Could be a very long engagement."

Clara gave a gentle laugh, feeling affectionate towards her brother and Annie, their housekeeper and friend, who seemed to epitomise the saying 'taking their time'. Then her face fell into a frown.

"Then there is this other business. The bit that sticks in my throat. The trouble in the backstreets with this gang, which Park-Coombs has told me to keep away from. And the Inspector has a fair point, that sort of crime is beyond my abilities to deal with, it is something you need an entire police division working tireless on for years to crack apart. So, why do I feel I have failed by walking away?"

Clara was thinking of a previous case, one where she had stumbled into a criminal gang, though she had only ever been at the periphery of their activities. They were dangerous people and she was not in a position to deal with them. She just didn't like feeling that she had to ignore what they were doing and trust that someone else would sort it out. That was not in Clara's nature.

Clara turned her gaze back to the road outside, just in time to see an older man, loaded with a towering pile of boxes, slip on a section of thick frost and tumble backwards. All the boxes crashed down around him, some spilling open, and the poor man smacked his head on the pavement.

Hastily putting down her teacup, Clara rushed down her stairs and outside to assist the unfortunate man. He was sitting up and rubbing the back of his head, his eyes closed as he winced with pain. Clara crouched beside him.

"Are you hurt badly?"

The man opened his eyes, they were a startling blue, like the colour of the ocean.

"That was a bit unexpected," he smiled sheepishly, embarrassed rather than hurt. He started to reach out for the boxes nearest him. His eyes fell on one which had exploded its contents into the road, leaving everything wet and filthy. "Just look at that!"

Clara helped him to his feet and then assisted in collecting up the boxes and restoring the items to those that had shed their load. She found she was picking up strange and wonderful things; brightly coloured clothes, astonishingly tall wigs and articles that looked out of a child's box of toys. An idea sprang to mind.

"Are these stage props?"

The man's eyes twinkled.

"For the pantomime at the theatre," he nodded. "Just arrived on the train from London. I am Rupert Maddock, director and dogsbody for the Stratford Company. We have been engaged to put on a pantomime in Brighton during the festive period."

Rupert suddenly winced and groaned, tipping his head forward and touching the back of his skull tentatively.

"I think I should look at that bump," Clara told him

firmly. "We can stack these boxes in the hallway to my office."

Rupert Maddock didn't seem inclined to resist; he was looking a little pale suddenly. Having worked as a nurse during the war, Clara knew that head injuries sometimes took a while to affect the patient. Often the initial reaction to a fall was to get back up, shake off the embarrassment and try to act normally. Only as the shock wore off, did the full effects of the blow kick in.

Clara opened the front door to her upstairs office, ushering Rupert inside to sit on the stairs while she collected the boxes and stacked them as best she could in the tiny foyer. They perched precariously in a pile, as Clara pulled the door shut and put the cold weather firmly outside.

"There are not a lot of boxes," Clara observed.

"Oh no, the rest is on a cart already heading to the theatre, these are just the things I like to keep a special eye on," Rupert pointed to the top box, which had spilled open to reveal a blue and gold costume. "That outfit has been worn by the actor playing Buttons in every pantomime the company has performed since 1909. It has had so many repairs and adjustments it is more darts, darns and stitches than original fabric, but no one wants to see it replaced by a new costume as it is deemed lucky. You know how actors are superstitious."

Rupert was slightly shy about the statement, though Clara suspected he was as conscious of theatrical superstitions as the rest of his company.

"I always fetch that costume myself, to make sure it gets to the theatre. Occasionally costumes and props go missing, and no one would want that to happy to the Buttons outfit."

"What about that giant red wig with the red glass beads and fake pearls?"

"That belongs to Mr Hutson. He is our Dame, he always plays the part, has done so for the last twelve years. Marvellous actor. Has never missed a performance. That wig is the one he wears in the final scene, after everything has worked out and the Dame, who is always a poor widow, has either married the old baron or come into some fortune in another way," Rupert chuckled. "That is the posh wig, to show how far up in the world the Dame has gone. Those might be glass beads and fake pearls, but they sparkle under the lights like diamonds and dazzle the children watching. A little bit of theatrical magic."

Rupert had brightened up and no longer seemed in danger of passing out, which was what Clara had initially feared. She suggested they go upstairs so she could make him a cup of tea and take a look at his head. Rupert was reluctant at first, glancing at a pocket watch to assess the time, but the throb in his head inclined him to stay put for a while.

Clara escorted Rupert to her office and offered him the old, but comfortable daybed, where he could lay back if he wished. He gave a small groan as he rested, and Clara made tea. She had time to get a better look at him as she went about her task.

Rupert Maddock was in his fifties but had worn well. His fair hair was barely touched by grey and still fell about his head in flamboyant locks. He had a sculpted, strong face, the sort an artist might like to study. His age showed in the deep laughter lines at the edges of his mouth, and the crow's feet at the corners of his eyes suggested a man used to being happy. It was overall a handsome, friendly face, one that made Rupert seem very approachable.

His suit was well-cut, though not of the most expensive sort and there were a few places of wear that indicated it got plenty of use. He had the first hint of a paunch pushing at his waistcoat buttons, but otherwise he was a man who clearly took care of himself and stayed in shape. It was a shame that the back of his suit was now wet, dirty and speckled with tiny fragments of stone and the odd leaf. Clara didn't think Rupert was the sort to like his clothes getting messy.

She took over his cup of tea.

"Sit up and I shall look at that bump. I used to be a nurse," she told him.

Rupert obediently sat forward. The wound was fortunately minor, Rupert's thick hair having taken the brunt of the fall. After assuring herself there were no cuts or grazes, Clara was satisfied it was just a bad bang which would leave Mr Maddock feeling sore and dizzy, but nothing much else.

"You'll live," Clara pronounced. "Just take it easy for a few days, and if you get a really bad headache, go to the hospital."

Rupert grimaced.

"That would be inconvenient," he rubbed at his head. "Damn weather. Why do pantos always have to fall in winter?"

Rupert chuckled at his own joke.

"Thank you very much for your help and kindness," he added. "I have been terribly rude and not asked your name?"

"Clara Fitzgerald," Clara replied, smiling.

"It is a delight to meet you and for your assistance I would like to offer you tickets for the first night of our panto, which will be this weekend."

"That is really not necessary," Clara assured him.

"I insist," Rupert refused to be deterred. "I shall take your address and have them sent over at once."

Clara tried to explain she expected no reward for her assistance, but Rupert would hear none of it. Finally, she gave him her address, which he wrote down in a small notebook he kept in his pocket. He then started to take a better look at his surroundings.

"What is it you do here, Miss Fitzgerald?"

"I work as a private detective," Clara said with a hint of pride. "This is my office."

"A private detective," Rupert's eyes widened. "What a fascinating career choice. I have never met a private detective before."

"Most people have not, unless they require one to help

them," Clara answered.

"Fascinating," Rupert muttered to himself. "Well, I must get on, those boxes shall not transport themselves and I have to make sure Aladdin's magic lamp is still in working order. It glows, you see, if you put a candle inside and there are glass lenses the actor can switch with a button to change its colour. The audience are always impressed."

"The panto is Aladdin then?" Clara asked.

"Yes. Aladdin is being played by Miss Burns, as it is traditional for a lady to take the lead male role. Mr Hutson is playing Dame Wishy-Washy, and the character of Buttons is to be her dreamy and slightly inept son, played by the delightful Mervyn Baldry. Slightly controversial casting choice as he has not been on stage for some years. But we don't mind a bit of controversy if it gets people talking," Rupert was enthusiastic about his panto, which was natural. "You shall see for yourself how they have all come together. We are in dress rehearsals for the rest of the week and then we open on Saturday afternoon."

"Must be a very busy season for you," Clara nodded.

"It is. The panto runs every afternoon and evening from now until the second week of January. Except for Wednesdays, when the cast have a rest day. We shall even be performing on Christmas Day, though only in the afternoon."

"Very busy," Clara repeated politely.

She helped Rupert check over his boxes to make sure nothing was missing, then loaded him up with his cargo. He looked only just able to manage the packages and there seemed constant danger of everything tumbling to the ground again.

"If you want to come back for some, you can," Clara told him.

"Do not worry, I am used to this," Rupert cast her a confident grin. "If you would just open the door?"

Clara obeyed and Rupert stepped outside. There was a brief moment when he found another patch of thick frost and his foot slipped, but he maintained his balance this time.

"Thank you Miss Fitzgerald, I won't forget the tickets!" He called out cheerfully as he headed down the road, barely able to see where he was going and having to apologise to those who he bumped into as he went.

Clara shook her head; what an impractical man – determined, but impractical. She closed her door, smiling to herself. It was years since she had been to a pantomime. She had gone to see Mother Goose in London with her parents. She had been scared by the giant goose with its wild, rolling eyes that was wheeled on stage as part of the performance. She had had nightmares afterwards and had never been to a panto since.

She supposed she had been about ten. Ever since, she had thought pantomimes rather an alarming thing to take children to, although they may have changed. It might be interesting to see a modern one.

Amused by the thought, she headed upstairs and back to her accounts.

Chapter Two

Clara reached home in time for dinner. Her own house was beautifully warm and she took off her coat with a sense of satisfaction as the cosiness of her home engulfed her. Tommy, Clara's brother and assistant in the detective business, was sitting in the front room, working on some papers that he put aside as soon as she came in.

"Evening, old thing," he grinned. "Been busy?"

"Mr Carter is still outstanding on his invoice from last month," Clara grumbled. "Sometimes I regret finding out if Mrs Carter was fooling around with someone else for him."

"He was not delighted when it turned out she was actually just volunteering for a local soup kitchen in the evenings," Tommy recalled.

"He was hoping he had found grounds for divorce," Clara shrugged. "He wants to marry his secretary. However, it is not my fault his wife was merely keeping her charitable activities from him, and he has the money to pay me. I shall write him another sharp letter."

"Threaten to tell Mrs Carter what he paid you to do," Tommy suggested.

"That would be blackmail," Clara threw up her eyes.

"That would hardly be good for my reputation."

"Blackmail?" Annie appeared in the doorway. "Is someone being blackmailed."

"Not currently," Tommy said darkly.

Clara poked his shoulder with her finger. Annie frowned, knowing she had missed something, but swiftly shrugged off her consternation.

"This came for you, Clara," she handed Clara an envelope with her name neatly spelt out on it.

Clara opened the glued flap and drew out four tickets to Aladdin at the theatre on Saturday. She was impressed by Rupert Maddock's generosity, she might have expected a pair of tickets, but not four.

"What are those?" Tommy asked.

"I helped a man who slipped on the pavement today and banged his head. He turned out to be the director for a company of actors, who are putting on the panto this year. He has sent me tickets for the show in gratitude."

"That was nice of him," Annie said. "I have not been to a panto since… well, since I was a child."

"I used to go every year as a boy," Tommy was eyeing up the tickets. "Until Clara had a nervous breakdown over Mother Goose and the parents refused to take us ever again."

"The goose was scary!" Clara said defensively.

"You screamed the theatre down and stopped the performance," Tommy reminded her with a flicker of amusement in his eyes. "It was dreadfully embarrassing. We were asked to leave."

"I am sure others were scared too," Clara pouted. "They probably just internalised their fear. I am not one for leaving my opinion unheard."

"That is for sure," Tommy laughed.

"I don't like geese," Annie reflected, twisting her lips into a worried scowl. "They attack you for no reason, and I can't see the point of them. They don't lay as many eggs as a good hen and, if you ask me, they are not much for making a nice roast out of either."

"No wonder geese attack you if you go around saying such horrid things about them," Tommy teased her.

Annie ignored him.

"Well, I have four tickets to the pantomime on Saturday. It is for the evening performance. I shall ask Captain O'Harris if he would like to come, which leaves two spare tickets."

She left the information hanging in the air. Tommy was quick to grasp it.

"I'll gladly go to the panto, what is it?"

"Aladdin," Clara handed him a ticket. "Annie?"

Annie glared at the ticket in Clara's hand.

"Which one is Aladdin?"

"Arabian nights," Tommy explained. "Boy gets shut in a cavern by wicked uncle, or vizier, depending on the version, and finds a magic lamp with a genie inside. Genie helps him escape and grants him wishes, which he uses to save the kingdom from said evil uncle-slash-vizier and marry the princess."

"That sounds all right," Annie said cautiously, taking a ticket also. "I shall have to rearrange dinner, if we are out in the evening."

Clara could see that the thought of upsetting her cooking schedule had almost over-ridden Annie's desire to see a pantomime.

"Well, if that is settled, I am going to write my sharp letter to Mr Carter," Clara told them.

She moved to the table where Tommy had been working and was laying out some paper when she caught a glimpse of some documents sticking out of a book on cricket that Tommy had apparently been reading. She could not help but read the last few lines of the text and her heart sank a fraction. She said nothing, however, until Annie had departed the room.

"I could take that letter to Mr Carter in person?" Tommy was offering her.

Clara was only half-listening.

"Why is there a police report sitting in that book?" She

asked.

Tommy glanced at the book and she was sure he had a slightly panicked expression on his face, that evaporated in the next moment.

"I was just using one as a bookmark, shouldn't have done, I know..."

"The report is about criminal gang activity in Brighton," Clara said firmly. "The bottom corner is sticking out and I can read that quite clearly. You are investigating the gang who hurt Private Peterson, aren't you?"

"No!" Tommy did not lie well. He cringed. "I was just looking up some information. One of my pals from the trenches now works for the police in London, he was able to provide me with some papers as a favour. I was just trying to get my head around what happened."

"Inspector Park-Coombs insisted I not investigate this," Clara pointed out, not entirely sure why she was so angry. "He made me promise."

"I was just looking to see if there was any danger from these people towards us, towards you," Tommy had gone a little red.

Clara did not know quite what to reply. She felt people had been going behind her back, but perhaps that was unreasonable. The gang situation had unsettled her, left her questioning her own abilities. It was rare for Clara to be confronted by a mystery she could not solve, or rather, one it was too dangerous for her to attempt to solve and it left her feeling uneasy. That made her sharp and cross about anything relating to the affair.

"You should have told me," she snapped. "Were you going to tell me?"

Tommy turned his head away, the answer altogether obvious.

"No, you were going to keep quiet, because you thought I would go off looking into this matter. You didn't trust me," Clara did not raise her voice, but her anger was plain.

"Clara..."

"Don't!" Clara held up a hand to stop him. "Park-Coombs asked me to keep away from this and I promised I would. I don't break my promises. It hurts that you think I would."

Clara rose and headed out of the room.

"Where are you going?" Tommy asked, his words anxious.

"For a walk," Clara replied, barely keeping her tone even. "To clear my head."

Clara stormed out the front door while Tommy protested behind her. She stepped onto the pavement and began to walk, heading for nowhere in particular.

She knew her anger was unnecessary. She was hurt though, hurt that Tommy was keeping secrets from her. All through her career as a private detective she had felt as if people did not entirely trust she could take care of herself, that she would get into trouble. She thought she would have proved by now that she could handle any situation thrown at her, and she knew when to seek help if an affair was getting beyond her. It stung that people questioned her judgement.

Would people be so concerned if she was a man? Would they doubt her so?

And it wasn't just Tommy, no, that was the tip of the iceberg. It was this whole business with the trouble in Brighton which she could not touch. She was sensible enough to realise this was outside her expertise, that she had to stand back, that didn't stop it from rankling like a fishbone in her throat.

It would pass, she told herself. She would calm down and this trouble would be consigned to a memory of another time, like all such events. It might occasionally come to mind and annoy her, but that was all. As long as the police could resolve the matter, she should be able to live with her lack of involvement.

Clara was beginning to lose the edge to her temper, the cold weather having a suitably cooling effect, when she heard a car horn behind her. She turned and saw a luxurious red sportscar pulling to a stop beside her. It was not the sort of car you saw in Brighton and not one she recognised. Clara paused and glanced to the driver's window. She scowled when she saw who was there.

"A delight to meet again, Miss Fitzgerald," said Brilliant Chang.

Brilliant Chang was a Chinese gangster, one who had done exceptionally well for himself and had, conversely, found his way into upper-class English society. He wore smart suits, drove flashy cars and was invited to all the best parties, the hostesses charmed by his manner and his danger, the hosts feeling his presence added a little spice to the occasion. Brilliant Chang was photographed with actresses dripping off his arm, standing next to dukes and earls, eating caviar at the best restaurants. He was a celebrity criminal, and he was clever. He kept himself safely removed from his various nefarious activities, causing the police endless frustration. They had cracked some of his operations and rounded up gang members, but they could not make the important connection back to him. And they had to be careful, for Chang knew the right people and could easily make life hell for a police detective who pushed him too hard.

"I would like to talk," Chang continued, his smile revealing neat white teeth. He was only in his thirties and handsome, which made him all the more popular. He was not a typical backstreet thug, and there was something enticingly dangerous about him that aroused the curiosity of the foolish.

"I don't see what we have to talk about," Clara said, though she did not turn and walk away. Chang was here for a reason, she wanted to know what that was.

"We have a mutual problem," Chang grinned. "Would you care to join me?"

He motioned to the passenger seat of his car.

"Certainly not," Clara laughed at the idea. "I don't trust you, remember?"

Chang pulled a sad face.

"I am hurt you would think I should be anything other than a gentleman," he purred. "You have my word you shall be safe."

"All the same, I shall stay here on the pavement," Clara replied.

Chang gave a snort of annoyance; it was not often people refused him. He tapped his steering wheel with his fingers, then came to a decision and turned off the car engine. He stepped out of the car and strode towards Clara. He was only as tall as her, which made her feel somewhat better. Clara faced him with her arms folded across her chest and a frown on her face. She would give no quarter.

"You are stubborn, Miss Fitzgerald," Chang said.

"You mean I don't do exactly as you say?" Clara remarked. "Shockingly, Mr Chang, I see you for what you are, a criminal. No doubt a charming and affable one, but a criminal. You can sweet talk me all you like, I shall not change my opinion."

Chang's grin had returned.

"This is why I like you, Miss Fitzgerald, you are honest. People lack honesty these days, don't you think?"

Clara started to deny this, then thought of how she had snapped at Tommy for hiding things from her.

"People are complicated," she shrugged. "Now, why have you tracked me down in this cold weather?"

"My car is warm," Chang motioned behind him. "I have fur rugs in the back, to keep my passengers cosy."

"I already said no," Clara reminded him.

Chang gave a sigh to indicate he was finding her frustrating, then carried on.

"As I said, we have a mutual problem. Brighton is beset by a gang; you have already encountered them briefly."

Clara was not surprised he had learned of the situation. The story concerning Peterson had been in all the papers, and the usual rumour mill had been spreading plenty of gossip far and wide. London had close ties with Brighton with criminals regularly journeying between the two. Chang was bound to hear about everything, what intrigued

Clara was why he cared.

"Why is this a problem for you?" Clara asked him

"Business," Chang replied. "And betrayal. I do not want to say more until I can be assured you will not speak of what I say to anyone. I believe private detectives are rather like doctors and priests, with what their clients saying remaining confidential?"

Clara wondered at him referring to a Roman Catholic priest's parishioners as 'clients'.

"While that is correct, and I am protective of my client's privacy, you are not a client."

"Yet," Chang interjected. "If I hire you, will you keep everything I say private?"

"I shall not work for a criminal, Mr Chang, surely that is obvious?"

Chang tilted his head and spread out his hands in a gesture of understanding.

"Of course, I forget you have a very stout moral code. That is why I feel I can trust you. If I cannot hire you, would you agree to cooperate with me upon the understanding that we would be assisting each other with a mutual problem?"

"I'm not sure," Clara admitted. "Working with you rather goes against the grain."

"Even the police have informants in the underworld to assist them," Chang pointed out. "It depends how much you fear this gang that is operating in Brighton. I have information that will be vital in bringing them down, but I cannot go to the police myself. Obviously. I shan't insult your intelligence by suggesting I am doing this out of a sense of public spiritedness. I am doing it because this gang threatens me too, and because their leader has personally offended me. It is pure selfishness on my part."

"At least you are honest," Clara shrugged. "But why should I even consider working with you?"

"You won't get this gang without me," Chang said, and it was not an arrogant statement, it was pure honesty. "You need inside information, that just won't come from any other source. But I shall offer you more, for this gang is a big problem to me. Work with me on this and I promise I shall have no criminal dealings in Brighton again."

Clara's frown deepened. She didn't trust Chang, but she knew this gang was beyond her and likely beyond the police and they needed to be dealt with.

"All right, let's talk."

"In my car?" Chang said.

"In my office," Clara replied. "And we shall walk there."

Chapter Three

Brilliant Chang took a long look around Clara's office. She could not read his face to see what he made of it. She set about making tea for them both.

"Do you drink tea?" She asked over her shoulder. Tea making was a comfort habit Clara had picked up from Annie, it gave her time to think. She needed time right then.

"Green tea only," Chang replied. "Though I do like coffee."

Clara gave up on tea making and motioned for Chang to take a seat before her desk.

"Who is that?" He asked, pointing at the painting on the wall.

"My late father," Clara replied.

Chang nodded, as if this explained something to him.

"I expected your office to be…"

"Grander?" Clara suggested.

Chang grinned.

"I like this place," Clara shrugged. "It's where it all began."

"My career began in a slum in Hong Kong," Chang said. "I was ten or eleven. I am not sure as no one ever bothered to tell me when I was born."

"We all have to begin somewhere," Clara replied nonchalantly. If he had expected pity, he was not going to receive it.

Chang seemed amused.

"Why don't we get down to business," Clara said.

"I need your assurance you shall not repeat what I say, other than what I am happy for you to repeat," Chang had become serious.

Clara paused to consider. Chang was a criminal and she didn't like him, but his help was likely to be essential in her current problems. This would not make them friends, or associates, just temporary allies. Sometimes you had to work with old enemies to deal with an immediate threat. Besides, Clara was still not satisfied that Peterson's attackers had been brought to justice – oh, they had got the man who had wielded the knife, but he was but the instrument of another, and she wanted that man.

She wanted to put Chang in prison too, but he was not going around terrorising Brighton residents and murdering people in the town. She had to do something to restore order here. It might be selfish, but Brighton was her priority and she would leave Chang to a London detective.

"You can talk freely, I shall not repeat what you say," she agreed at last.

"You are wise," Chang bowed his head. "There are worse than me out there."

"Really?" Clara said in obvious disbelief.

"Oh yes. I may be ruthless, I may be a criminal, but I have certain standards. I avoid hurting the innocent, for a start. I remember when I was a boy, I remember the gang wars in Hong Kong. I recall vividly what it was like to be a child mixed up in that and perpetually afraid," Chang's smile was now ironic, his voice tainted with bitterness. "I kill people, yes, I have people murdered. I supply drugs, I run a string of brothels, but I do have a conscience. I don't employ children, for a start."

"Look, I am not going to feel any better about this than I already do. I am ignoring my instincts because I want revenge. Revenge for Peterson and for Jenny who was slaughtered by this gang. I want my town free of this pestilence," Clara told him bluntly.

"And you are angry that you can't conquer these thugs?" Chang guessed astutely. "You don't like being defeated any more than I do. That is what makes you dangerous Miss Fitzgerald."

"Well, I don't feel very dangerous right now," Clara snorted. "This gang is running amok and I can't do much about it. They are too powerful for me."

Chang nodded his understanding. His smile had faded to a business-like stern expression.

"We are more akin than either of us would like to admit. It pains me to be here, as much as it pains you to welcome me. We are both risking our reputations, I am not blind to that. That is why I am grateful for this audience."

For once Clara felt there was no acting from Chang. He was not just saying these things to get her on his side.

"You better explain why this gang is such a problem that you are prepared to come to me," Clara said.

Chang leaned forward over her desk.

"It all began a year or so ago. Some of my people took this idea in their heads that they could do better without me. Not in London, of course, for I am everywhere in London," Chang sounded proud at this statement, "but here, in Brighton. Near enough to the Capital to get a slice of the action, but far enough away to not attract my attention too soon."

"I am guessing this is about drugs," Clara added.

"Yes, mainly," Chang agreed. "I have been using various seaside resorts as drop sites for drug deliveries. Opium, mostly, but some other varieties too. The drugs come aboard pleasure craft, yachts, and so forth. The supplies are smuggled into the towns, transferred to my people and then sent to London. The police have no idea."

Clara said nothing.

"These traitors decided they wanted a piece of my pie and they would take over the drugs coming into Brighton. They plotted against me, taking out my associates here in town and filling their places. Then they started to lure the smugglers to them, offering larger shares in the profits. It was dangerous for these men, I would have them killed for their treachery, but smugglers like money."

"This was happening right under your nose?" Clara said, somewhat surprised.

Chang looked grim.

"You have picked up on what shames me the most. Yes, this was going on without me realising what was happening. I was blind to it all until it was too late. This new gang had consolidated, made itself strong and put down sturdy roots in Brighton. By the time I realised what had happened, they were big enough to threaten me and, without launching a full-scale war against them, I could do very little," Chang scowled angrily. "Oh, I killed the odd smuggler, tried to scare them back to serving me, but I couldn't reach enough of them. And my rivals only increased the money they offered. The danger is spreading, smugglers at other seaside resorts are switching sides. I have increased the money I pay, but so have my rivals. This simply can't go on."

"You are losing to them?" Clara said in astonishment, she had never thought she would hear such a thing. Brilliant Chang seemed at the top of his game.

"I am, but in part that is because I am scared to act. Yes, Miss Fitzgerald, I admit I am scared. For I no longer know who I can trust among my subordinates and I feel lost. I have been betrayed by someone close to me, and I feel impotent to react."

"That's why you came to me?" Clara asked.

Chang briefly smiled.

"You are honest. It might sound odd, but I am a criminal who values honesty. I think I can trust you, as long as we have a cause in common."

Clara knew that to be true. He had picked up on her own weakness – that she wanted to take down this gang and not simply leave it to others to deal with. She had her own pride wrapped up in all this.

"Who betrayed you?"

Chang folded his fingers together. He suddenly seemed shy to speak. It took him several moments to find his voice.

"Her name is Jao Leong," he said. "She is my half-sister."

And finally the last piece fell into the puzzle. This was why Chang had felt it impossible to act. The traitor was family and the usual tactics he would employ against any other associate who betrayed him could not be used against her. Chang was right, he did have a conscience.

"Your sister?"

"Half-sister. Same mother," Chang explained quickly, as if it pained him to speak too much about the situation. "She is a year or two younger than me. We left Hong Kong together and we have been working as a partnership ever since. No one ever saw Jao, she is private. Barely anyone knows she exists. I doubt the police are aware of her. She is like a shadow and she is ruthless."

A notion came into Clara's mind.

"She has been the driving force behind your criminal activities," she said.

"No!" Chang spluttered, then he relented. "She is very clever, maybe some of the ideas were hers, but we were a team. The thought that she wanted to usurp me never crossed my mind."

"What happened? What triggered this all?" Clara queried.

Chang simply shook his head.

"I do not know. I wish I did."

It was the first time Clara had ever seen Brilliant Chang looking defeated and it sent a chill down her spine. To think there was someone out there who would trouble him, leave him feeling useless, was disturbing.

"How dangerous is she?"

"Jao is very dangerous," Chang groaned. "She is not tempered by my own ethics. For her, there are no rules, no lines that cannot be crossed. Sometimes I think that is why she betrayed me, because I would not consent to her utter ruthlessness and disregard for anyone. I don't know. Since this all occurred I have doubted myself, felt I am no longer the man I thought I was. I seem crippled by indecision in this affair. I don't know how to stop her.

"But I do know this. My sister will destroy anyone who opposes her, and she will ruin this town gladly. She has no qualms, no sense of right or wrong. I have always known this, but I thought I could keep her in check. Now… now she is loose and acting as she pleases. She is a monster, Miss Fitzgerald, but she is also my sister."

There was pain in Chang's voice. Clara actually felt sympathy for him.

"I don't want her to die," Chang continued. "I have looked after her since we were children, taken care of her. Even after what she has done, she is my kin. I need to stop her, but I cannot go about this in my usual way. She needs to go to prison. Her gang must be destroyed. Do you see? I must rely on the police to help me, yet I doubt they have any clue about my sister, and even if they did, they would be useless in capturing her."

Clara didn't argue with him. She suspected he had a point. Jao Leong had been working with her brother all these years and the police had never been able to touch them, why would that change now she was working alone?

"You make me feel a little hopeless," Clara said. "If you can do nothing, what good am I?"

"The police must arrest her, to do that they need information about her and evidence. I can provide that," Chang insisted. "I need you as a go-between."

Clara was uneasy about the arrangement. She would still be working with a wanted criminal.

"She has a route through Brighton for her smuggled drugs," Chang continued, aiming to convince her. "This route will be kept clear of witnesses, so that when the goods are smuggled there is no one to see them or interfere. She will rule by fear and remove any who threaten her."

Clara thought of the alleyway where Peterson had been stabbed. That was part of the route, kept purposefully clear and witness-free. Peterson had been a potential witness and they had dealt with him brutally.

"What do you propose we do?" Clara said carefully.

Chang smiled at her use of the word 'we'. It was not a snide or satisfied smile, it was a genuine look of relief.

"Now I am in town I shall begin collecting information. I have not done so before because I had to know you would help, if you would not, then I would be exposing myself to dangers unnecessarily."

Clara was brought up sharp by his words.

"Your sister is a danger to you?"

Chang winced.

"She would kill me if she felt I was in the way. I am her weak brother," he lowered his head. "I have failed her."

"I don't see how you have failed her," Clara said pointedly.

"That is because we walk in different worlds, Miss Fitzgerald," Chang said softly. "I have failed her because I have been unable to teach her that ruthlessness is not a strength. That cruelty and intimidation is a short-term solution. She rules by fear, no one is truly loyal to her. This I am sure of. Eventually, she will push someone too far and they will kill her."

Chang paused thoughtfully.

"I have not been the leader of a criminal organisation all these years without knowing how to handle people, how to ensure my own safety. I don't fear the police, but I do fear my rivals and my subordinates. I am not even English, yet many of my followers are. I have been clever to keep myself at the top and safe," Chang gave a weak smile at this statement. "Jao does not appreciate all this, does not appreciate that when I am merciful, when I am restrained, it is as tactical as when I am fierce."

Clara could offer him nothing, no response felt suitable. He was right, they walked in different worlds.

"How will you get this information and evidence to me?" Clara changed the subject, as Chang became solemn.

"I am renting a house," Chang took a piece of paper from his pocket with an address. "When I have news, I shall send you a message and I would appreciate it if you would come to me. I do not think it wise I come to you. I would prefer if Jao has no idea we are associates, for you own safety."

"I am grateful for the consideration," Clara said, thinking that she would not fancy Jao's thugs on her doorstep. "I shan't let on to anyone we are working together."

"Hopefully the arrangement will not be for long," Chang nodded. "Jao is careless because she is cocky, that shall be her weakness."

He rose from his chair, glancing once more at the portrait of Clara's father on the wall.

"You do not know how much you are aiding me, Miss Fitzgerald, or how grateful I am for your assistance."

He turned around and left the office, Clara heard the door downstairs open and close. She sat still at her desk, wondering what she had agreed to. Had she just made a very foolish decision?

Chapter Four

Saturday arrived and they were dressed for the pantomime. Clara wore her favourite green dress, the one with a pretty pattern of sequins. Captain O'Harris looked devilishly handsome in a smart black dress suit, with a white scarf tossed about his neck and a top hat on his head.

O'Harris had been a pilot during the war and had found settling down to normal life after 1918 challenging. The only thing that really kept him grounded was Clara, who he adored. They had met when she was investigating the mysterious death of his uncle and had remained friends ever since. He was hopeful one day they would be more than friends, but they were in no rush.

O'Harris ran a convalescence home for former servicemen who had suffered, (and were still suffering) mental trauma during the war. There were far more men out there with problems than there was space in his home for them, but he helped those he could. Private Peterson was one of his tougher cases, and things had seemed to go from bad to worse when the young man was nearly fatally stabbed, and then accused of murder. Clara had been Peterson's saviour, and O'Harris could never fully express how grateful he was to her.

As for Tommy and Annie; he looked charming in a new suit he had bought for the occasion, including a dark red bowtie, which he kept tweaking. Annie was wearing a cream dress, with silver edging, slightly more flashy that she would normally pick, but she had been persuaded to try the outfit by Clara who didn't want Annie to appear at odds with the others. Annie might be inclined to dress humbly, still clinging to her notions of station – she considered herself of a lower station to Clara – but Clara would not hear of it. Annie was an equal to them, she just had to start believing that.

"I haven't been to a pantomime in years," O'Harris grinned at Clara, looking boyish in that moment, the strain of the war falling from him briefly. "I have been practicing my hiss."

"Hiss?" Annie asked in surprise.

"For when the evil villain comes upon the stage and we must all hiss at him," O'Harris laughed.

"I forgot that part," Annie looked bemused. "Oh, I won't have to shout out things, will I?"

"Only if you want," Clara promised her. "I am sure there will be plenty in the audience to do the shouting for you."

"You'll soon get in the spirit once you are there," Tommy took Annie's hand and squeezed it.

Annie looked a little mollified. O'Harris offered Clara his arm and she took it gladly. They stepped outside towards the waiting car, with Jones behind the wheel. He glanced at them and there might have been a look of surprise at the sight of everyone dressed so smartly, but he was too professional to comment.

The drive to the theatre was not far, they were soon on the steps leading up to the doors and sweeping inside. There were a lot of people crowding the foyer, keeping out of the cold night air. Clara pointed out a poster for the panto, a garish blue and purple affair, with an illustration of a young man and woman in Persian costume (or at least the sort of Persian costume pantomime writers envisioned) sailing through the air on a magic carpet. Behind them loomed a hunched and evil looking vizier and the hulking bulk of a green skinned genie. Blazoned in big black letters at the bottom of the poster was the sentence – Stanley Hutson as the Dame! There was no illustration of Mr Hutson, but as he happened to be the only performer named on the poster, he probably was unconcerned that he lacked a picture.

"Let's buy some sweets," O'Harris said, waving to a girl going around with a tray of boxed sweets.

They were soon each supplied with their favourite confectionary; Annie had pear drops, Tommy aniseed balls, O'Harris had a packet of liquorice and Clara had strawberry bon-bons. Now all they needed was to find their seats and they would be settled for the evening.

Rupert Maddock had been generous with his tickets, not only in how many he had given Clara, but in their position in the theatre. They found they were in the front row of the balcony, right in the middle, providing them with a brilliant view of the stage. Clara leaned on the railing and gazed down at the people filling the seats below. The theatre looked packed, a good sign for Mr Maddock and his company.

"This year's Aladdin shall be the most spectacular performance since 1914," O'Harris read aloud from a programme he had bought. "Technical wizardry will dazzle you and the performances of Miss Audrey Burns and Miss Grace Allen, as Aladdin and Princess Zara respectively, will whisk you away to a land of fantasy and illusion like you have never seen before."

"Big claims," Tommy said, slightly sceptical about the panto living up to the programme.

"What does it say about the actor playing Buttons?" Clara asked, thinking of the lucky costume that every actor in the role had to wear.

O'Harris flicked through the programme.

"Ah, Mr Mervyn Baldry," he read out. "'Many of the audience shall recall Mr Baldry for his performances at the Theatre Royal before the war, where he was best remembered for playing the spectre in Oscar Wilde's The Canterville Ghost. More recently he has appeared on radio programmes, supplying the voices for numerous entertaining characters. 1922 shall see a welcome return to the stage for Mr Baldry.'"

"I always feel sad for Buttons, he never gets to marry the principal girl, though he never fails to be undyingly devoted to her," Annie said with a small sigh.

"It's just a panto," Tommy reminded her gently.

The lights then dimmed, and the talking of the audience settled down to the quiet expectation of the curtain rising. Clara felt an unexpected sense of anticipation running through her as she gazed down upon the stage. There was a long pause, that seemed to drag on and on, then the red curtains rolled back and a spotlight fixed a point in the middle of the stage.

Stood before a scene of Arabian houses and with suitably Eastern props all around 'him' was Aladdin.

"Why, I am so hungry!" Declared Aladdin. "I have not eaten in days, what is a poor boy to do?"

The stage filled with other people, milling around and pretending to go about their daily tasks, while Aladdin stood at the front of the stage looking miserable. From stage left emerged Mr Hutson as Dame Wishy-Washy, followed by Buttons. Hutson was dressed in an enormous patchwork gown with a staggering orange wig that must have been quite the feat to balance on his head. As he emerged onto the stage and began to speak his lines there was a loud, long booing from someone in the audience.

There was a slight hesitation on stage, Mr Hutson paused in his dialogue.

"Seems someone does not know their dames from their villains," he said caustically. "For future reference, I get the cheers."

The audience laughed at this interlude, and the event was brushed off as someone getting carried away. Hutson continued the scene, talking to Buttons about the arrival in town of Princess Zara, and then chasing Aladdin away.

There were no further unexpected outbursts from the audience. The story unfolded much as it always did. The evil Vizier talked in asides to the audience about his plans to overthrow the Sultan and was treated with the appropriate hisses and boos. Aladdin was sent down a rope ladder into a shimmering cave full of treasures and then found himself trapped inside. Stumbling across a magic lantern, he was able to unleash the genie who would help him to escape and save the day.

Dame Wishy-Washy made regular appearances on stage, always in a different but grandly elaborate dress. She was the comic interlude, especially at the darkest moments when anyone unaware of the story might have feared Aladdin was doomed. Buttons ran around the Dame, demonstrating his devoted love for Princess Zara and generally getting lots of sympathetic coos from the audience when it was plain he was unappreciated. He was never going to be the hero and he played up to this, with the audience firmly on his side.

The interval seemed to come around altogether too quickly. Aladdin had just escaped the cave and was wondering what to do next, the following scenes would allow the panto writer's imagination to work overtime and there was no knowing what might occur. They would have to wait fifteen minutes to find out, however, for the stage sets needed to be changed while the curtain was down.

"Shall we go for a drink?" O'Harris suggested.

They headed to the upstairs bar where a crowd had already formed around a barman who was taking and preparing orders as fast as he could. Annie flapped a hand before her face, feeling flushed by the heat of so many people close together.

"Enjoying it?" Clara asked her.

Annie smiled.

"Very much," she said. "The Dame is stealing it, of course."

"That's what Dames do," Clara chuckled.

O'Harris managed to push his way through to the bar and they were soon enjoying cold drinks of gin and tonic water. Clara pressed the cool glass to her cheek.

"It seems exceptionally warm tonight," she remarked. "Considering outside it is freezing."

"I rather wish I had not worn my thicker suit," O'Harris concurred. "These places have no windows, that's the problem, all the hot air gets trapped."

There was a loud shout from the staircase, as if someone was angry about something. It reminded Clara of the sudden boo that had greeted Mr Hutson's arrival on stage.

"Do you think the person who booed the Dame really did not know she was not the villain?" She said.

"Such things happen, old girl," Tommy replied. "Not everything that occurs is sinister."

There was another shout from the staircase and someone protested at being pushed. A man appeared in the bar and Clara recognised him as Rupert Maddock. He looked wild-eyed and slightly crazed.

"Fire!" He screamed at them all. "Get out! Get out!"

Panic immediately commenced as people fled for the staircase. Clara did not react at once, seeing that any attempt at flight would result in being crushed on the stairs. She glanced around her and noticed that the barman was exiting via a door behind him.

"I wouldn't be surprised if there is another staircase that way, one for staff to use," Clara pointed. "He has gone somewhere at least, and I doubt it is to wash up dirty glasses."

They headed for the door behind the bar and pushed through to find themselves in a narrow corridor, with a staircase at the end. This was the domain of the theatre staff, rather like the servants' stairs found in large country houses. Clara ran to the stairs, the others following, and could hear the distant footsteps of the barman clattering down. The steps were bare wood sandwiched between two walls. Clara raced down them and came to another door which opened when she pushed it. She found herself stepping out into the foyer, the people who had come down the main stairs were filing through the front doors to escape.

Annie coughed. There was a thin haze of smoke floating through the foyer, catching at the back of their throats.

"Come on," Clara grabbed Annie's hand and ran for the doors. People were pushing and shoving to get out, some were stumbling to the ground in the crush. Clara tutted to herself and wondered that no one was attempting to coordinate the escape. The staff seemed to have vanished. She managed to push Annie outside before rising to the challenge herself.

"Everyone calm down! We shall all get outside, but if we push and shove someone will get hurt!"

O'Harris and Tommy joined her, bringing the rush of people to a temporary halt.

"Women and children first!" O'Harris barked. "And anyone old or infirm! Don't shove, sir, I saw that and it shall not get you out any quicker!"

Within a matter of minutes the escaping audience was sorted by the priority of age and gender, then they filtered out in an orderly fashion. Forcing people to wait their turn had a calming effect on everyone and it did not take long for the whole audience to be outside on the pavement, staring back at the theatre with a slight look of disappointment. There was no sign of leaping flames or a fiery blaze. Just a slight mist of smoke that was not much more than you found in a smoking room. People were starting to question if they had been rushed outside for no reason.

"Have you ever noticed, Clara, that when we go out for the evening it always ends in some emergency?" O'Harris said.

Clara could not think of a suitable reply to that.

"Why is the fire engine not here?" Annie said, glancing around. "Has it not been called?"

"I don't know what is happening," Tommy shrugged. "We seem to have departed the theatre under false pretences.

"There was definitely smoke," Clara said.

They milled around for a while longer and then Mr Maddock appeared at the main doors.

"I do apologise wholeheartedly for this drama," he told the grumbling audience. "The fire has been contained, it started in the prop room. Thankfully, very little has been destroyed and the theatre is already clearing of smoke. I felt it was prudent to evacuate you all to ensure no one was hurt. However, you may all now return and the panto shall continue as before. Also, you are all entitled to complementary drinks. Now if you will come back to your seats?"

The phrase 'complementary drinks' was enough to rally the spirits of most and the press to get back in was almost as bad as that to get out. Clara and the others headed back to the balcony to be seated ready for the second half.

"What a performance!" Tommy snorted. "Rather an over-reaction!"

"But if the fire had spread with everyone inside it would have been awful," Annie reminded him.

Tommy gave another snort to indicate he thought there had been a lot of fuss over nothing.

"Let's hope the Buttons costume didn't get singed," Clara changed the subject. "The cast might never recover from fear of bad luck befalling them."

Tommy rolled his eyes at this laughable superstition.

"Theatre folk!" He groaned.

The curtains were rolling back, a new set was revealed, this time of the palace of the Sultan. The evil Vizier strode onto the stage.

"My plans are coming together!" He declared. "Aladdin is doomed and that awful Dame Wishy-Washy is consigned to prison and shall never be seen again!"

Chapter Five

The panto writers had clearly enjoyed the liberty of imagination the scenes after the arrival of the genie now allowed. Aladdin went after the vizier, was nearly cut in half by angry palace guards, ended up in the dungeon with Dame Wishy-Washy and Buttons, and was pursued by ghosts and skeletons. There were gasps of alarm and the odd scream as the monsters of the dungeon prowled across the stage. In time-honoured tradition, the audience cried out 'it's behind you!' while the lead actors feigned sudden deafness and pretended they did not understand what was being yelled at them. Everything had started to become very loud and raucous.

"Hutson is certainly giving it his all," O'Harris chortled as the unfortunate dame found herself confronted by a skeleton with a sabre and cowered with exaggerated, shaking knees. Down in the orchestra pit, someone rattled a wooden instrument that made suitable 'bony' sounds to emphasis the jitters of Dame Wishy-Washy. There was a mock fight scene, carried out in slow motions and again with sound-effects from the orchestra. Hutson ducked and dodged beneath the sabre, before suddenly rearing up with a left hook that struck the skeleton with a corresponding clash of cymbals from the pit. The audience cheered.

The heroes escaped the dungeon and headed for the royal palace, there they were reunited with Princess Zara, but only briefly, for the vizier struck and seized the girl, holding her hostage. Now it was the genie's turn to make a dramatic entrance; smoke and an explosive bang from the stage announced his arrival and made Clara uncomfortably aware of the recent mysterious fire that had nearly stalled the panto. Fires happened, of course, especially in theatres where there were a lot of unguarded candles and gaslights mixed with flammable props and costumes. It just seemed a little unlucky on the first night.

The vizier put up a good fight and there was lots of 'magical' activity on the stage as he battled the genie. Dame Wishy-Washy was hit by a levitation spell and began to rise up, flapping her arms and shrieking, much to the amusement of the audience. It all came to an end when Aladdin entered a swordfight with the vizier and fought him into a corner. The vizier begged for mercy and Aladdin, being a worthy hero, granted it. The vizier was arrested, the sultan saved, and it all ended with an elaborate wedding scene for Aladdin and Zara. Dame Wishy-Washy used a hidden hose to cry streams of tears onto the audience, while Buttons kicked his heels to one side and earned sympathetic 'ahs' from those watching.

Finally the cast took their bows, the curtains came down, then rose again for another series of bows. This was repeated several times, to the point where Clara was becoming irritated, then the curtain closed for good and the house lights came on.

"I really enjoyed that," O'Harris grinned as they stood from their seats and stretched their legs. "I thought it was very good, or maybe I just haven't seen a panto in such a long time that anything would amuse me."

"They certainly put a lot of effort into it," Tommy remarked. "How many costume changes did Hutson have? I started to count and then lost track."

They began to shuffle from their seats, following the

rest of the departing audience, but a figure pushing in the opposite direction brought them to a halt. Rupert Maddock was blurting out hasty apologies to everyone around him as he squeezed through the crowd, he reached Clara's party looking a little dishevelled. Captain O'Harris was ahead of Clara, the narrow aisle of the seats preventing them from doing much but follow one another. Maddock peered around him with another unconscious apology.

"Miss Fitzgerald, might we talk a moment?"

Clara felt her heart sink. The look on the man's face, his clear unease and the fact he wanted to catch her before she left the theatre all suggested one ominous thought to her mind. Clara masked the sigh that almost escaped her lips.

"Yes, of course."

"If your party would wait in the bar area, please, I shall return in a moment," Maddock departed as abruptly as he had appeared, forcing his way through the crowd.

"What is that about?" O'Harris snorted.

"Probably the fire that happened earlier," Tommy suggested. "He wants to know how it started. Fires scare theatre producers."

"Wouldn't they scare you if your entire livelihood was liable to make excellent kindling?" Annie remarked. "But surely it was just an accident?"

"I suppose he thinks otherwise," Clara shrugged. There was a niggle at the back of her mind – that strange interruption from the audience member earlier in the evening. It had been out of place and O'Harris was probably right that it was an error, but supposing there had been someone here tonight with a grudge against the production? Or could it be that the unexpected boo had sparked Maddock into hysterical suspicion about the fire and it was really all just a coincidence? Sometimes you could read more into a situation than was truly there.

They headed to the bar, as they had been requested. The barman had clearly been primed for their arrival and instantly set about preparing complimentary drinks. Clara fanned herself with the programme, the theatre was still sweltering. O'Harris loosened his bowtie and looked in half a mood to kick off his shoes. Clara smiled at him; it was not often that they had these quiet, relaxed moments together. She couldn't help but think how handsome he looked in his suit, with his slightly wavy dark hair and playful grin. Clara almost blushed as the thought crossed her mind and O'Harris looked at her at the exact same moment, as if he knew.

He reached out for her hand.

"Thank you for inviting me, this has been such a..." O'Harris frowned for the right word. "I suppose it has been a release for me. A chance to get away from the everyday worries and just laugh. We must do something like this again, very soon."

Clara stepped closer to him, feeling the warmth that radiated from him engulf her like a blanket. She looked up at his face.

"I would like that."

O'Harris grinned.

"Here comes Maddock," Tommy announced from Clara's left.

Clara allowed herself to sigh this time. She rested her head for a second on O'Harris' chest, then she drew back and prepared herself for whatever drama the director was about to unleash upon them.

Maddock looked as stressed as before. His own bowtie was twisted to one side and the top button of his collar was undone. A film of sweat glistened on his forehead and there was a look of fixed horror in his eyes, as if he had seen something truly awful and would never be able to un-see it. Clara felt her earlier annoyance with the man's interruption of her evening fade. This was more serious than a small fire in the prop room.

"Thank you for staying behind," Maddock said quickly. "I know it is an inconvenience, but I really had to ask."

"What has happened?" Clara enquired.

Maddock shook his head.

"In a way I am not sure I can say what happened. I know

that sounds odd. I can see the result. I just don't know how the thing occurred."

"Is this about the fire earlier?" Tommy asked.

Maddock shook his head.

"I wish it was as simple as that. Would you mind following me? I think it would be easier to show you than to try to explain further."

Maddock turned away without waiting for an answer, seeming wrapped up in his own thoughts. Clara shrugged to her companions and then followed him. Mr Maddock led them downstairs and through a door that was painted black and marked as private. They entered the backstage area of the theatre. Here the walls were either plainly whitewashed or left bare to reveal the red brick they were built from. The floor was scuffed wood and lightbulbs hung from the ceiling unshaded. There was no glitz or glamour, all that was reserved for the front of house. Instead this was a world of plain practicality.

Maddock led them through a warren of corridors, past store cupboards, empty dressing rooms, basic offices for visiting directors and producers and of course the prop room which was a cavernous space filled to the ceiling with oddities, including old scenery, forgotten costumes and enough stage swords and guns to have worried an army – had they been of any use, that is.

They finally came to a smaller room at the back of the theatre which contained several enormous wicker baskets on wheels. They were laundry baskets, industrial size ones. Considering the number of costumes the performers went through, it was no wonder they needed such giant containers to carry it off to the unfortunate laundress who must clean it and do repairs. Clara hoped there was more than one woman in charge of the task.

Maddock had paused inside the room. Clara stepped in behind him, wondering if someone's costume had gone missing. Could it be the lucky Buttons outfit had vanished? That would certainly fill Maddock with horror. This thought was quickly put aside when Tommy nudged her shoulder and pointed to a basket with its lid open. Lying on the top of a pile of clothes was the famous costume, awaiting a repair to a nasty rip in the crotch of the trousers. Mervyn Baldry was clearly not quite as slender as the previous Buttons' performers and had managed to tear his costume during the performance.

"Why are we here?" Clara asked Maddock who had grown alarmingly silent.

He jumped.

"Sorry, I… I still can't quite believe it," he was stood before a laundry basket in the middle which, oddly, had been padlocked shut. "I feel as though it is a terrible joke. Not the sort of thing that could really happen."

"You are not explaining yourself," Clara told him gently, recognising a man baffled by shock. "You said you had something to show me?"

With shaking fingers Maddock dug into his pocket and produced a key. He fitted it in the padlock and there was a click as it released.

"I didn't want anyone else seeing this," he mumbled. "It would have upset everyone so badly. We might not have been able to carry on with the performance."

Clara wondered if he was about to show her some burnt precious stage prop or costume, something that had been the cause of the fire. Maybe someone had come into the theatre to deliberately set fire to an item.

Maddock lifted the lid of the laundry basket, and there was a distinctive waft of burned cloth, making Clara's assumptions seem even more likely. Maddock was breathing in short, sharp gasps, he seemed frozen with the lid of the basket raised up above his head, staring in at the contents. That look of horror had returned to his face.

O'Harris stepped forward and took the lid from the man's hands, as it seemed he was unable to move. For a moment Maddock remained standing with his arms up in the air, though his hands no longer grasped anything, then O'Harris let the lid fall backwards and the thud jerked Maddock from his thoughts.

"Ah," O'Harris said as he stared into the basket.

Clara peered in for herself. She had expected to see an item burned to nothing, something precious to the company. She had not expected to be confronted by the pale face of Stanley Hutson. The great Dame still wore his make-up from the night's performance, but he was wigless. He had been shoved into the cramped space of the laundry basket like a doll, his legs were stuck up in the air, his stage shoes level with his face, while his arms flopped by his sides. His eyes were shut, his mouth set in a peaceful line that might have suggested he was asleep, had you not been able to see the nasty red slash across his throat. Someone had cut him almost from ear to ear and blood had poured down the front of his frock.

Stanley Hutson was very, very dead.

Clara took a moment to grasp what she was seeing.

"He was only just on stage," she said.

Annie and Tommy had crept closer, curious about the contents of the basket. Annie peeked over Clara's shoulder apprehensively. She had seen a few more dead bodies than she would like to admit to since being in Clara's employ, but they still shocked her. She caught a glimpse of Hutson and grimaced, but a moment later she glanced again.

"That is the costume from the Arabian Bazaar scene," she declared.

Her words seemed to rouse Mr Maddock.

"Very well observed," he said, his face strained, his eyes looking as if he would never blink again. "Yes, this is the final costume Mr Hutson wears before the interval. Then he is supposed to change into his birds and bells costume, for the scene where Aladdin returns and everyone is caught up by the vizier's men."

Clara pulled at the edge of the costume, getting a better look at the ensemble. She had to admit she had lost track of the dame's changing dresses and could no more have said when a particular outfit was on stage than she could have predicted the outcome of a horse race. She didn't doubt that Annie or Maddock was correct however, that just led to a very odd circumstance.

"But Dame Wishy-Washy was on stage all night, we saw her," Clara said, already guessing the explanation.

"Mr Hutson has an understudy, all the main characters do. In Hutson's case, his understudy is his own son, Donald," Mr Maddock explained. "We lost track of Stanley after he came off stage before the interval. He was nowhere to be found. With time running out, Donald took over. I thought maybe Stanley had been caught up in the commotion of the backstage fire and kept looking for him. The only reason I looked in this basket was because I had picked up some of the discarded costumes from the performers and was throwing them in here. Had I not happened to glance over, I never would have realised..."

Maddock gave a very honest shudder at the memory of the discovery. O'Harris had been quietly examining the body while this conversation took place, now he attracted Clara's attention.

"The costume includes a white apron sewn to the skirt," he said, pointing out the apron which had fallen back on itself when the body was shoved in the basket. O'Harris had touched the edge of the apron and glimpsed something. "Someone has written on the apron."

O'Harris scowled.

"In blood."

Chapter Six

The word was clear, even if the letters had blurred due to the blood soaking into the weave of the apron.

Thief.

There was no question that the accusation had been daubed using the blood that had poured from Hutson's neck. Clara examined the apron for several moments.

"What a shame the killer could not have kindly left a fingerprint behind in this blood," she said, before realising how that must sound to the anxious Maddock. She glanced in his direction, but he did not seem to have noticed. "Mr Maddock, you must call the police at once."

"Police?" Maddock said, managing to look even more horrified than before. "I can't have the police here! The cast would be traumatised. Policemen are terrible bad luck in a theatre."

"I would say Mr Hutson has used up all the bad luck going around," Clara said grimly. "The fact remains, Mr Maddock, this is a murder and the police must be summoned."

"I thought you could solve it without a fuss," Maddock said with a pleading tone to his voice.

"I am willing to assist in this matter, if that is what you

desire, but it would be against the law for me to do so without reporting this incident to the police. There is no question in the matter, the police must be summoned."

Maddock looked miserable, then he slowly nodded.

"I suppose you are right, but I must allow the cast to leave first. They are always tense after a performance, especially on the opening night. This would upset them terribly."

"What about Donald Hutson, he must be wondering about his father?" Tommy said.

Maddock had wrapped his fingers together and turned his fists into a ball, he was unable to take his eyes from the laundry basket.

"We… that is…" Maddock cleared his throat. "It is not unheard of for Stanley to… disappear."

Maddock was clenching his hands together so tight his knuckles were going white.

"Stanley, in recent years, has suffered from a very slight drinking problem," he said, downplaying the information. "It has never interfered with his work before, but he has been known to go off on a binge when he is… upset. The incident earlier this evening with the audience member who booed him, led to Stanley having one of his more dramatic moments. We had trouble convincing him to go back on stage. When he was nowhere to be found during the interval, we all assumed he had gone to get a drink to calm himself. When he did not return, we were concerned, but only because it was unlike him to miss a performance. Fortunately there was Donald."

"Well, you can safely say he was not getting a drink," Tommy observed dryly.

"Strange to think that a person accidentally booing him could have caused Mr Hutson such anxiety," Clara said, staring at the sad face of the dame. With the make-up smudged and the wig missing, all the magic of the performer had evaporated and what was left was an old, bald man who had once been racked by demons. "I would have thought he could brave such a storm, he seemed so confident in himself."

"That is actors for you," Maddock replied. "They act. Upon the stage they are heroes, bravely projecting themselves to the audience. Backstage they are nervous wrecks, riddled with doubts about their abilities and talents. Stanley Hutson was the greatest dame of his generation, yet he was never happy, always finding fault with his performance. Actors need constant reassurance, you see, they need applause and adoration to keep them going. Even the villains feed off the audiences enjoying their performance and hissing and booing at them. But for a hero to be booed, that is like swearing at a vicar, it is just something you would not do. So shocking, so upsetting. It cut through Stanley straight to the part of him that was holed with self-doubt."

"Might it be possible he took that upset to an extreme?" O'Harris said. "Might he have felt so bad he slit his own throat?"

"He hardly threw himself in here," Clara answered before Mr Maddock could speak. "And there is simply not enough blood for him to have died in this basket, nor a knife."

"So, he killed himself and then someone dumped him in here?" O'Harris suggested. "To keep the show going."

His pointed gaze settled on Maddock.

"Me? I would never…"

Clara stopped him.

"We are missing the vital thing that makes this an unlikely suicide. The accusation on the apron," Clara spoke. "Mr Hutson could not have written that. Aside from the difficulty of writing upside-down while dying, he was hardly likely to make such a statement. If he felt guilt about something and wanted to confess, why not leave a note? This word 'thief' indicates plainly that someone else was with Mr Hutson when he died. But he did not die here."

Clara stepped away from the laundry basket.

"Do you have any thoughts on where this murder took place, Mr Maddock?" She asked the director. "There has to have been a lot of blood, this would have been messy."

Maddock nodded uneasily.

"I understand, but I can't offer an answer. I went to Stanley's dressing room and there was no sign of blood there. I searched most of the used rooms backstage too."

"What about unused rooms?"

"I haven't had a chance to look everywhere," Maddock admitted. "And I stopped once I had found Stanley."

Maddock winced as his words brought back to him the moment of discovery yet again.

"How much time passed between the moment Mr Hutson was last seen coming off the stage and you found him?" Clara asked.

Maddock shrugged.

"Stanley is in the final scene before the interval, when Aladdin returns triumphantly with the lamp. He is also in the first scene of the second half. But Donald had to take over for that. I would say it was not long after that scene started I found him. That makes about fifteen or twenty minutes he was missing."

"Roughly the length of the interval," Clara said.

Maddock nodded.

"That is a relatively short time to murder a man and dispose of his body," Clara stared sadly at the deceased dame. "I doubt Mr Hutson was killed far from here. The murderer would not wish to be seen dumping this body. I suggest we look at those unused rooms."

Maddock nodded again, his face forlorn.

"There are some dressing rooms along this corridor. They are out of use for the moment due to a problem with the ceilings. And there is a small room that contains ropes and pulleys that raise and lift the scenery. We don't use those as there is a newer system of ropes backstage. No one would have gone into that room during the show."

"They seem as good a place as any to start looking for our crime scene, but Mr Maddock, you must send for the police at once."

Maddock looked truly despondent. His shoulders

slumped and you might have imagined he had been accused of the crime himself.

"I suppose it won't be so bad," he muttered to no one in particular. "The cast will have all gone home, but, Miss Fitzgerald, you will keep looking into this, won't you? I have never had much faith in the police."

"I think you are wrong to doubt the police's capabilities, but of course I shall continue to assist you, if that is what you want."

"I do," Maddock agreed swiftly, a look of hope returning to his face. "Do you think you can solve this quickly, before it becomes a scandal?"

Clara did not care to ask him what he meant by 'quickly', he might be under the impression she could name the killer before the morning and she was not going to commit herself to any time scale.

"I shall do what I can to find the murderer," her assurance was necessarily vague.

Maddock seemed to accept it.

They departed the laundry room, Maddock heading for the front of house to find a telephone to summon the police, and the others heading the opposite way to explore the unused rooms and hopefully find the crime scene.

"Makes you wonder about that fire," Tommy said once Maddock was out of the way. "Was it a lucky coincidence for the murderer, or a deliberate distraction?"

"I had been thinking about that too," Clara said as she pushed open the door to the first unused dressing room. "It was convenient. That is for sure. What better way to have the backstage near deserted than to have everyone think there is a fire? Actors are certainly not going to hang around in their dangerously flammable costumes."

The moment Clara stepped into the room she saw why it was currently avoided. When Mr Maddock had said there was a problem with the ceilings, he had not mentioned that they were largely absent. There was a gaping hole above their heads, revealing the beams of the floor above. By the looks, there had been a burst pipe that had flooded through the plaster and ripped out the ceiling. The room smelt nastily damp and there was an ominous patch of black mould growing on a wall. Due to the lack of a ceiling, there was naturally no electric lighting in the room. Clara had to use the light from the corridor to examine the small room. It was obvious no crime had been committed here. Wherever Stanley Hutson was killed, there would be a lot of blood.

"You know, going backstage of a theatre rather destroys the veneer of glamour it tries to project to the audience," O'Harris looked grimly at the ceiling.

"I imagine, like a lot of places, this theatre is still recovering from the bleak years of the war," Tommy replied. "Most theatres were closed for the duration. I know this one was. That's a lot of lost income."

They exited the room and went to the next. The story was the same with the ceiling here, though remarkably the damage was even worse. The old dressing room mirrors, fixed to the wall, had been smashed possibly when the ceiling caved in. Clara glimpsed a dozen versions of herself reflected in the broken glass, but there was no blood.

They moved on again, finding the same story in the two dressing rooms on the opposite side of the hallway. Finally, they came to the room Maddock had described as containing the old pulley system. It was not precisely a room, more a corridor leading off the hallway that ran straight to the stage. At some point, someone had put a curtain up to mask off the ropes and winches for anyone walking past. Presumably it was to please the aesthetics of the actors using this corridor.

At one time the stage had been set further forward, the theatre being much smaller and then these old pulleys would have been in the right place to haul up and down scenery. Then the theatre was expanded, the stage moved back and these ropes were redundant. It would have taken more time and money to remove the old system than just to leave it where it was, so it was curtained off and forgotten about.

Clara pulled back the curtain and discovered the hallway was too dark, even with the light from the parallel corridor, to see anything. She shook her head.

"I need a lamp, or something."

They returned to the inhabited dressing rooms searching for a light. It was there that Maddock found them.

"Any luck?" He asked with a little too much optimism in his voice. It sounded wrong to be so keen to find the place a murder occurred.

"We were going to explore that old pulley room, but it is too dark," Clara explained. "We were hoping to find a candle or something."

"Oh," Maddock said, then he darted into the corridor. They could hear him opening a door, before he returned with a torch. "There is one in the emergency cupboard, in case the lights go out. These corridors are pitch black without the electrics."

Clara gladly took the torch, only wishing Maddock had mentioned it before, and headed back to the pulley room. She pulled back the curtain and shone the light into the dark, narrow space. There was several feet of empty floor before the rope system started, but Clara did not have to go that far. The torch beam caught the edge of something glinting on the ground – a shard of glass. It looked like a piece of the broken mirror from the unused dressing room, and it was covered down one edge with a burgundy red substance.

There was more blood just beyond where it lay, a great pool of it on the floor, and streaks spattered up the narrow walls. There could be no doubt that here was where Stanley Hutson, the greatest Dame of his age, had met his end.

Clara shone the torch slowly over the scene, only able to take in fragments at a time. Maddock pushed back the curtain beside her and stared in horror, the colour draining from his face at the ghastly sight before him. He suddenly stumbled backwards and O'Harris stepped forward thinking the man was going to faint. Maddock kept his feet, but he looked sick to his stomach.

"Who knew about this old corridor?" Clara asked him.

Maddock seemed dazed as he answered her.

"Anyone who has walked down here, most of the cast, certainly all the stagehands. Most are employed by the theatre and are completely familiar with its secrets. I have a few I employ for the company, they have been doing this for years. They know this theatre inside and out too."

Not a secret place then, which ruled out one means of discovering who was behind the murder. Clara was still casting her light about the small space. There was something sinister about the old ropes hanging under tension and in perfectly vertical lines. They made her think uncomfortably of nooses, though she considered it unlikely there was any such symbolism for the killer when he chose this place to kill Hutson. No, it was just a convenient place, out of the way, unused and dark – very dark. Hutson probably never saw the attack coming.

"You think the killer could have been kind enough to leave us some clue," Tommy grumbled, his words partly said to alleviate the tension in the air. "A bloody footprint or handprint would have been helpful."

"He left us the murder weapon," Clara pointed out, shining her torch on the glass shard. "I dare say that were we to pick up that fragment, it would fit one of those broken mirrors we glimpsed perfectly. And that tells us something."

"It does?" Mr Maddock looked both baffled and hopeful in the same instant.

"It tells us the murderer did not bring their own weapon. It suggests this was a spontaneous act of violence, using a weapon near to hand…"

Clara was interrupted by the sound of boots coming down the corridor.

"I left the front doors unlocked," Maddock explained quickly.

Clara stepped back into the corridor. The police had arrived.

Chapter Seven

Inspector Park-Coombs was a worthy and valiant ally to Clara in her detective work, but he could also be grumpy and surly. He was a man in his early fifties, who liked his routines, his sleep and a biscuit with his morning cup of tea. He did not like being called out late on a Saturday evening – just when he was looking forward to his day off – to be confronted by a crime scene that, as one constable put it, looked like an episode from Alice in Wonderland. In short, he was in a bad mood before he reached the bloody corridor and his moustache was twitching on his face. Clara greeted him politely.

"Hello Inspector, you shall find the murder was committed through here. We have touched nothing."

Clara pulled back the curtain and kindly shone her light into the hallway. Park-Coombs took several moments to absorb the scene.

"And the body?"

"Dumped into a laundry basket a few rooms down. There was a message written on the murdered man's clothing. It describes Mr Hutson as a thief, though I don't understand the significance."

Park-Coombs gave a familiar groan. He was always

gloomy at the start of a murder case, fearing that he might face insurmountable odds in attempting to solve it and end up with no solution to the crime.

"Mr Stanley Hutson," he said solemnly. "I saw him play Widow Twanky in London once. Never would it have crossed my mind I would be coming to the place he was murdered years later."

"This is Mr Maddock, the director of the Stratford Company," Clara introduced the unfortunate man, who had regained a little of his composure.

Inspector Park-Coombs turned and nodded at him in acknowledgement.

"You found the body?" He asked Maddock.

"Yes, Inspector," Maddock replied.

"When was that?"

Maddock blinked fast, as if the question had been completely unexpected.

"Oh, well, what is it now?" He glanced at his watch and for the first time Clara felt there was something odd about Maddock's demeanour. "About... about quarter past eight."

"That's over two hours ago!" Park-Coombs blustered. "Why was I not called sooner?"

"We had to finish the performance..." Maddock became uneasy.

"You mean you went on with the pantomime when one of your cast was lying dead in a laundry basket?" Park-Coombs' appalled tone reminded Clara that she had not thought to ask the same question. Perhaps she was a little more familiar with the nature of theatrical folk – the show must go on, even when one of the main stars was dead.

"I didn't want to upset people," Maddock replied, as if that was obvious. "The cast would have been so shaken. Besides, Mr Hutson would not have wished for the panto to stop."

"I don't give a damn what Mr Hutson might or might not have wanted," Park-Coombs snorted. "You know it is a crime to delay reporting something like this to the police?

It can be seen as interfering in police business."

"Well, I didn't want you here at all," Maddock snapped, his words imprudent. "If Miss Fitzgerald had not insisted I summon you, I would have gladly not done so!"

Clara felt it was wise to intercede at this point, before Maddock ended up incurring the inspector's wrath and potentially incriminating himself.

"The matter has been reported now," she told Park-Coombs. "And I doubt the delay has made much difference. Whoever the killer was, they were long gone before Maddock came across the body."

The inspector grumbled under his breath, but he moderated his tone when he next spoke.

"I best see Mr Hutson, then."

Maddock led the way to the laundry room, agitated and jumpy. He seemed to half-expect to be arrested at any moment. Clara wondered what had occurred in his past to make the theatre director so wary of the police.

They arrived at the laundry room and Maddock lifted the lid of the central basket. Mr Hutson was still inside, his bald head slumped to his right, looking as if he had just dozed off, if you did not take into account the bloody gash across his throat. His skin had taken on the grey, waxy appearance Clara had seen too often upon a corpse. His lips were devoid of colour and it would be impossible to consider him a living person, no matter how peacefully his head seemed to repose.

Park-Coombs carefully pulled down the edge of the apron to read the accusatory word 'thief' written upon it.

"Whoever wrote this can spell. Lots of people are caught out by the word thief and misspell it," he said conversationally, some of his ire had dissipated now he was involved in the case. "Any thoughts on the relevance of the word?"

Maddock shook his head.

"I can't think of the logic. Mr Hutson made a lot of money as a performer. He would not have to steal anything."

"Might not mean a material thing he stole," the inspector persisted. "Anyone among your company have a grudge against him?"

"No," Maddock shook his head even harder. "Mr Hutson was well respected among us. He had been loyal to the company, even during the slim years of the war."

"No one looking to take his place, maybe?" Park-Coombs pushed.

"No one would even consider it!" Maddock said in horror at the thought. "Mr Hutson was the greatest dame of our age! I would never think to replace him!"

"What about his son," Clara interjected. "He clearly possessed his father's talent and was able to mimic him perfectly during the second half. He was indistinguishable from his father."

"Donald is very good," Maddock agreed. "But he would never think of replacing his father, not like that."

"Rather makes you think Donald was walking in his father's shadow," Tommy whispered in Clara's ear. She gave him a look that said she had thought the same.

"When was Mr Hutson missed?" Park-Coombs now asked.

"Shortly before the curtain was due to go up on the second half," Maddock explained. "I have an assistant who makes sure all the performers are present and ready to go on the stage before each scene. She noticed that Mr Hutson was absent and informed me. When I could not find him and discovered that his first costume of the second half was sitting in his dressing room, I had to make a split-second decision. I asked Donald to take-over while I looked for his father."

"Donald did not know where he was?"

"No," Maddock was struggling to take his eyes off the recumbent figure in the basket. "Donald said his father had been upset after the first half and wondered if he had gone to get a drink. I should emphasise, Inspector, it was extraordinary for Mr Hutson to miss a curtain call."

"Then you must have been worried about him?" Park-Coombs pried.

"I was. There was some unpleasantness at the start of the panto. An audience member booed Mr Hutson when he entered on stage as the dame. I rather felt Hutson had taken the comment to heart. It was probably just an accident."

"And Mr Hutson liked to drink when he was upset?" Park-Coombs was not giving Maddock any leeway and the director was starting to sweat.

"He had been known to drink when a performance had not gone well," Maddock admitted. "But I had never known him to miss a show. That was why I was worried, but I never suspected he was dead. I thought I would find him in a pub, drinking away his woes. I only found the body by chance."

The inspector seemed to accept this answer.

"Anything else unusual happen tonight?"

Maddock gave a small, uncomfortable cough.

"There was a fire, in the prop room," he confessed. "I'm not sure how it began, but a papier mache rock we use in the cave seen was at the centre of the trouble. It was blazing away and a number of other props caught light. I evacuated the theatre while a couple of stagehands doused the flames."

The inspector was clever enough to suspect the two events – the fire and the murder – were connected, just as Clara had done.

"Any idea how the fire began?" Park-Coombs asked.

"Not really, but I was rather distracted from that after I found…" Maddock waved his hand in the vague direction of Mr Hutson's corpse and fell silent.

"I'll need a full list of everyone in your company," Park-Coombs said casually, starting to move away.

"What?" Maddock startled.

"I thought that was plain enough? I'll need to speak to everyone, find out if they saw or heard anything."

"But, Inspector, if you do that, how shall I ever get them to perform?" Maddock said desperately. "Actors are such precious creatures. A murder investigation shall have them falling to pieces."

"What you have to bear in mind, Mr Maddock, is that among your 'precious creatures' is a murderer. For all we know it was one of Mr Hutson's fellow actors," Park-Coombs was blunt. "This was a personal attack, someone out for revenge, and they wanted people to know about it, hence the message. Strikes me, that is the sort of thing a rival actor might do."

Clara almost corrected the inspector for jumping to conclusions, then changed her mind. He was pushing Maddock, seeing what he could get.

"Your company is likely harbouring a murderer. Until this matter is resolved, every person at this theatre is a suspect and that includes you, Mr Maddock."

Maddock looked like he might faint at this information. He gulped hard and had to excuse himself from the room, rushing to the nearest bathroom to be sick. The inspector shook his head and tutted as the man departed.

"These theatrical types are so sensitive," he said.

"Mr Maddock has been under a great deal of strain," Clara reminded him. "He has lost one of the main members of his crew, discovered a corpse, had to deal with a fire in the prop room and is now contemplating that among those people he has known and worked with for years is a murderer. I think he can be excused his reaction, under the circumstances."

Park-Coombs was duly chastened by her gentle rebuke and had the decency to blush a little.

"You are right, I am being harsh. I'm tired, that's all," Park-Coombs' moustache did one of its little twitches that suggested its owner was feeling thoughtful. "We have been working our fingers to the bone trying to sort out this business with the mysterious alley gang, the one who attacked Private Peterson."

Clara nodded, not daring to speak. Her mind had flicked

back to Brilliant Chang.

"Progress, if you can call it that, is slow. No one is talking and anytime we try to interview someone they seem to have magically disappeared. Honestly, I am frustrated," Park-Coombs scratched at his ear. "Does it sound awful that I actually feel better to have just a run-of-the-mill murder to solve?"

"I understand," Clara promised him. "If I can do anything..."

"You stay out of this gang business, Clara, it's far too dangerous," Park-Coombs told her firmly.

Clara chose not to argue, even if she was not precisely staying away from the matter.

Maddock returned, wiping his mouth with a white handkerchief.

"The panto can carry on, can't it, Inspector?" He asked desperately.

"I don't see why not," Park-Coombs replied, his tone kinder. "Once everything has been investigated here, you can return to normal, well, as normal as possible under the circumstances."

Maddock looked relieved.

"I don't know what we will do without Mr Hutson," he said miserably.

At that moment Dr Deáth, the police coroner arrived, humming to himself in the happy-go-lucky fashion that seemed so at odds with his job. He smiled at everyone; clearly, he did not hold a grudge for being disturbed from his sleep. The coroner was one of the kindest and gentlest men Clara knew. Some might find his cheerful attitude to death disrespectful, but it was nothing of the sort, Dr Deáth simply saw no reason for being morbid about such things. He had utter respect for the dead, which was why he did not mope about around them. He had a job to do and he would do it to the best of his abilities.

"Well, well," he said, peering in at Stanley Hutson. The coroner was not an overly big man and he had to pop up onto his toes to get a good look. "This is unexpected.

Though, very seasonal."

Inspector Park-Coombs muttered something under his breath, Clara suspected he was finding the coroner's jolly demeanour irritating when he was craving his bed.

"You know what is very curious, Inspector?" Clara said to him.

Inspector Park-Coombs looked at her with an expression that indicated he did not know.

"Considering the amount of blood Mr Hutson lost, and that his killer must have had to carry him here, the culprit ought to have been positively covered in blood. Yet, no one witnessed a person so drenched," she elaborated.

"Clara is right," Dr Deáth emerged from him work. "When you cut a man's throat you don't instantly kill him. The heart keeps pumping and it causes blood to shoot out from the wound. And a big, deep wound like this, that would cause a lot of blood to splatter around. The killer must have been stained."

"And yet we are in a theatre, with lots of potential changes of clothing," Park-Coombs pointed out grumpily. "The killer does his messy work, then changes into a different costume."

"And with the fire as a diversion, he would have been able to work without too much fear of being spotted," Tommy added.

"What are the odds the killer dumped his soiled clothes somewhere around here?" Clara said quietly to her brother.

"Not a lot of time to hide them, what with disposing of the body. He had to lure Hutson to the old pulley room, kill him, start a fire, hide the body and then get rid of the clothes."

"And, as far as the killer knows, the body has yet to be discovered," Clara reminded him. "Maddock told no one aside from us of his discovery, and I bet these laundry baskets are not collected until the morning."

"You mean, maybe the killer left his blood-stained clothes hidden here, hoping to retrieve them later?"

"It's worth a shot, isn't it?"

Chapter Eight

Clara explained her idea to the inspector, hoping to distract him from grilling poor Maddock, who the policeman seemed to suspect of being the murderer. The fraught director was beside himself with alarm and looked fit to collapse. Clara's second suggestion, after she proposed searching for the murder clothes, was that someone take Maddock to a quiet place and get him a stiff drink. Annie volunteered, as she was beginning to feel queasy hanging around a corpse. Park-Coombs sent a constable to accompany her and Maddock, just to be sure, as he put it.

That left several people to go through the large laundry baskets that contained a vast amount of clothing. The number of costume changes during the panto, not just for the main cast, but for the chorus, was immense, and over the course of the night the costumes were torn, frayed, ripped and stained in the actors' haste to don them or remove them.

Clara found herself elbow deep in sweaty linen, searching for an outfit that looked bloodstained. The simplest means of making sure each basket was thoroughly searched was to tip it over and empty the contents, then return each item one by one. The process went quite smoothly until one constable discovered that his laundry basket contained several items of feminine underwear and he was so embarrassed he could barely continue. Clara shut her ears as Park-Coombs barked at the prudish constable and dragged a sequined tunic from among her pile. It had some dark patches on the sleeve, but when she sniffed them she discovered they were unmistakably wine stains – someone had been celebrating the first night in their costume.

In the background, Dr Deáth continued his work with cheerful disregard for what was going on around him. He was talking to himself as he examined Hutson, making comments under his breath about skin discoloration, temperature changes and wound patterns. Clara had one ear on him, not meaning to, but finding it hard to tune out the man's steady conversation with himself. She finished searching through her pile of clothes and threw the last item back in the basket with a despondent look. Glancing around she saw her fellow searchers were also nearly done, and no one had found a bloody outfit, not even one solitary item that could be linked to the crime.

"Maybe the killer took the clothing away, after all," Tommy shrugged to her as he discarded a pair of blue tights, the sort Aladdin wore, into his basket.

Clara bit on her lower lip, thinking. The killer had had so little time, it seemed logical that he would abandon his clothes somewhere in the theatre to retrieve later. But if not in the laundry, well they could be anywhere. Clara thought of the holes in the ceiling of the abandoned dressing rooms, those would make good hiding places, no one would think to look there. Then, as she let her mind wander, she found herself imagining all sorts of places you could hide something in a theatre. You could spend weeks searching this place and never uncover all the hidden nooks and crannies. And that really worried Clara.

"Hmm, that was a dead end," Inspector Park-Coombs said moodily, before noticing Clara's forlorn expression. "It was a good idea though. Killer had to have changed his clothes. Anyway, I want to look at the remains of this suspicious fire."

"May I come?" Clara asked.

Park-Coombs raised an eyebrow at her.

"Surprised you asked permission, you don't normally, and, of course," Park-Coombs walked out of the laundry room door and stood in the corridor. "Where is the prop room, anyway?"

They ended up having to ask Maddock for directions, and it turned out there was more than one room used for storing props, since the theatre had far too many of them. When the inspector mentioned perhaps throwing some away, Maddock looked at him as if he had suggested cutting off the man's hands. Clearly you did not 'throw things away' in the theatre business. The place where the fire had been discovered was actually the largest of the prop rooms. It was a vast space filled with shelves and a few clothes racks, though Maddock was quick to explain that most clothing items were kept in a separate space known as the wardrobe. He showed them into the room and down a central aisle. It was easy to spot the remains of the fire, no one had bothered to clean up the ashes or remove those items charred by the flames. No doubt that was another job being left until tomorrow. Clara got the impression that the second a performance ended, everyone was altogether too glad to get home to their beds and tedious tasks were left for the next day.

"It was fortunate we spotted it before it caused a lot of damage," Maddock remarked, nudging the ashes with the toe of his shoe. "It happened we needed a spare sabre, the tip of the vizier's having snapped off during the cave scene. If not, the fire would have spread a lot further before we realised. As it was, it damaged these shelves nearest it."

Park-Coombs gave a whistle.

"This place is like a tinder box. So much wood and fabric. A flame in here is a frightening thought."

"Inspector, I near enough had a heart attack when I was told what was occurring," Maddock grimaced. "I had people rushing to put it out, but there was a possibility we would not succeed. That is when I evacuated the audience and cast. I wasn't going to take any chances."

Park-Coombs picked up an old lamp from a shelf, it was a big policeman's bull's eye lamp and when he sniffed it, he smelt paraffin.

"Had this been touched by the fire, things would have been a lot worse," he handed it to Clara, who smelt the oily aroma.

"A lucky escape," she shook her head. "What is a full paraffin lamp doing in here?"

"It's another prop," Maddock explained. "Not sure for what play, but sometimes you have real lamps on stage and the actors cast light on the audience, or something like that. I suppose no one thought it important to empty it afterwards."

Clara turned her attention to the charred debris from the fire. Most of the items were burned beyond recognition, but she noticed what might have been the handle of a wooden sword, and a dummy block of cardboard books.

"This was deliberate," she said, poking about in the ashes and producing a used matchstick that had miraculously escaped the worst of the blaze.

Maddock was gnawing on his lower lip, enough to make it bleed.

"I feared as much. I mean, sometimes accidents occur. A stray cigarette thrown down thoughtlessly, for instance, or a fault with the gas or electrics, but I saw all these things on the floor and thought to myself 'someone meant to start a fire here'."

Clara worked through the remains, trying to work out what the items were and if they were at all useful to her. She assumed most of the burned objects had been added to the fire as fuel and had no real significance to the case at hand. She poked about in a clump of items with the remains of the wooden sword and suddenly noticed something.

"There is cloth here!"

She pushed aside a sheet of wood cut into the shape of a giant mushroom and revealed a black lump. Pulling carefully at its edge, she dragged out a bundle of material. It was badly burned, but where it had been folded on itself, the fabric had been protected and it was possible to see the original pattern. As Clara gingerly unfurled the costume, she revealed a set of trousers and a jacket. Maddock was peering over her shoulder.

"That's a royal guard costume," he remarked, sounding astounded by what she had found.

"A bright red jacket," Clara observed. "Not bad for hiding blood stains, but look here Inspector, at the cuffs."

She indicated where the material was stiff with dried blood and a slightly different colour. Much of the jacket was too badly destroyed to reveal where Hutson's blood had spattered upon it, but Clara had no doubt this was the outfit the killer had worn during the murder. It made sense; the killer burned the stained costume to destroy evidence, along with creating a distraction sufficient enough to give him time to dispose of Hutson. Knowing that the missing dame would be looked for, the killer hoped to place the body somewhere it would not be found until morning, giving him time to slip away. He could have left him in the pulley room, but he might have been discovered there too soon. He had to take a chance that someone might notice the blood, but with the body hidden it would buy precious time.

"How many royal guards are in the panto?" Inspector Park-Coombs asked Maddock.

"Four," he answered.

"Well, that narrows down our suspect list considerably," the inspector looked pleased. "I'll need the names of those actors."

The inspector paused.

"How do you know who has which guard outfit? They are different sizes, I imagine."

"They have a label sewn into the collar with the name of the relevant actor," Maddock said uneasily, struggling to picture one of his own cast as a killer.

Clara lifted the collar of the uniform and looked for a name tag.

"It's badly burned," she said. "I think the end of the name is 'son', such as in Johnson."

"Jorg Erikson and Jasper Smithson play two of the guards," Maddock said obediently, though not looking happy about it. "Neither have been with the company that long, I can't think they would wish Stanley harm…"

"If we look at the name tags in the remaining costumes, then we can work out whose uniform this is," Park-Coombs said with sudden enthusiasm. "Where are those other costumes, Mr Maddock?"

Maddock looked defeated, he mumbled something about them either being in the backstage clothing racks or the laundry, before the inspector instructed him to find them. The two gentlemen left the prop room.

Clara studied the burned uniform for a while longer, willing it to offer her an insight into this mystery. Would a man be stupid enough to wear his own costume to murder another? Perhaps, if the killing was a sudden act of violence, a moment of passion with no thought of the consequences. But why? What reason could there be for someone to hate Stanley Hutson so much they chose to kill him? And what of the bloody message – why was Hutson a thief?

Clara gave up on the costume which was offering her no solutions and headed for the corridor. She located the inspector and Maddock backstage going through a rack of clothes where two guard uniforms hung.

"We've found Smithson's," Park-Coombs said in delight. "Looks like our culprit is Mr Erikson. Name sounds Scandinavian."

"His grandparents came to England from Denmark," Maddock shrugged, the evening had taken its toll on him and his voice sounded cracked and weak. "I can't see why he would do such a thing."

Park-Coombs was too over-the-moon with his

discovery to listen. It appeared he had solved the case in record time. Clara decided to bring him back down to earth.

"You know, a clever man would wear someone else's costume to shift suspicions from themselves," she remarked.

Park-Coombs scowled at her.

"What supposes our killer clever? He murdered a man during the middle of a performance with a shard of glass."

"Yet he had the sense to somehow lure Hutson to an unused room to commit the crime, then create a distraction and hide the body somewhere it would be unlikely to be found soon. It also should be noted that it is terribly convenient the royal guard costume jacket is just the right shade of red to mask blood stains," Clara folded her arms and awaited the inspector's rebuttal.

He twitched his moustache in clear irritation.

"You must always make things complicated," he grumbled.

"I only wish to make sure the right man is caught," Clara consoled him. "As do you."

Park-Coombs muttered under his breath.

"Well, this Erikson still seems our best suspect and I shall be interviewing him in the morning," he said aloud. "We have plenty of evidence, after all; the murder weapon, the killer's outfit, just need a motive to wrap it all up."

Maddock had hung his head as the conversation continued, Clara surmised he was picturing the ruination of his pantomime. One of his stars was dead and it looked like one of the chorus had killed him. How could a performance carry on after that?

"Mr Maddock, maybe you should go get some rest?" Clara intervened, knowing she was stepping on the inspector's toes by doing so.

Park-Coombs shot her a look, but Clara caught his eye and her expression said they were done for the night. Maddock looked fit to collapse, and he would be no use to them if he was taken seriously ill.

"I think I could do with lying down," Maddock said quietly. He pressed a hand to his head.

"Is your hotel far?"

Maddock shook his head.

"I'll have Tommy escort you, all the same. You need to keep your strength up, you have a pantomime to run," Clara reminded him.

A flicker of a smile crossed Maddock's lips and then he weakly agreed to the arrangement.

Maddock was safely on his way home when the inspector caught up with Clara.

"You can't go around sending my suspects home without asking me first," he snapped at her.

Clara had expected the response.

"The man looked like he was going to faint," Clara said calmly. "We didn't need another problem on our hands. Besides, you have your suspect."

The last sly comment stroked Park-Coombs' ego, until he recognised the edge to her tone.

"You think I am barking up the wrong tree?" He accused her.

"I merely think you should remain open-minded on the matter. Until we can say for certain that Mr Erikson had a motive for murdering Stanley Hutson," Clara appeased him.

Park-Coombs snorted.

"Why can't these things ever be simple?"

"Because they involve people, Inspector, and people are never simple," Clara patted his arm. "I am going to go home and begin again in the morning. I want to have a long chat with Donald Hutson."

"The son?" Park-Coombs seemed to have forgotten about him.

"The man who is about to take over a prestigious role due to the death of his father," Clara said pointedly.

Park-Coombs' annoyance faded, replaced by a slight

grin.

"Now that is a very good motive for murdering someone," he said.

"Exactly what I was thinking, Inspector."

Chapter Nine

Clara rose later than she had intended the next morning. The night's adventures had taken their toll, with the result she had over-slept. Not that she supposed it mattered a great deal, since Donald Hutson would undoubtedly also rise late, exhausted from his performance and (presumably) anxious about his father's whereabouts. Unless he was the murderer, of course.

Whether Inspector Park-Coombs had dispatched a constable to inform the younger Hutson of his father's demise she could not say. The inspector had been extremely busy at the theatre, gathering any information he could and ensuring the staff and cast could resume their normal activities the next day without interfering with a crime scene. He would have accompanied the body back to the morgue, sent men to search the area around the theatre for clues and, shorthanded, as he usually was, he may have allowed the task of informing Donald of his father's death to slip his mind. For the moment, at least.

Clara glanced at the hallway clock, which was alarmingly close to chiming nine o'clock. Surely the inspector would have visited Donald to tell him the news? Clara would have liked to have seen the young man's face, to gauge his reaction. Of course, he was an actor, so any reaction could be feigned, but still, it would have been interesting. But now the chances of her reaching Donald before ten were slim, and Park-Coombs would not be so lax as to wait beyond then to alert Donald, would he?

Clara brushed off the thoughts. In reality, though seeing Donald's reaction would have been interesting, it would have only been a small part of the investigation. There were many more avenues to explore as yet.

Annie appeared in the hallway as Clara was putting on her hat.

"You have had neither a cup of tea nor any breakfast," she puttered, thrusting a teacup into Clara's hand as she spoke.

"I overslept," Clara protested, though she knew the answer would garner her nothing from Annie, who considered there to be no excuse for missing a meal.

"You still have time for a cup of tea and some toast. You can't go around on an empty stomach, it isn't healthy," Annie forced the teacup into Clara's hands and departed to fetch toast.

Clara obediently sipped the tea, trying to consume it as fast as possible. She knew that defying Annie would only result in a lengthy argument. Annie was technically the Fitzgeralds' housekeeper, though such a short description failed to encompass all she did for them fully. She had originally come to the house to help look after Tommy when he returned from the war badly injured but had slipped into the role of housekeeper without anyone really noticing. Annie liked fussing around people, and she felt that no one needed more fussing around than Clara, who could be careless about both her eating habits and her wellbeing. If it was going to rain, Annie made sure Clara had an umbrella with her, for she knew full well Clara would not remember it alone. If it was cold, she made sure there was a warm fire waiting for Clara from wherever she had been traipsing about after a criminal. And she monitored Clara's eating like a hawk, insisting she have four meals a day and getting quite incensed if Clara missed one. Some might have thought Annie a touch overbearing, Clara knew that it was because Annie cared so much about the Fitzgeralds that she badgered them.

She finished the tea and was placing the cup on the hall table when there was a rap on the door. Clara didn't mean to startle at the sound, in fact, she was surprised at herself, but her mind had instantly jumped to the notion that the person at the door might have been sent by Brilliant Chang. She quickly composed herself and went to open the door.

"Who would it be at this time of day?" Annie was walking briskly towards her with a plate of toast. "The milkman always comes to the kitchen door, as does the delivery boy."

"I imagine it is someone for me," Clara replied to her, pulling back the door with a little flutter of anxiety.

It was not a messenger from Brilliant Chang. Not unless Rupert Maddock was moonlighting. The director looked pale and dark rings beneath his eyes indicated he had not slept well. He looked sorrowfully at Clara.

"Thank goodness, I hoped I would catch you. I want to come with you to speak with Donald."

Before Clara could protest, Annie had intervened.

"Mr Maddock, you look terrible!" She said in the blunt manner she was renowned for. "Come in at once and have some tea and toast. No, don't protest, I shan't let you refuse. You carry on like this you will be laid up in bed before long."

Clara shrugged at the fraught director.

"Best not to argue," she whispered. "It is easier that way."

Maddock was ushered into the front parlour and tea and toast magically appeared before him. He looked a touch stunned by Annie's attention, but he did not protest further.

"I thought you would be at the theatre," Clara said to him gently.

"The cast won't appear until noon, at the earliest," Maddock ate his toast quite keenly once he began. "And I thought it was more important I accompany you to speak with Donald."

"I would prefer to go alone," Clara said carefully.

"Donald is as much my responsibility as any of the cast. And his father was a friend," Maddock took a shaky breath, the memory of last night returning. "I think it would be better for all involved if I was present. Donald might not even consent to seeing you unless I can speak with him first."

Clara pulled a face, certain she would find a way to persuade the man.

"Mr Maddock, I don't normally allow those who have hired me to become part of the investigation."

"No, I suppose that is prudent, but I am going to insist," some of Maddock's resolve had returned. "I need to be there. Donald is going to be upset, he needs a friend and, to be brutally honest, Miss Fitzgerald, I cannot afford to lose my replacement dame. If Donald loses his head over this, then I might not have a pantomime by teatime."

Clara wanted to point out that Donald's father had been murdered but reminded herself that for men like Maddock – and for all the cast of the panto – the success of a show meant the difference between eating or not. No one could afford for the panto to be cancelled. It might ruin the company completely, depending on how much of a financial outlay Maddock had banked on the success of Aladdin. No, of course he was thinking about the monetary consequences of the show failing, and what that might mean for his cast. Clara decided to go against her better judgement.

"Very well, Mr Maddock, you shall accompany me. But I must insist that I be allowed to conduct this investigation as I see fit. You understand?"

"Of course," Maddock finished his tea.

"There is one other thing."

Maddock looked worried again.

"If Donald Hutson murdered his father, then he must be tried for the crime, even if that jeopardises your pantomime," Clara told him firmly.

Maddock's lips twitched into a grimace of despair. His eyes seemed to become distant as the impact of this statement hit home and he envisioned the consequences.

"I would understand if you wished to cancel my services," Clara continued. "Then this could be left to the police."

Maddock fought a wealth of indecision, the battle plain on his face, before he turned to Clara.

"No, I want you to carry on. The police are going to blunder all about this, I need someone I can trust looking into things," Maddock looked bleak. "I endured the police last night, pulling apart the theatre, tampering with the costumes and props. They are talking about arresting Erikson, one of the chorus, because of the finding of his costume."

"I know," Clara said. "I was there."

"I don't know what to think anymore. I need someone who I know is on my side. Please, Miss Fitzgerald, work with me."

Clara sensed his desperation was genuine and nodded.

"As long as we understand one another. Now, we best see Mr Hutson."

Donald was residing at the Imperial Hotel, where he shared a suite with his father. As the star of the panto, the name that was going to draw the crowds, Stanley Hutson had been housed in better accommodation than most of the cast. His fellow performers either had humbler rooms in the Imperial or were residing at a local boarding house. Maddock remarked to Clara as they approached the hotel that even his room did not cost as much as that of Hutson's.

"You have to keep a man like Hutson happy," he explained. "He knew his worth. He could have stayed in London for the season, performed in some of the most prestigious pantos. We all knew that, but Hutson has been my friend for more years than I care to remember and he always supported the company during the festive period. I was never in any doubt that it was because his name was on the posters that we sold out for every performance."

"And now, without him?" Clara asked.

Maddock shook his head.

"We shall see. Some might want a refund on their tickets, others will still come to the panto anyway," Maddock looked shyly at Clara. "I was hoping we could keep this quiet for as long as possible. Donald really does impersonate his father perfectly, and people need not know…"

Clara understood his implication.

"I am not going to declare anything to the press, if that is your concern," she told him. "That is not my place. But I would suggest you think carefully about attempting to fool your audiences, you might end up offending people."

Maddock thought about this for a moment.

"I think that is a chance I shall take. No one ever said I have to make a general announcement when an understudy takes over, after all."

Clara said no more, even if she did think Maddock was taking a big risk. Some people could be very upset if they thought they had been gulled into watching a mere understudy, instead of the real Hutson.

They walked up the wide steps of the hotel. The Imperial was one of the smartest establishments in the town and was known for attracting famous guests, including royalty. A doorman in a smart red uniform nodded to them and held open the door as they entered.

"How long have you known Hutson?" Clara asked Maddock.

"I was trying to think about that last night," Maddock replied. "I think it was in 1897 we met. I was just getting started in the industry. I know it was before the turn of the century and I was working as a stage manager at the time. Hutson was already famous, and I was responsible for ensuring he had everything he needed while at the theatre. It was another panto, Hutson's bread and butter.

"Anyway, I noticed Hutson was not quite himself. I mean, I knew who he was, had heard all about him, but meeting the man in the flesh was another matter. I expected this idol, this actor I had envisioned with superhuman abilities to act and sway an audience. Instead he seemed… broken. That was around the time Hutson lost his wife, I imagine you are too young to remember that."

"I believe I read about it once," Clara tried to remember. "It was a road accident?"

"Yes. Mrs Hutson was hurrying on an errand for her husband. The favourite legend was she was fetching one of his wigs that was being cleaned and mended. I know she was actually buying him a male corset. Stanley was always sensitive about his appearance on stage and liked to hide his girth," Maddock blushed a little at the confession. "In any case, the rest is true enough. She was crossing the road early in the evening, thick London smog was making it impossible to see a thing and she was struck down by a coach and four travelling far too fast for the conditions. She lingered longer than was right. Hutson always thought she would have suffered less had she died at once. Anyway, Stanley was left bereft. He spiralled into depression and he began to drink."

"Not an uncommon story, sadly," Clara said with true sympathy.

"Well, there I was, a young stage manager trying to cope with a star performer who was drunk more often on stage than he was sober. I had to do something," Maddock winced at the memory. "I played it tough. Took away every bottle of alcohol in Hutson's dressing room and locked him inside. I even went so far as to escort him back and forth to his hotel rooms and locked him in there too. I would pay one of the boot-boys to stand outside and keep an eye. Stanley could have hated me, instead he thanked me. I got him clean, well, mostly, and he started to wake up to the world again. He remembered he had a young son who needed taking care of. That was how we became friends. I knew his secrets, you see, but I didn't pander to him like most would. That was why he liked me, respected me.

"When I became a director, the first panto I was in charge of Stanley insisted on playing the dame. He turned down two London theatres, and a great deal of money, to act for me. He was a true friend."

Maddock's eyes glistened with unshed tears and Clara suddenly realised how personal this case was to him. It was not just that an actor in his company had been killed, it was that a friend, a good friend, had been murdered.

"It sounds like Stanley was a decent man," she told him. "I will do all I can to find his killer."

"Thank you," Maddock smiled. "I owe that man. I owe it to him to bring him justice."

Chapter Ten

Donald Hutson was sitting on a long, low leather sofa in the sitting room of his father's suite. The furniture all around him was very modern and Clara felt it rather too artsy for her liking. Not the sort of furniture for cosy comfort, that you might snuggle into when disaster has occurred. But maybe she was being old-fashioned in her thinking, perhaps the low arms and backs, which looked very difficult to sit in nicely, were really rather pleasant.

Donald was hunched before a white and gold coffee table with spindly legs. It looked fit to collapse if you so much as placed a cup of tea on it. When they had knocked on the room door, he had called them to enter, saying it was not locked. He seemed disappointed that his visitors were Maddock and a woman he did not know, instantly losing interest in them.

Donald was still dressed in the clothes he had worn when he left the theatre, except he had disposed of his suit jacket, so he sat in his shirt sleeves and braces. He still had his shoes on, and Clara guessed he had not slept at all.

He was a robust young man, not of the girth of his father, but carrying a few more pounds than was fashionable. He had chestnut brown hair, that was ruffled about his head, as if he had been running his fingers through it a lot. His eyes were big and deep blue and his face had a handsome aspect, though the extra weight he carried tended to make his features appear puffy. Clara could see faint traces of make-up around his ears and jawline, where he had not quite removed all the greasepaint from the night before. The way he clutched his hands together, huddled over and seemingly distraught made Clara think he was genuinely concerned for his father – either that, or he was worried he would be caught out as the murderer.

"Donald," Maddock moved to a chair close to him. "Have the police been to see you?"

"Police?" Donald looked alarmed, suddenly all his anxiety for his father's safety was unleashed. It had been possible to pretend that nothing bad had happened, to keep the worry at bay, until the mention of the police. "Is father all right?"

Maddock didn't know where to look as he spoke the bad news.

"Your father has been found dead, Donald."

The colour drained from Donald's face and his mouth went slack. The horror the news caused him convinced Clara this young man was not a murderer. Unless his acting skills were of such a calibre he had trained his unconscious responses to perform on cue.

"What happened?" Donald asked, his voice tense and quiet. "Was he drinking again?"

Maddock struggled with the next words.

"Your father has been murdered Donald. I found him at the theatre, after you were all gone."

Donald dropped his head into his hands and his breathing came in a whistling rasp. Clara glanced around the room for something to offer him, and finally discovered a pot of tea that had been brought up by room service not so long ago. It was still warm and had not brewed itself to slurry in the pot. She poured out a cup, laced it well with milk and sugar, then placed it before Donald.

"Try that," she said softly.

Donald took several moments to react, then he lowered his hands and looked at the teacup as if he was seeing something alien. He reached out a hand to it, but when he noticed how much it shook he withdrew it and clutched his hands in his lap.

"I don't understand any of this," he said weakly.

"Honestly, Donald, nor do I," Maddock sympathised. "Which is why I have asked for Miss Fitzgerald's assistance. She is a private detective and I trust her more than I trust the police to figure this all out. She is going to find out who did this and bring them to justice."

Donald's eyes wandered up to Clara's face and seemed for the first time to register her presence.

"Nice to meet you, Miss Fitzgerald," he said out of habit, rather than real sentiment. His eyes glazed over again. "Why would anyone harm my father? He had no enemies."

The question appeared to be addressed to Maddock.

"That's what Miss Fitzgerald is going to try to discover," Maddock spoke in the gentle voice you adopt when addressing a distressed child. "She needs to ask you a question or two. It will help her."

Donald was trembling all over. Clara recognised shock when she saw it. She fetched up a blanket that was thrown over a nearby chair and slipped it around Donald's shoulders. Then she nudged the tea towards him again.

"Try to take a sip."

Donald didn't move. Clara sat down in a chair opposite, satisfied to discover it was as uncomfortable as she had suspected, and waited. Several minutes ticked by and then Donald's shivering eased, and he slowly reached out for the teacup and took the sip of tea as instructed. The tiny act seemed to be the breakthrough that brought him back to life.

The dazed look passed from his face, and his eyes focused on Clara. Shock and grief were being replaced by something else, something fiercer – rage.

"My father was a good man. He did not deserve this. All these years he has brought laughter and joy to the nation, he went to the Front and performed for the troops! This is not how a man like him should have ended his days!"

Donald was changing, waking up and becoming a young man with spirit and a forceful personality. Clara could finally see the true man beneath the layers of exhaustion and fear.

"Why would anyone do this to him?" Donald demanded of Clara.

"At this moment, I cannot offer you an answer to that question," Clara explained. "A message was left with your father. The single word 'thief' was written on the apron of the costume he was wearing. Do you know why anyone might have written such a thing?"

Clara avoided mentioning the message had been written using Stanley Hutson's blood, that seemed unnecessary.

"Thief?" Donald spat the word, his face had hardened, the slackness of shock had disappeared. "My father was no thief! What would he need to steal for? He had a fortune! We lived humbly, most of the time we were performing, and our accommodation was provided by the theatre company. We have a house, but we barely live in it. No servants, no point. Neither I, nor my father, have expensive tastes. My father had no need to steal anything!"

"The killer may not have been suggesting Mr Hutson stole money or even an object, it could be a metaphorical act of theft," Clara explained. "For instance, someone might feel that Mr Hutson stole a part in a production from them."

Donald snorted.

"My father did not audition for roles. He has not auditioned since 1882. People asked him to be in their cast. I can show you piles of letters requesting he take on this role or that. He has never asked for any part, he has had no need. He has never stolen a role from anyone, because there has never been an opportunity for it to happen," Donald was adamant. "Besides, actors replace other actors all the time. You won't last long in this business if you can't handle rejection."

"That is a fair point," Maddock interjected. "People are always being replaced for one reason or another. Take our Aladdin, Audrey Burns, she was recruited after our original Aladdin discovered she was pregnant. I've replaced people because they were late for rehearsals or did not get along with other cast members. As director that is my prerogative and you get a hard skin to the abuse it always produces. If anyone was worthy of revenge over a lost part in a panto, it should surely be me."

"Then that leaves us with no real explanation for the strange message, and yet the killer clearly thought it would mean something. They were making a point, trying to tell us something," Clara said. "I do hate it when criminals become cryptic."

Donald's anger had dimmed again as the reality of the situation slowly overcame him once more.

"How did my father die?" He asked.

Maddock cleared his throat and glanced pointedly at Clara. He was not going to be the one to answer the question. Clara sighed to herself, she hated this part.

"Mr Hutson was attacked with a shard of broken mirror. His throat was cut. I imagine it was very quick."

That was a lie, of course, Clara knew that bleeding out from the throat could take several minutes, depending on which veins the blade struck. However, no one wanted to hear that about a loved one's demise.

Donald rocked back on the sofa, he was fading back into a glazed stupor and Clara wanted to prevent that happening.

"When did you last see your father?" She asked quickly.

Donald blinked, the question rousing him from whatever dark place he had been falling into.

"It was just at the start of the interval. He had been in a foul mood since the first act, when that stupid man booed him," Donald spoke the word 'stupid' like it was a curse. "He stormed off stage and said he needed some air. He walked off without even changing his costume. I thought he might be going to get a drink. There is a pub just around the corner. Father didn't drink so often these days, but when something rattled his nerves, he would have to have a whisky to settle him again."

"You thought he went to the pub in his dame costume?" Clara asked, picturing what sort of reaction Stanley Hutson would have received walking into a pub in his full stage costume.

Donald shrugged.

"I didn't give it a thought," he admitted. "You forget the costumes are strange to others after a while. I'm so used to them. They are just clothes."

"When did you realise he had not returned?" Clara continued.

"When Mr Maddock came to the door of my father's dressing room and told me I was taking father's place. I assumed father had drunk too much. Sometimes that happened," Donald was sheepish at confessing his father's weakness. "Father would have these moments when he drank as much alcohol as he could during an interval and then end up good for nothing. He would still try to go on stage. We have had to lock him in a spare dressing room before now."

"That's true," Maddock confirmed. "When I could not find Donald after the fire, I assumed he had gone off to drink and hastened to prepare Donald to go on stage."

"You told the Inspector Hutson never missed a performance," Clara pointed out.

Maddock looked sheepish.

"He would always return in time, that was no lie. Just sometimes he was not fit to go on stage."

"All right," Clara said thoughtfully. "Donald, if you could describe to me what you did during the interval, it would help me to understand what might have been going on during that time."

Donald shrugged.

"After father stormed off, I went to the dressing room to prepare his next costume. I act as father's dresser when he is performing. There are eight costume changes in the second half alone. He usually comes to the dressing room, touches up his make-up and puts on the first dress for the second half. The other costumes are set up in order of when they need to be worn in the wings of the stage. When father did not appear within the first five minutes of the interval, I suspected I would have to take his place. I started to put on make-up."

"That was slightly presumptuous of you," Clara observed.

"Not really," Donald shook his head. "I knew my father's habits. If he disappeared during an interval he was drinking and he would not be fit for the second half."

"Stanley never quite freed himself from the demons of his alcoholism," Maddock added. "Most of the time he was fine, but occasionally he would binge. The trigger was usually something happening during a performance he could not cope with. That booing member of the audience was deeply unfortunate."

"Father can't cope with criticism," Donald said, sounding as if it was a mark of pride, not something to be ashamed of.

Clara also noticed he was still referring to his father as if he was alive.

"What about when the fire occurred?" She said to Donald.

"Maddock knocked on the dressing room door and said we needed to all go outside as there was a fire in the prop room," Donald replied. "I left with the others and stood outside until Maddock said it was all clear. I suppose it was a few minutes after I was back in the dressing room that he told me I was performing in the second half."

"Did you notice anyone missing as you stood outside? Or maybe someone appeared later than the others?" Clara persisted.

"Not really, I suppose I wasn't paying attention," Donald answered. "I did walk down the alley behind the theatre and look in the direction of the nearest pub, just in case I could see father. I didn't see him."

"And then you were back inside," Clara nodded, understanding. "What about Erikson?"

"What about him?"

"Did you notice him standing outside?"

Donald paused to think about that strange disruption to his evening. Slowly he responded.

"He was there. I glanced over and saw him with his arm around Audrey. She had rushed out in her Aladdin costume and was cold. Why?"

"His costume was one of the things that was burnt in the prop room," Maddock said before Clara could speak.

Donald did not know the significance of this and merely frowned.

"How does this help find my father's killer?" He demanded, his fury abruptly returning. "I want to know who did this, who hurt him! I want to wring their neck!"

"You are not alone," Maddock grumbled. "We…"

He was interrupted by a knock on the room door. A voice from outside echoed into the room.

"Mr Hutson, this is Inspector Park-Coombs of the Brighton police. I need to speak to you about your father."

Clara glanced at Maddock.

"He isn't going to be pleased we arrived first," she hissed.

Donald was quick to catch on.

"Go hide in the bedroom," he said, louder he called out. "Coming, Inspector."

Clara and Maddock disappeared into the other room and closed the door behind them. Maddock raised his eyebrows at her.

"Such subterfuge! It is like the plot of a bad play."

"You wouldn't be saying that if you had seen the

inspector when he is annoyed," Clara whispered back.

Maddock, despite the grimness of the day, managed to grin.

"Do you do this often?" He asked her.

Clara raised a finger to her lips and indicated they should be silent as in the next room they heard Donald greeting the inspector.

Chapter Eleven

The inspector was with Donald Hutson for almost an hour. Enough time for Clara and Maddock, stuck in the bedroom, to get restless. Maddock looked at his watch every few minutes, which started to irritate Clara considerably. She pulled a chair quietly to the door and listened to what the inspector and Donald said. She admitted to herself this was slightly underhanded, maybe even a touch deceitful towards Park-Coombs, but she was certain he would have lost his temper had he discovered she had reached Donald first. Not that it was her fault he had been lax with reaching out to Stanley's son.

Donald reacted to the news of his father's death, coming from the lips of the inspector this time, with a similar level of stunned shock as he had shown earlier, followed by outrage. His voice was low when he spoke, answering the inspector's many questions, most of which were in the same vein as Clara's. After forty-five minutes of intense talking, Maddock pulled a face and flopped back on the bed he was sitting on. Clara glared at him as he made the bed squeak, but there was no reaction from the other room.

Finally, the inspector thanked Donald for his time, spoke suitable words of condolence, and then departed.

Donald rose and opened the bedroom door.

"He's gone," he said solemnly. "He thinks I did it, I could tell from his voice."

Donald's face was flushed, as if he was feverish. Maddock stepped forward.

"Donald, I don't think that at all, I…"

"I would like to be left alone now," Donald said quietly. "Don't worry, I'll be at the theatre on time."

Then he pushed past them into the bedroom and shut the door behind him. Maddock looked grim. Clara took his arm and led him towards the door of the suite.

"He needs to grieve," she said. "This is difficult news to absorb."

"That damn inspector, making Donald think he is a suspect," Maddock's eyes flared with indignation. "I am glad I hired you, Miss Fitzgerald, you have to solve this mess before that inspector upsets my whole cast!"

Clara said nothing. The odds were, as she went about her job, she would upset a few people on the cast, especially if one proved to be a killer.

She separated from Maddock on the steps of the hotel, arranging to come to the theatre once all the cast were present. She had more people to interview, specifically Erikson, whose costume had been found so conveniently blood stained and burned. In the meantime, she was going to go home and update Tommy on what was happening.

Almost since she became a private detective, Tommy had been involved, largely in the background at first, but these days he was a partner in her work. Admittedly, Clara sometimes forgot she had a partner and carried on by herself. Not this time, however, there were lots of angles to this case and if she was going to discover who had a big enough grudge against Stanley Hutson to want him dead, she was going to need to know more about the man himself. And since Stanley spent most of his time in London, it seemed logical that someone was going to need to go to the capital and find out more.

She hoped Tommy would be amenable to a train trip,

while she continued delving closer to home.

Clara reached home just as a heavy rainstorm struck. She hastened in the door to be greeted by Bramble, their small poodle, who had distinctly wet paws. Clara sighed at the marks on her skirt, then patted the little dog's head.

"Where is your master?"

Bramble scampered off to the morning room, and Clara was about to follow him when she noticed there was a letter for her on the hall table. She grabbed it up and headed to Tommy. Her brother was sitting by a window, making use of the wan winter light, as he worked on some papers.

"What are you doing?"

"Compiling a list of potential suspects," Tommy announced, showing her the papers. "Seemed to me there were a lot of people present backstage last night. There are fifteen cast members, including the chorus and Donald Hutson who was understudy to his father. Then there was Maddock, the stage manager, numerous stagehands and the musicians, who have a room backstage to relax in during the interval. That is a long list of suspects. I thought we ought to start coordinating them all."

Clara looked at the long list of names and felt a wave of despondency. She rather wished he had not made the list. It made the task seem overwhelming.

"How did things go with Donald Hutson?" Tommy asked.

"He was upset, genuinely as far as I could tell. He says he was outside the theatre in the alley when the fire happened. If we assume the fire was a distraction to enable the killer to hide the body, then one way of eliminating people is to discover who was in that alleyway during the commotion."

Tommy nodded his agreement.

"You know what intrigues me?"

Clara motioned she did not and that he should carry on.

"The mysterious audience boo-er," Tommy declared. "Think about it, was he just a fool? Or did he have a reason for deliberately booing Mr Hutson? And if it was deliberate, does that mean he was somehow involved in the man's death."

"Finding out who the man was will be tricky. I never saw him."

"No," Tommy agreed. "But we know roughly where the sound came from and if we can work out who was seated in the area, someone must have noticed the man. That's the sort of thing people remember."

"You are talking about a lot of legwork for what is an unlikely lead," Clara said. "How would a member of the audience get backstage unnoticed?"

Tommy dipped his shoulders, a gesture that indicated he understood her thoughts.

"Just a coincidence then, that the night Stanley was killed someone disrupted his performance?"

"I won't say the possibility does not exist it was something else, but I think there are more promising avenues to pursue as yet," Clara answered him. "Which brings me to an idea I have started to formulate. I was wondering if you would be prepared to go to London and dig into Hutson's background? There is something there that sparked his murder. His son does not think he had any enemies and could not fathom what the word 'thief' meant, but there must be something that triggered this killing."

"You think there was someone in his past who held a grudge against Stanley," Tommy rubbed his chin. "You know, the world of theatricals is pretty cutthroat at times. I suppose someone could feel that Stanley Hutson wronged them, cost them a part or something?"

"It has to either be something pretty dramatic, or someone with a very disturbed nature to have led to him being violently murdered," Clara observed. "You know, it strikes me that this was a very deliberate crime. There was more meaning to this than just that bloody word on the apron. Hutson could have been killed at a location and time that would have been more convenient for the killer. Maybe as he walked home from the theatre. Certainly there must have been occasions when he was alone and the murderer could have struck and then vanished. Surely the worst time to kill him was during the middle of a performance, with lots of people around and a bare minimum of time before Hutson was missed?"

"You mean there could be a symbolism to Hutson being killed while he was playing a dame?"

"It has crossed my mind," Clara dropped onto the sofa and looked at the letter in her hand. "The Inspector seems to think Donald a promising suspect, at least that is what Donald believes."

"And you?"

Clara shrugged.

"He seemed upset over his father's death and shocked too. I like to think he is not a good enough actor to fake such emotion. I could be wrong."

Clara slipped her finger under the envelope flap and ripped open the upper edge. Tommy drew his papers back towards him.

"I was going to draw a plan of the theatre next, so we can look and see who would have been around the area where Hutson died. You are right, the killer took a big risk attacking the man when anyone could have discovered him. If Hutson had just cried out… Did he know his killer and allowed himself to be lured to the old pulley room, or was there another reason he was there?"

Clara was not listening to him. The letter in her hand had a distinctive script upon it, the script of a hand that has not always held a pen and to who the letters of the alphabet are not as familiar as the symbols of another written language.

Clara had been summoned by Brilliant Chang. He had something for her.

She folded up the letter and returned it to the envelope without saying a word, hoping her demeanour had not revealed what she had just read, or the nerves fluttering in her belly. She had made the decision early on to keep her arrangement with Chang a secret from Tommy and Annie, for their own sake, and she did not want to now ruin that.

"Are you listening?"

Tommy's demanding question broke her thoughts. Clara glanced up, her mind working fast.

"Donald Hutson is too big for the royal guard uniform," she threw in the comment, something that had rattled about her brain for some time. "We assumed the killer was wearing the uniform as it appeared to have stains of blood, and why burn it other than to hide the evidence? Donald Hutson takes after his father and would not have fitted into that uniform."

"Good point," Tommy agreed. "And the costume contained the name of Erikson, the man from the chorus. Seems case closed, doesn't it? Except you don't like things so simple."

Tommy was grinning at his sister. She did not take his words as an insult, or an implication that she saw complication where there was none.

"I am not ruling out the possibility that Erikson is that stupid, and failed to remove incriminating evidence about his role in killing Hutson," she replied. "It would be nice to have such a simple case. Trouble is, we don't know any motive for Erikson to kill Hutson. I'm going to speak to him this afternoon and maybe that will give us an idea. Oh, and Donald saw him in the alley with his arm around Aladdin during the fire, which makes it less likely he is the killer."

"But not impossible. Depends how quickly he hid the body after he set the fire."

Clara conceded that.

"Just seems a lot of trouble to go to, only to leave your very identifiable costume behind."

"He might have thought it would be destroyed entirely in the fire," Tommy reminded her. "People make mistakes."

"True," Clara nodded.

The envelope was feeling hot in her hand, as if the words were burning her. Chang had asked her to come to him as soon as she could. There was time now before she returned to the theatre.

"You are happy to go to London?" She asked Tommy to distract herself.

"Sounds like an opportunity to take Annie for a bit of Christmas shopping in the city. And I am sure if I pick the right theatre companies I shall learn a secret or two about Hutson. There is a list in the programme of who he has performed with before," Tommy began rifling through his papers again. "Good place to start. There is always someone prepared to speak ill of the dead."

Clara had risen from the sofa. She was calculating how long it would take to get to the address Chang had given her. Should she take a direct route or meander her way there? Depended on whether she feared being followed or not. Clara was not used to this level of skulduggery and wished she could say something to Tommy. He would no doubt have read about such activity in one of his many American books about private detectives, but she felt happier with him ignorant. The fewer people who knew about Chang and his sister, the better. In any case, Tommy might start saying this was all too dangerous, and it was dangerous. But she could see no other way to finally stop the mischief that was happening in Brighton.

If Chang was correct (and she had no reason to doubt he was) that his sister was behind the troubles, then things would likely get a lot worse before they got better, and the police would struggle to do anything. She had seen enough of how Chang operated to know there were certain levels of criminality the police could not penetrate, at least not easily.

In her darkest moments, she envisioned people being hurt trying to stop Jao Leong. Policemen being stabbed or shot, innocent people getting caught up in violence. If she could nip this all in the bud by working with Chang, then surely she had to at least try? Brighton was in danger of becoming a hotbed of gang crime, she could not allow that to happen.

"I am going to my office, I left some paperwork there," she said casually to Tommy over her shoulder, leaving the room before he responded.

He was already back on his list of suspects and only half-heard what she said. He mumbled something as she headed into the hallway, but she was not sure what it was.

Clara collected her hat, coat and an umbrella. Chang's rented house was some way out of town and would require her to change buses at least once. She doubted she would be followed, but, just in case, she would use the slow bus, which stopped at numerous villages along the way. She could even get off at one and wait for the next bus. Her hands were trembling as she walked outside and popped open her umbrella. What was she doing? She had promised everyone she would stay out of the alley gang business.

Then again, maybe it was because everyone kept saying she was over her head, and that this was a step too far for her, that she could not resist becoming involved. Clara's old stubbornness, the part of her that was known to get her into trouble, disliked being told she could not do something. She was trying to pretend that was not why she was helping Chang, but deep down she knew what this was really about.

She wanted to prove Park-Coombs wrong.

She wanted to prove she was not afraid.

Chapter Twelve

Several bus stops later, Clara found herself stood before an old house set on a slight rise in the land. The house was lonely and isolated, the nearest property was a rotting windmill, with only one sail, that looked as though it had not been used in decades. The windows of the house looked out on open pastures, one filled with black and white cows, and beyond them, just visible in the curve of the land, the rooftops of a village. If Chang's intention was to be as remote as possible while still within reach of civilisation, he had certainly achieved it.

The bus did not go past this house, instead the driver had dropped Clara at a crossroads and pointed her in the right direction. According to him, the house had been empty for years, rumours being that it was haunted, though he was more inclined to think damp and a leaking roof, along with a lack of internal plumbing, was the reason no one with any sense wanted to rent it. He could not fathom why Clara was heading in that direction, and when she remarked that a friend was renting the house she might as well have said she was going to commune with the fairies, the look on his face was so incredulous.

The house itself was early Victorian in appearance,

made from a greyish stone Clara did not recognise as common in the district and with the woodwork painted a similar shade of grey to match it. The paint had peeled and there were large parts of bare wood exposed to the elements. Clara thought about what the bus driver had said concerning damp; she suspected much of the wood was rotten too.

The house was set back from the road, a rough lawn stretching up the curve of the rise and badly in need of being cut. Straggly bushes obscured the ground floor windows and there were numerous thorny brambles looping over the garden wall and forming a dense hedge several feet thick. Stray ornamental shrubs battled through the decay to remind the world of what had once been. They were in their winter clothing, but Clara recognised the dead, bulbous heads of hydrangeas and the teardrop shaped leaves of old English tea roses.

Clara pushed open the worn iron gate, which creaked loudly on its hinges and stuck halfway. No amount of shoving, or even kicking, would entice it to open further and she had to lever herself through the narrow gap available to her, hoping she would not end up with rust marks on her clothes. The gravel path was rapidly being eaten up by the encroaching grass either side of it, but Clara could still hear its crunch beneath her feet. She wondered if anyone had noticed her arrival. If there were lookouts posted in the windows, they were well hidden. As far as she could tell, each aperture was shrouded by heavy curtains and not a soul peered out.

She was not surprised, however, that a man opened the front door and glowered at her long before she was close to the house's porch. He was one of Chang's thugs, an Englishman with a badly smashed nose, scars across his cheeks and a completely bald head. One of his eyes had a glassy look, that suggested he had sustained some permanent injury to it. He was dressed in a dark suit, well cut and not what you might expect such a man to wear. Clara guessed Chang made sure his highest-ranking men dressed smartly.

The man had not asked her anything, just scowled at her. Clara stopped before him and refused to speak first. She had no idea who he was or how much he knew about her arrangement with Chang. Silence seemed wisest until she had properly assessed the situation. The man's scowl deepened, his mouth twisting into a grimace, still Clara waited for him to make his move. She stood upright before him, her face neutral and her hands before her showing she was unarmed. The stalemate seemed to drag on for a considerable time, both reaching a stage where it would feel awkward to say something. Neither wanted to lose face before the other.

At last the thug got impatient.

"We don't want any Bible passages, or knitted socks or clothes pegs, or anything else you are trying to hock."

Clara snorted.

"Do I look like I sell socks or clothes pegs? As for distributing Bible passages, I think if that was my intention, I would have unloaded my entire lot on you and disappeared as quickly as possible," Clara gave the house a careful look. "Besides, everyone thinks this house is unoccupied. Why would they come to an empty house to sell anything?"

"All right, so you are clever," the thug snarled. "How do you know we are here?"

He had gone from annoyed to threatening in a matter of seconds. Clara decided it was time to answer him and stop playing games.

"Mr Chang sent for me," she produced the letter from her handbag and showed it to him.

"Oh, so you are Clara Fitzgerald," the thug's demeanour changed again, this time mellowing. "Why didn't you just say?"

"I was waiting for you to ask," Clara replied simply.

The thug muttered something rude under his breath.

"You could have been in a lot of trouble, you get that?"

"That is a normal state of affairs for me," Clara said with

the hint of a smile. "I believe that is why Mr Chang employed me."

The thug's scowl had returned.

"I don't like women with attitude."

"And I don't like gentlemen who scowl all the time, therefore we are even. Can I see Mr Chang now? I do have other things to get on with, and this house is miles outside of Brighton. Do you know how many buses I was required to take to get here?"

"You sound like my sister," the thug grumbled, moving back so Clara could step into the house. "And I don't speak to her."

"Does that please your sister?" Clara asked in her sweetest tone.

The thug cast her a look.

"If you weren't a guest of Mr Chang…"

"Yes, yes, you would threaten me with violence," Clara brushed off the comment. "This is not my first encounter with men of your calibre, Mr…?"

"His name is Rodney Blunt," Brilliant Chang's voice purred from his mouth as he stared at them both in amusement. He had appeared at the doorway of a downstairs room. How long he had been watching the exchange was difficult to say. "Rodney, the reason I have always had a soft spot for Miss Fitzgerald is her peculiarly irritating nature. She masks her fear with sarcasm. Also, she is surprisingly stubborn in the face of danger, it makes her quite belligerent."

Clara was unsure if she was being complimented or insulted. She chose not to respond.

"Rodney is my bodyguard, Miss Fitzgerald, and very good at it too. I consider him exceptionally loyal; it is his most endearing quality. Please do not upset him, we are all on the same side, after all," Chang continued.

Clara cast a look at Rodney who was managing to look both confused and surly at the same time. She decided to ease the tension.

"Nice to meet you Mr Blunt," she held out her hand to

the baffled bodyguard.

"Yeah, well..." Blunt took her hand a little harder than necessary and shook it.

She was aware of the implication; Blunt wanted her to know that he was a tough and nasty man, and she was only being tolerated because Chang needed her.

"Come into my sitting room, Miss Fitzgerald," Chang ushered her through the doorway and Rodney disappeared back to his duties. Chang made sure the door behind them was shut. "I have attempted to make this place somewhat bearable. You will forgive its shabbiness, under the circumstances."

The room was long and once would have been a stunning reception room, but now the big bay window was masked by the overgrown garden and the wallpaper was faded and peeling from the walls. Plaster was missing from the ceiling, revealing the joists of the floor above. The room was dark and smelt of damp. Chang had brought his own furniture and the modernistic pieces sat uncomfortably in the middle of the sullen decay.

"I'll be glad to get back to London," Chang read her mind, shuddering at the sight of the room, as if he had just seen it afresh. "But this serves my purpose. Remote, with easy views of all the approaches and few knowing anyone is even here. Its terribleness is all part of the charm."

"You are making the best of things, then?"

"What else can I do, Miss Fitzgerald?"

Clara walked to the old fireplace and noticed that a dead pigeon lay in the hearth.

"Why did you send for me?"

"I have news," Chang sighed. "But it is not of a good nature."

Clara turned back to him. There was an iciness to the room that made her shiver. Chang was wearing a thick fur coat. Lighting a fire would give away his presence, so he was bearing up under the conditions. Clara thought the situation must grind on his nerves, considering he was used to luxury and comfort. He had been brought to this impasse by his sister and she could see the resentment festering in him.

"Have you located your sister?" Clara asked.

"No," Chang shook his head. "Jao is still hidden from me. I have had to move carefully to avoid revealing myself. It is a tricky business. However, I have discovered something that I felt it was imperative you know."

Clara felt worried now. She stepped a little closer.

"You have my attention."

"Good, because my quiet investigations have revealed that Jao has a policeman in her pocket. She is paying someone to cover up her tracks. I'm afraid, I suspect this person is highly placed, probably Inspector Park-Coombs himself."

Clara could not stifle the laugh that escaped her lips.

"Mr Chang, while I am not fool enough to suppose that corruption does not exist within the police force, after all, you had a policeman, as you put it, in your pocket, but to suppose Park-Coombs the traitor, well, it defies all reason."

Chang looked at her sadly.

"I had feared you would say as much. The inspector has been your friend these past years. But no man is immune to corruption, in one form or another. After all," Chang looked at her darkly, "you are prepared to ignore who I am and work for me if it suits your own ends. Some could call you corrupt."

Clara was staggered by the implication, but when the initial shock passed, she saw, with alarming clarity, how accurate his statement was. Anyone looking at her actions from a distance might perceive she was corrupt, working with a criminal she should be summoning the police to arrest. She had convinced herself it was all for the greater good, but she had to admit it was a morally vague situation. Even so, there was a difference in working with a criminal to destroy another and helping such a fiend for profit.

"The circumstances are different," Clara said, a touch defensive. "In any case, Park-Coombs is an honest man and would not accept money from anyone to cover up a crime."

"Perhaps you are right," Chang conceded, but there was an air of disbelief in his tone. "But my point remains. The talk among Jao's people and those who associate with them is that a policeman is being paid off. That is why no progress is being made with arrests."

Clara had a sick feeling in her stomach as Chang finished speaking. It reminded her too painfully of a previous case where a corrupt policeman had almost murdered another copper. Chang had been behind that scandal, but she had not been able to touch him. If anyone was to know about dubious policemen it was Chang, but could he be saying these things to unsettle her? She still didn't entirely trust him, but what would he gain from trying to trick her?

"How reliable is this information?" She asked.

"I believe it," Chang shrugged. "Jao was present and knew of my operations in Brighton. She knew I was paying a policeman and saw the advantages. I imagine she decided to try the same. This situation is big Clara, bigger than I first imagined. If Jao is allowed to persist, then she will turn Brighton into her town and there won't be an honest copper left to stop her."

Clara might have accused him of being overly dramatic, but she saw the look on his face, one that was full of despair and shock. He had also slipped and used her first name, when normally he was carefully formal with her. The slip hinted at his emotional turmoil and the anxiety that was bubbling beneath the surface.

"If Jao carries on, she will be able to seriously threaten your organisation," Clara nipped to the root of the matter. "Brighton and London have always had strong ties, what happens in one, tends to affect the other, and no more so than when it comes to criminal activity. For years now we have seen the gangsters of London come to town for their 'holidays' and to run their businesses by the sea. But they have always left again. Now we have a permanent gang, and one that if it is allowed to grow will start to cause problems for the London gangsters who like to come to

Brighton."

Chang was nodding along.

"And when a gangster is threatened, he reacts violently," he said. "Jao is challenging the status quo and that can only lead to an all-out war. Brighton will be the battleground. Neither of us want that."

Clara knew what he was saying. The gangs of London had stayed largely in their own territories, occasionally violence erupted and turf wars ensued, but it was mainly kept in check by the gangs' various alliances. Jao was above all that, coming at things from a position of isolation, wanting to destroy them all. And all the innocents of Brighton would suffer as a consequence.

Jao was insane, she didn't understand the politics of the criminal underworld, but that did not change things.

"Thank you for the information," Clara told Chang without revealing the turmoil it had created within her.

"I hope you can do something about it," Chang replied, his face grim. "As much as I hate to admit it, we need the police and we can't afford for them to be corrupt."

Clara had no more to say. What could she anyway? She hoped he was wrong, that the information had somehow been incorrect.

She feared, however, that he was right.

Chapter Thirteen

Clara felt a strange sense of dread looming over her as she headed for the theatre. The thought that another policeman had forgotten his duty and taken to accepting bribes was upsetting enough, to suppose that policeman could be the inspector was simply shocking.

Park-Coombs and Clara had worked together since 1920, an initially challenging relationship, where neither quite trusted the other, developed into a friendship that, though sometimes turbulent, had certainly been mutually beneficial. They had worked together on numerous cases and Clara had never once doubted the inspector. Why should she begin now? Because of a sly comment from Chang? She had no way of knowing how reliable the information he had received was, or how honest he was being with her. She had far less reason to trust him than she did the inspector.

Yet…

There was this nag at the back of her mind. How quickly and with frightening determination had Park-Coombs sought to condemn Private Peterson in a murder that was actually committed by this new gang. He had spoken about pressure from above to resolve the case – had that been the truth? And was it purely concern for her wellbeing that had caused him to cut her off from the gang investigation entirely? She had accepted that at first, having been shaken and scared by her experiences. Now, with time mellowing what had happened and giving her a chance to work up her anger, she felt frustrated at being on the outside looking in.

If Park-Coombs wanted to keep her from discovering the truth, the best way he could do so was to tell her it was not safe, that he was protecting her. And yet that was also the action of a good friend.

Clara mentally shook herself. All this gang business was warping her thinking. Park-Coombs was a good policeman and she would not have Chang making her doubt that. She feared there was corruption within the force, for that would explain how Jao had been able to find her feet in Brighton with no one taking any notice, but it was not the inspector. It had to either be a subordinate or, worse, someone senior to him.

Clara blinked as the thought struck her like cold water to the face. Yes, if Jao had gone beyond her brother's level of corruption and bribed a senior police official rather than just a constable, that would be very serious indeed. It would also explain that 'pressure' Park-Coombs had felt to arrest Peterson. However, as tantalising as the idea was, Clara had no idea how she could go about unravelling such a mess, at least not at that moment.

It was almost something of a relief to arrive at the theatre and be able to concentrate on a murder that was not swamped by conspiracy and nefarious criminal dealings. Well, at least she hoped that was the case.

Tommy was waiting for her on the steps of the theatre.

"Annie was concerned you missed lunch," he said, handing her a parcel wrapped in greaseproof paper.

Clara opened it to find two thickly cut slices of bread sandwiching a portion of ox tongue. There was a liberal spread of mustard, just as Clara liked it. She smiled.

"I got distracted."

"I supposed as much. Lots of paperwork at your office?"

Clara sensed a hint of something in his tone. Her brother always seemed to know when she was lying. She just shrugged her shoulders as she bit into one half of the sandwich. A full mouth was always a good excuse not to answer a question. Still giving her a suspicious look, Tommy walked with her to the theatre doors and they were allowed in by Mr Maddock, who was waiting impatiently.

"All the cast are here, including Donald. I have had to break the news to them of Stanley's death. It's put the wind up them," Maddock explained as he escorted them through to the auditorium. "I don't think we shall get much of a rehearsal today. Besides, I fear the inspector shall arrive at any moment to question everyone."

Maddock was beginning to look very careworn; it was not just the murder of a friend, bad as that was, it was the fear that he would not be able to hold the company together and salvage the pantomime. While grief for a friend was a powerful emotion, life went on, and Maddock was envisioning debt and bankruptcy if the panto failed. Such immediate concerns were overshadowing the terrible thing that had happened the night before, and Clara could not blame him. There was nothing more terrifying than the thought of losing the roof over your head and not being able to eat.

"Mr Maddock, please do not fret, I intend to do everything in my power to resolve this matter swiftly."

Maddock looked at Clara, a mix of gratitude and despair on his face, the warring feelings twitching his lips into odd shapes.

"You are my only hope, Miss Fitzgerald," he declared. "My only hope."

The pantomime cast were all assembled on the stage, where they had received the news of Stanley Hutson's death. They were clustered in small groups of two and three, some talking in low whispers, others just standing and looking bleak. Aladdin was sitting on the very edge of the stage, hands either side of her and head forward as she battled her inner thoughts. The only other person sitting alone was Donald, who was in one of the red velvet auditorium chairs, staring at the carpet and ignoring everyone else.

Maddock took a deep breath as he approached the stage and put on as bright and positive a face as he could.

"Everyone, this is Miss Clara Fitzgerald. She is a private detective and is going to find out who hurt poor Stanley," Maddock's voice cracked a little as he spoke the dead man's name. "I know you will all be most cooperative with her."

No one stirred among the cast of actors. Clara scanned her eyes across the stage.

"Mr Maddock has hired me to give Mr Hutson justice. This is a terrible thing to have happened, but I will work tirelessly to find answers. I will need to speak to you all, probably more than once, to understand what occurred last night. You can also always seek me out, if you need to. I will listen to any concerns you have, and you can tell me anything. If you want to just talk, that is fine too. Please consider me someone you can confide in, if you need to," Clara paused and cast another look across the assembled company. A few people were looking at her, while the rest seemed lost in their own sombre thoughts. "Naturally the police are involved in this matter and will wish to speak to you at some point. While I work with the police, consider me an independent agent. If I find that the police are going in the wrong direction, I shall certainly say so. My only purpose is to find out the truth.

"Lastly, I am not someone who will blab information to the press. I have little time for the newspapers, and I know how to hold my tongue. If you have a secret you wish to tell me, it shall go no further, unless it is vitally important to solving the crime. You can trust me."

Maddock clapped his hands.

"Right, as rehearsals are something of a washout today, I suggest we allow Miss Fitzgerald to ask a few questions," he said.

Donald Hutson had lifted his head and was listening with narrowed eyes. Clara guessed he was already sick of questions.

"Firstly, I would like to establish who was the last person to see Mr Hutson before he disappeared," Clara strode towards the stage, she had been careful to avoid using the word murdered, as she was trying to keep everyone calm. "I know you all ended up in the alley when the fire broke out, but which of you saw Mr Hutson before then?"

A series of hands slowly reached into the air, hesitant and reluctant, the act of one caused others to follow suit.

"Several people were in the final scene before the interval," Maddock interjected helpfully. "Let's see, the last scene involves Aladdin, Buttons, Princess Zara and the chorus. Perhaps those people could step forward?"

Eight people stepped forward. The three principal actors, and the five members of the chorus who were involved in that scene. That included three men and two women. However, one of the male chorus put up his hand as he reached the edge of the stage.

"Erikson?" Maddock said the man's name.

Clara's eyes shot to the man whose costume had been covered in blood before being consumed by fire.

"Mr Maddock, I'm afraid I was not present in that scene last night," Erikson said sheepishly.

Maddock stared at him.

"Why ever not?"

Erikson glanced at his chorus fellows and looked decidedly unhappy.

"I took ill in the second scene," he confessed slowly. "Must have been something I ate. I spent the majority of the first half in the toilet. I had only just returned when the fire happened, and we all went to the alley."

Clara wondered if this was true, or a good cover story.

"Can anyone confirm you were unwell?" She asked Erikson.

"I can confirm he was in the toilet most of the night," another of the male chorus interrupted. "I went to use the loo myself and found him locked in there groaning. We had to perform the last scene minus one royal guard."

Clara shot a look at Maddock who blanched as the significance became plain to him.

"Erikson, in the second scene you play a street vendor, I believe?" He asked.

"Yes, Mr Maddock," Erikson ducked his head, a red flush coming to his cheeks. "I'm very sorry, but the costume was somewhat… stained. I was so ashamed, I took it home to wash myself. I brought it back tonight."

"I saw him in the alley in the street vendor costume," Donald spoke up in a dismal voice. "I remember that."

"Are you feeling better now, Erikson?" Maddock asked his cast member.

"I do," Erikson nodded. "I've never missed a performance before, you know I haven't. But then, I have never felt that ill before. I'll be fine to perform today."

"Well, you won't be in the palace scenes," Maddock remarked without thinking.

"But, Mr Maddock, it was not my fault..."

Maddock cut off the fraught actor.

"That was not what I meant," he was about to offer further explanation when Clara jumped in.

"During the fire, your costume was badly burned, Mr Erikson," she said.

"What?" Erikson stared at her as if she was speaking another language. "I don't understand, the fire was in the prop room, how did it damage my costume?"

"Your costume was also in the prop room," Maddock said calmly. "I suppose you don't know how it got there?"

"No," Erikson was baffled. "It was meant to be backstage, with the others, ready for a quick change."

There was no need to pursue the matter further. Clara was satisfied by Erikson's reaction that he had no idea about the burnt costume, and while Donald's testimony that Erikson was in his street vendor outfit in the alley, could be a red herring – Erikson had to switch costume when he burned the bloodstained one – the witness who heard him in the toilet added weight to the man's story.

"Have you got the street vendor costume?" Clara asked.

Erikson gave a small nod.

"Can I see it?"

The actor looked surprised by the question. After a moment he strode off the stage and then returned with a canvas bag in the style of a satchel. He unfastened two catches, rummaged among pages of script, stage make-up and several combs, before producing the costume. It was still a little damp from Erikson's attempts to wash it.

"I wasn't as successful as I had hoped," Erikson admitted, as Clara held up the costume.

"Cleaning stains from fabric is a skilled business," Clara reassured him. "Soap and water are not always enough."

The street vendor costume consisted of a pair of white pantaloon trousers with a yellow sash, matched by a light shirt with puffed sleeves and a red waistcoat. There were faint stains on both the shirt tails and the pantaloons that indicated how ill Erikson had been. He winced as Clara examined them.

"You had a rough night, Mr Erikson," Clara handed back the costume, convinced the man had been as ill as he said, and sorry she had had to embarrass him before the others.

"I don't think I have ever felt that ill in my life before," Erikson grimaced. "You don't realise how far to the back of the theatre those toilets are until you are in desperate need. I was lucky to survive the second scene."

"I did think you smelt a little when we…" Audrey Burns, or rather Aladdin, started to speak then stopped herself. "Of course, with that awful smoke stench in my nose I hardly considered it."

The red hue on Erikson's cheeks deepened. Clara decided it was time to stop tormenting the poor man.

"When did you last see your royal guard costume?"

Clara asked him instead.

Erikson shrugged.

"During the afternoon matinee. I wore it in the very last scene, when Aladdin and Zara get married in the palace. Then I put it on its hanger and left it on the rail backstage, ready for the next performance."

"You didn't notice it that evening?"

"No time to look," Erikson replied. "The dressers are supposed to keep track of the costumes."

"Yes, that's correct," Maddock added. "They make sure all the costumes are present and in the order they are required on the rail before each performance. It makes things run far more smoothly."

That made sense to Clara, and she would need to speak to the dressers and see if they had noticed the costume missing. In the meantime, she wanted an answer to her original question – who was the last to see Stanley Hutson alive?

After considerable discussion, the cast agreed that that honour went to Mervyn Baldry, who played Buttons. He had followed Stanley off the stage and had last seen him in the backstage corridor before he went to his dressing room.

"And in a fine state he was," Baldry said. "Ranting about that person who booed him, as if it was deliberate. I tried to talk to him, but you could never get Stanley to see sense when he was riled. He walked away from me."

"In which direction?" Clara pressed him.

Baldry considered this for a moment, conjuring a mental image of the theatre in his mind.

"Actually, that was a little odd now I think of it," he mused. "He walked away from his dressing room. He went the wrong direction."

Chapter Fourteen

There were two dressers working backstage during pantomime season, with so many costumes and quick changes required, a single dresser was not enough.

"And Mr Hutson near enough needs a dresser just to himself," Maud Dobbins explained to Clara. She was blissfully unaware that Mr Hutson was dead. "He has so many costumes and they are all so big!"

She expanded her arms to indicate the elaborate skirt of one of Mr Hutson's many dame outfits.

"They have all these bits attached to them. One has toy wooden ships fixed to the skirt, another has giant pretend lollipops and sweets sewn to the cloth. That's for the scene where Mr Hutson casts sweets into the audience."

"Not to mention the wigs," piped up Dolores Smith, the second dresser. "We have to keep them on a special stand, and they can be quite the effort to fix securely to Mr Hutson's head. We have this sticky tape we can use, but it gives the poor man a terrible rash and is ghastly to get off between changes."

Maud and Dolores were both in their forties and had worked with the company for the last decade or so. Dolores had taken the job in 1910, when another dresser retired.

Maud had arrived in 1912. They had been firm friends ever since.

Though neither was highly educated, they were intelligent women who paid attention to their surroundings and enjoyed watching the plays performed. They were also both skilled seamstresses, a necessary talent when disaster could strike a costume at any moment.

Maud, the slightly younger of the two women, had been put in charge of ensuring Hutson's costumes were always ready to wear. While Donald was his father's personal dresser, the women made sure everything was ready for each change. They took pride in their work.

"That reminds me, Mr Maddock, I am missing a costume. I have looked all over for it and asked the ladies who do the laundry. They say they have not seen it. It is the cook's costume, the one with yellow stripes and a white pinny," she said to the director.

Care had been taken to remove Mr Hutson long before the laundry ladies came to collect the soiled costumes. Maddock had persuaded the police that it was best if only a handful of people knew about the actor's death. As far as the laundresses were concerned, it was just another day of collecting clothes to wash.

"There was an issue with that particular costume," Maddock said uneasily to Maud. Clara wondered if he was going to attempt to keep up the pretence that Hutson was alive. "We shall have to consider a replacement. Also, Donald Hutson will be taking over the dame role from this afternoon."

Maud did not seem unsettled by this remark.

"Oh, like last night. Then we shall need to adjust the costumes. He isn't as comfortably built as his father."

Clara was amused at how politely she avoided calling Stanley Hutson fat. Maud and Dolores were too discreet to ask the obvious question; why was Donald replacing his father? They were the sort of ladies who assumed that if they needed to know something they would be told about it, and that was why they were perfect for backstage work where all manner of scandalous secrets were bandying about. Maud and Dolores knew how to keep their mouths shut and their noses out of others' business. Which was delightful for the actors, and a nuisance to Clara.

"You should know," Maddock cleared his throat nervously, "Mr Hutson has suffered an accident and, well, he passed away last night."

The dressers both froze as the news hit them, but there were no hysterics or signs they were taking the revelation badly. They were saddened, but they were also robust ladies.

"That is terrible for poor Donald," Dolores said with appropriate sympathy to her voice. "And to think he must take over his father's role."

"We must make sure there is lots of hot tea ready for him between scenes, Dolores," Maud told her friend with firm resolve. "And those lemon biscuits he likes. He will need the sugar."

"Yes, my dear, and we shall run everything as smoothly as possible, for his sake."

"What of the other costumes?" Maddock asked them. "Are they all accounted for?"

It was a leading question, one to which he knew the answer very well.

"Now you mention it, we are missing a costume for Mr Erikson," Dolores replied. "His street vendor outfit."

"Mr Erikson was taken unwell last night and, ah, his street vendor costume became rather stained," Mr Maddock pulled a face as he explained. "Also, his royal guard uniform appears to have been burned in that silly fire last night."

The women exchanged glances again.

"That happened in the prop room," Dolores said. "What was his costume doing in the prop room?"

"You ladies did not take it there? Perhaps for repairs?" Clara suggested.

"Any repairs we do in our little sewing room," Maud told her. "Besides, the fire happened in the interval and the uniform should have been back on the rail."

Maud suddenly paused and a flicker of insight filled her eyes.

"That was why the costumes didn't tally, Dolores! I told you I was sure one was missing, but I couldn't think which one it was," Maud turned her attention back to Clara. "There are so many costumes and the chorus have a lot of similar ones, so it is harder to remember them all. Each rail holds twenty outfits and the chorus have four rails alone, they have so many costume changes and only a few of the outfits are reused more than once. I said to Dolores last night, I was sure there should be thirty-four costumes on the chorus rails, but I could count only thirty-three. We went through the rails repeatedly, trying to work out what was missing and could not."

"I thought Maud had made a mistake," Dolores confessed with a slight look of shame in her eyes. "She is not the sort to make errors, but when we could not think which costume was missing, it seemed we must have at some point miscounted the number of chorus clothes. Bear in mind, with all the principal costumes and Mr Hutson's many changes, we have close to a hundred outfits to keep track of."

"I was worrying all night, waiting for the moment when we would discover a costume was missing, but it never happened. So, I came to the conclusion I had been mistaken on the number," Maud added. "Now I know I was not mistaken and the reason the missing costume was not discovered was because its wearer was not performing."

Maud looked satisfied with herself. She had been vindicated.

"I still don't understand, why was the costume taken and put in the prop room?" Dolores looked baffled.

"Did you notice anyone who should not have been there walking among the costume rails yesterday afternoon?" Clara asked.

Again, the ladies exchanged a look.

"I can't say we did," Dolores spoke up for them. "Miss

Burns' Aladdin costume needed some repairs. I took it away to work on immediately after the performance."

"I placed all the costumes on their rails in the order required," Maud said. "Everything was ready for the evening performance."

"You didn't notice there was a guard uniform missing then?" Clara asked.

Maud frowned. She took pride in her work and it pained her that a costume had gone missing right from under her nose.

"Now you mention it…" she glanced over to the rails to her right. They were stood in the wings of the theatre, among the many costumes. The ladies had been primed for the afternoon's performance. "Yes! There were three guard uniforms! That is why I was confused later on, Dolores! I counted four guard costumes back onto the rail, but when we returned that evening, there were only three!"

Everyone stared at the offending rail where the three surviving guard uniforms hung innocently. Clara was beginning to see how the murderer had tried to throw blame onto Erikson, but the missing costume, long gone before Erikson was due to go onstage, was the final proof that he had not been behind the killing. They had been meant to assume Erikson had worn the costume in the scene before the interval, then came off stage and murdered Hutson in a fit of rage. There would have been no need for Erikson to steal his costume before the performance if he intended to be wearing it when he killed Hutson. In fact, the deeper she looked, the more Clara concluded that this had been a carefully planned act of violence, made to look like something done on the spur of the moment.

Having obtained all she could from the dressers, Clara returned to the auditorium where Tommy had been trying to gather information from the shocked cast. He gave Clara a tight-lipped smile as she returned.

"They pretty much all vouch for one another," he said as she approached. "They all say they were in the alley during the fire, though I don't take that at face value.

People make mistakes about these things all the time and misremember. If someone says firmly enough they were in such-and-such a place at such-and-such a time, people have a tendency to suddenly recall them being there, even if it is not true. Memory is a tricky business."

"What about Mervyn Baldry? Did he remember anything else about seeing Hutson walk away?"

"Nothing terribly insightful," Tommy shrugged. "He said Stanley was in a foul mood and when he walked away he was muttering to himself. Mervyn did not think about the fact he was going the wrong way until you questioned him. He was busy getting back to his dressing room, downing a cup of tea and a sandwich, and retouching his make-up for the second half."

Another dead end. Clara was beginning to think the killer was either very cunning, or extremely lucky that no one had noticed anything odd.

"Did you ask them about the fire?"

"I did. Most of them knew nothing about it until Maddock knocked on their dressing room doors and urgently told them to get out of the theatre. Miss Allen, however, recalls smelling smoke and she thinks she might have seen someone around the prop room, but it was only a glance," Tommy was flicking through the notes he had quickly taken. "She suffers from cramp in her feet, and she was having an episode, as she states it, which came on at the end of the scene before the interval. She was walking up and down the corridor to ease it, when she noticed someone around the prop room. You can see the door from the corridor. However, she was not paying a great deal of attention. She thinks it might have been a man, as they seemed tall. She just thought it was one of the stagehands."

"That is what the killer was banking on, everyone being so busy and distracted, they took no heed of someone committing a crime under their noses," Clara thought it had been a risky, but clever ploy on the murderer's part. "Did you ask them if anyone had a grudge against Hutson?"

Tommy's face took on a despondent frown.

"They are all saying he was very loved by his fellow actors and the audience alike. I think they are being tactful and don't want to speak ill of the dead."

"I hate it when people do that," Clara grumbled. "They think they are being respectful, but really it helps shield the killer. Someone detested Mr Hutson enough to go out of their way to commit a bloody murder."

Clara cast her gaze across the pantomime cast. Mr Maddock was attempting to rally them for the afternoon matinee and she had no doubt he would succeed – the actor's mantra was to carry on no matter what.

"How many of the cast had worked with Hutson before?" She wondered to herself.

"I didn't ask that specifically, but I could garner from what they all said that for many of them this was their first time working with Hutson," Tommy answered her. "Mervyn Baldry had worked with Hutson on several occasions, but this was the first time since his return to the stage. Neither of the principal ladies said they had worked with Hutson before, but the fellow who plays the evil vizier did some pantomime in the early 1900s alongside Hutson. Donald might be able to offer more insight."

Clara was thoughtful for a while, then she made up her mind.

"Let's leave them in peace for the time being. Someone might think of something if we give them the chance. In the meantime, we need to find out more about Stanley Hutson's past."

"You are definitely ruling out Donald?" Tommy asked.

Clara's eyes drifted to the young man about to take over his father's role.

"He could never have fitted the guard uniform," she observed. "We also need to find out what caused Erikson to become unwell, that was not a coincidence."

"He doesn't have a clue, himself," Tommy said. "He ate the same food as several other members of the cast that evening, and they were all fine."

"What about food or drink he consumed here at the theatre?"

"He says he only drank tea from an urn in the communal dressing room."

Clara narrowed her eyes in Erikson's direction.

"Well, we have to believe him for the moment, but my suspicion is he drank or ate something different to the others. He either does not recall it or is lying about it."

"Why would he lie?" Tommy looked confused.

Clara gave him a sombre smile.

"Oh, lots of reasons. Maybe what he consumed he is not allowed before a performance? Or maybe he was given it by someone who he does not want to get into trouble."

Clara was watching the stage where Erikson was stood extremely close to Audrey Burns. Their hands were almost touching and their proximity was not by chance. Donald had mentioned they had been stood together in the alley and Erikson had his arm around Audrey. Were they lovers? They certainly seemed close.

Deciding there was no more to be done for the moment, Clara and Tommy left the theatre. Early arrivals for the afternoon performance were beginning to gather in the foyer. As Clara walked down the front steps, she noticed Park-Coombs heading towards her.

"The matinee is starting shortly, you won't have much luck questioning anyone," she said to him as their paths crossed.

The inspector had a miserable look on his face, as if he was doing something he really did not want to.

"I'm not here to ask anyone questions," he sighed deeply. "I'm here to arrest Mervyn Baldry."

Chapter Fifteen

"He could have at least waited until after the performance," Maddock's eyes sparkled as if he was perilously close to shedding tears. The strain of the last few days was clearly taking its toll.

They were stood at the backstage door that led to the alley. Inspector Park-Coombs had graciously agreed to escort Mervyn out the back, rather than through the foyer where the unfortunate man in full Buttons costume would be seen by the gathering audience. He had also agreed not to handcuff Mervyn, who had been cooperative with the police, while denying all their charges.

"It makes no sense," Maddock whimpered.

But to Clara it did make a certain, imperfect sense. Mervyn had admitted to being the last person to see Stanley Hutson alive and, as it turned out, they had some unpleasant history that offered him a motive. The inspector had made a few telephone calls to his colleagues in London, to see if any trouble involving Hutson had appeared on their radars. That was when he discovered that in 1913, the last time in nearly a decade that Mervyn Baldry had walked the boards, there had been a major upset during a performance of Red Riding Hood.

Mervyn had attacked Stanley Hutson with a prop sword. The weapon was no use for stabbing or slashing, but it was heavy enough that when Mervyn battered it repeatedly over Hutson's head he caused the dame to pass out. Worse still, the assault occurred within sight of the audience, though off to one side in the wings. There had been no question of the police being called. However, Hutson refused to press charges against Mervyn and though the authorities could have pursued the matter, it was ultimately agreed that nothing further would be done. Mervyn lost his role as Buttons in the pantomime and disappeared from the theatre scene altogether, reinventing himself for the new media of radio.

Yet, an argument that occurred nine years ago was hardly cause to arrest Mervyn. No, the nail in the coffin, so to speak, was that when Dr Deáth conducted his autopsy on Hutson he discovered the man was clutching a very distinctive button in his closed hand. A button from Buttons. When Park-Coombs had confronted Mervyn backstage, it had taken only a moment to identify where a button had been lost and a replacement, that did not match the others, had been sewn on. Mervyn could not explain how his lost button had ended up in Hutson's hand.

Nor could he answer why a witness, who the inspector would not name, had walked into the police station that morning and insisted they had seen Mervyn follow Hutson as they came off stage and appeared angry. It was all very damning and Mervyn had not been able to offer any innocent explanations for the evidence against him.

"Let's go inside and try to make some sense of this," Clara said gently to Maddock. "The pantomime will carry on without you for a bit."

Maddock was too stunned to argue. The formerly under-suspicion Erikson had been Mervyn's understudy and had taken over as Buttons. Being of the same height and build as the actor, he fitted Mervyn's costumes without adjustments, which also meant that Mervyn could fit his.

Clara had not mentioned that aloud, as it was another piece of circumstantial evidence that could condemn Mervyn.

She ushered Maddock to his temporary office in one of the smaller dressing rooms. Tommy was waiting for them. He gave Clara a hopeful look, but she quickly shook her head. They had at first thought they could persuade the inspector he was wrong, but even Clara could not argue with what Park-Coombs had presented to her. She had to admit, there looked a fair possibility that Mervyn was the killer and this case had been solved right under Clara's nose.

As Maddock sat down in a chair, Tommy presented him with a glass of brandy he had fetched from the upstairs bar. Maddock took a deep drink and choked.

"Well, what do we make of it all?" Tommy asked Clara.

She sat down on a padded stool and tried to focus on the case again.

"Much of the evidence against Mervyn is circumstantial," she began. "Though, we both know that many a murderer has been convicted on similar circumstantial evidence. The really damning part is that Mervyn attacked Hutson once before. Whichever way you look at that, it makes it appear he held a pretty serious grudge against the man."

Tommy whistled at the news.

"There was bad blood between them?" He mused. "What was it over?"

Clara glanced at Maddock, hoping he was paying attention and would explain the matter fully to them. He took another long drink of brandy.

"You probably think I should have mentioned that before," he said weakly to them. "I was aware of the situation, but both men assured me it would cause no issue for this year's pantomime."

"What was the cause of the grievance between them?" Clara nudged him.

Maddock wrapped his hands around the brandy glass, seeming to draw comfort from the feel of the solid tumbler in his palms.

"Stanley and Mervyn have worked in pantomimes together since... actually, I am not sure exactly when they first performed together, but it was certainly before the turn of the century. And they always played the same parts. Like a lot of stalwarts in the pantomime circuit, they had found their preferred roles and they stuck to them," he began uneasily. "Of course, Buttons and the Dame always play together, they are the comic staple and bounce off one another. You get a good Buttons and Dame combination going and you know the panto will be a hit. People don't come to see the hero and heroine, they come to see the larger-than-life dame and her hard-done-by sidekick. Year after year, that pair will steal the show, at least if you have good casting they will. I have seen pantomimes fail because of a poor pairing, even when the principal girls have been big names."

Maddock gave a long sigh.

"Up until 1913, if you could hire Baldry and Hutson for your panto, you knew you were onto a winner. Typically, one always came with the other. If you got Hutson, you knew you had Baldry and vice versa. Those two were no fools, they knew they were a good team and could ask for a premium rate when they worked together."

"What happened to so dramatically change things?" Tommy asked quietly.

Maddock's knuckles had gone white around the glass.

"Remember I mentioned that Hutson started to drink after his wife died? Well, he was not the only one with a vice. Mervyn was addicted to morphine. I think he hurt his back and was prescribed the drug originally to help him keep performing. Anyway, by 1913, he was taking a dose every few hours and always before he performed. Honestly, some nights neither man went on stage without a drink or a drug in their system," Maddock shrugged as if this was all very commonplace. "That night in 1913, Stanley had drunk a little more than he should have, and he accidentally knocked over Mervyn's morphine bottle when he visited him in the dressing room. The bottle smashed and there was no time to fetch more, so Mervyn had to go onstage without his usual dose.

"Things went downhill from there. Mervyn was in a state, jittery with nerves and then lacking his dose and feeling the withdrawal effects. If Stanley had not been so drunk, maybe the incident would have passed without anything serious happening, but Stanley was dropping lines and then adding new ones. Admittedly they were funny and all pantos revolve around a small amount of improvisation, but Mervyn was struggling to get through each scene and could not handle Stanley's audience stealing antics. By the interval, Mervyn was so twitchy and jumpy, a pin dropping would have him leaping into the air.

"Probably if someone had found him some morphine all would have settled. But no one did, and Mervyn was getting more and more erratic, while Stanley was slipping into the irreverent stage of drunkenness. He began to push Mervyn, enjoying seeing his reaction, and that was when it happened. Scene eight, the forest of Riding. Stanley made some joke about Buttons being only of any use when he was high and Mervyn snapped. It wasn't even a very funny joke. I don't think the audience grasped the point. Anyway, when Mervyn and Stanley walked off stage, Mervyn grabbed up a prop sword and started attacking Stanley.

"It was quite a mess. Stanley passed out. The audience caught glimpses of the chaos and the police had to be summoned."

"Certainly unpleasant," Tommy agreed. "But not something to hold a grudge over for nine years, surely?"

"You forget," Clara interrupted, "Mervyn did not work on the stage again after that, not until this year."

"That wasn't directly due to Stanley's involvement," Maddock said. "The theatre director decided Mervyn was not fit to be in his pantomime and told him to go seek help. Stanley got a warning too and made the effort to cut back on his drinking. Mervyn vanished for a while. I later learned he had gone to one of those special clinics that help a person with addictions. After he was clean, he found he could not face theatre work anymore. He had developed terrible stage-fright. That was why he went into radio, instead."

"What changed to make him agree to your pantomime?" Clara asked.

"A chance meeting between Mervyn and Stanley," Maddock replied. "I had already hired Hutson. I was still looking for a Buttons. Stanley bumped into Mervyn in London, seemed one of those lucky coincidences. They talked, reminisced about the old days and Stanley persuaded Mervyn to give panto another chance. Spoke about reviving their old partnership and Mervyn was taken in. We all wondered about his nerves, but he has been completely professional through the whole thing."

Maddock grew solemn. The brandy glass was empty, but he still clung to it.

"That's why I can't think he killed Stanley. They were friends and they had forgiven one another for their past failings. Because of Stanley, Mervyn was seeing his career revive. Why would you kill a man who was helping you?"

"It does seem an unlikely scenario," Clara agreed. "Unless something was said last night, something that stirred old grievances."

Maddock shook his head, unable to believe it all.

"Aside from this old argument from 1913, what evidence is there against Mervyn?" Tommy said. "Maybe there is something there we have missed."

"Mervyn admitted freely that he was the last to see Stanley alive," Clara said calmly. "Or, rather, the last before the killer. The only other physical evidence is that Hutson was clutching one of the buttons from Mervyn's costume when he died. I imagine the police theory is that he grabbed the costume as he died and tore a button off."

"There are other ways a button could have come to be in his hand as he died," Tommy pointed out. "Maybe it was lost earlier and Hutson spotted it on the floor, picked it up and intended to return it to Mervyn?"

"Maybe," Clara was not satisfied with the explanation, it was too vague and would Stanley really have kept hold of a button as he was attacked unless it was somehow important to pointing at his killer? "You know what troubles me? The witness who says they saw Mervyn following Mr Hutson."

"Why does that trouble you?" Maddock said, his tone dull even as he tried to keep up.

"Well, only a handful of people knew that Mr Hutson was dead until you spoke to the cast today," Clara explained. "Outside of myself, my companions and the police, the only persons in the theatre who knew Stanley had been murdered were you, Mr Maddock, and the killer. The cast were not informed until today and none have left the building since they heard the news, I believe?"

"No, you are right," Maddock nodded. "I told them at the start of the afternoon warmup rehearsal. No one has left since."

"And among the theatre staff, who knows of what occurred?" Clara persisted.

Maddock thought about the question.

"We only told the dressers just before the inspector arrived. I have not mentioned it to anyone else, though no doubt the gossip is doing the rounds by now."

"You only told the dressers Mr Hutson was dead, not that he had been murdered. Do you see my point?" Clara asked him.

Maddock frowned, then he shook his head.

"I'm sorry, Miss Fitzgerald, but I am struggling to think straight. You will have to spell it out."

"I think I know what Clara is saying," Tommy interjected. "If none of the cast or theatre staff knew Mr Hutson was murdered last night, then who went to the police station and said they had seen Mervyn follow Hutson? Only someone who knew he was dead and that someone had attacked him would have done that. And since neither myself, Clara or our friends could have provided information on what was happening backstage during the interval, that leaves a very small pool of people."

"One of which is you, Mr Maddock," Clara pointed out.

"Me?" Maddock blinked in alarm. "I did not tell the police any such nonsense! I not only never saw Mervyn follow Stanley, but even if I did, I would not accuse my remaining top named star of murder!"

Maddock looked stunned that Clara would even suggest it.

"I would not go out of my way to ruin my panto, even if I believe Mervyn had killed Stanley, which I don't!"

Clara believed him. His confession that the panto was more important than finding a murderer rang true. He didn't even seem to realise how terrible his admission was – that he cared more about a play than he did about a murdered friend.

"That leaves only one possibility," Clara continued. "Someone else knew that Stanley Hutson was dead and if we assume Mervyn is innocent, that implies this witness could actually be the killer."

"They might be attempting to frame Mervyn," Tommy said bluntly. "Throwing suspicion off themselves."

"In which case they have been foolish," Clara smiled, suddenly feeling better about the case. "They have revealed themselves to us. All we have to do is find out who this witness is and we shall be closer to the killer."

Maddock looked hugely relieved.

"You think so?" He groaned. "Oh, if that is true then at least all is not lost. You know, I can convince the audience that Donald is really his father. I can pretend that they are actually watching Stanley perform, but I can't mask the fact that Erikson is not Mervyn Baldry. He is a lot younger for a start."

"Don't you think it is slightly duplicitous to fool your paying audience into thinking that Donald is really Stanley?" Clara asked him.

Maddock looked shocked.

"My dear, this is theatre!"

Chapter Sixteen

The arrest of Mervyn Baldry had placed a new spin on the mystery. Clara considered going straight to the police station to try to speak with Mervyn, however she suspected it would be best to allow Park-Coombs time to conduct his own interviews and not barge straight in. Mervyn was going nowhere, after all, and there were plenty of other avenues to explore. She also had a prior engagement she did not wish to cancel. So, once more saying farewell to Tommy as he headed home, Clara set off in the opposite direction.

Her life being somewhat erratic as well as hectic, and Captain O'Harris being similarly busy, the pair had found it convenient to arrange regular times when they would come together and just enjoy each other's company for a while. Only an emergency would call off one of these rendezvous, and there had yet to be a cancellation. Clara was not about to be the one to break that trend.

She arrived at O'Harris' large house slightly bedraggled, her umbrella proving inadequate to the increasingly wet and windy weather. Orange leaves were whipping at her legs as she strolled in through the gates, trying to pretend she did not look like something the cat had dragged in.

The captain was stood on the steps of his Home.

"I should have sent the car for you," He apologised as Clara approached. He hurried down the steps and took her umbrella.

"I look wetter than I really am," Clara lied.

"I'm very sorry, I could have saved you getting wet at all."

Clara waved off his remarks.

"You didn't know where I was to send the car," Clara reminded him. "Anyway, I just need a warm fire and a towel or two, and I shall be right as rain. Oh…"

Clara laughed at her choice of phrase. O'Harris chuckled too, then guided her into his private sitting room where a warm fire was flickering in the hearth and a teapot was gently warming before it. O'Harris fetched Clara towels himself and then rang the bell to alert the cook that he wanted the cake and crumpets he had requested brought to his room. It felt like an afternoon for sitting by the fire and toasting crumpets.

Clara laid a towel on an armchair near the fire so she would not make it wet and then sat down. She used the other towel to dry her hair, while the warmth from the hearth started to sink into her bones.

"Are you investigating the pantomime case?" O'Harris asked.

"Yes. I was at the theatre before I came here. Park-Coombs arrived and arrested Mervyn Baldry."

"Baldry?" O'Harris said in stunned amazement. "Buttons?"

"Yes, it was quite a shock. I am not convinced myself, I think the inspector may have jumped the gun and arrested the wrong man."

"He has been doing that a lot, recently," O'Harris said darkly.

Clara knew he was referring to the matter of Private Peterson.

"In fairness to the inspector, he has to follow procedure

and there is some troubling evidence against Mervyn, even if I think it might be being misinterpreted."

"Evidence?" O'Harris asked.

"He had a history with Stanley Hutson, was in fact once arrested for seriously assaulting the man, that was many years ago, but it cost him the role he was playing at the time and he left the stage for eight years," Clara explained. "He fully admits to being the last person to see Hutson alive and Hutson was clutching one of the buttons from Mervyn's costume when he died. Lastly, someone has come forward and stated they saw Mervyn follow Hutson right before the fateful incident."

"That does sound quite serious," O'Harris agreed, reluctantly withdrawing his earlier snipe against the inspector. He would not forgive Park-Coombs in a hurry for accusing Peterson of murder.

"It depends upon whether you take those strands of evidence at face value or not," Clara replied thoughtfully. "The assault on Hutson occurred many years ago and was due to Mervyn being addicted to morphine. They were friends before that and I have heard no indications that there was any continuing animosity between them. That Mervyn was the last to see Hutson is hardly surprising, considering he was right behind him as they left the stage for the interval. The button is a mystery. How it got into Hutson's hand is an open question. The inspector is working on the theory Hutson ripped it from Mervyn's costume as he died.

"But the piece of evidence I find most troubling, is the witness who says they saw Mervyn with Hutson. Bear in mind, this witness came forward before Mr Maddock had informed his cast that Stanley Hutson was dead. That means the witness somehow knew about the murder before everyone else and that raises the question – how?"

"I see your point. Seems all very strange. An innocent to the crime should not have known anything about the killing, and certainly not have been suspicious of Mervyn Baldry. Aside from us, the only person aware of Hutson's death was Maddock, yes?"

"And whoever killed Hutson," Clara pointed out. "And it would be convenient for them if someone else took the blame."

They were both silent for a while. The cook arrived with crumpets and fresh current buns. She glanced at Clara and tutted over her wet hair. Promising to return shortly with a hot water bottle. O'Harris took up a crumpet and stabbed it onto a toasting fork. He offered the impaled crumpet to Clara and she propped it near the fire to start to crisp. As O'Harris prepared his own crumpet he voiced a thought that had been worrying Clara.

"Park-Coombs is not a stupid man, far from it. So why would he be so quick to make this arrest when the evidence is somewhat suspect? He would surely know that this witness was questionable, considering the circumstances?"

Clara had been wondering that too. Park-Coombs could have pursued the evidence further before making a decision. Rushing into an arrest without being certain the evidence was accurate was a recipe for potential disaster. He had no real motive, only an assault that happened eight years ago, and a missing button that might or might not have come off in an attack. On the other hand, there were people who would confirm Mervyn was in the alley at the time of the fire and then there was the oddity of the missing guard uniform. Whoever started the fire, tried to burn the costume, but logically they would only have done that after the body of Hutson had been hidden. Else they would risk getting blood on any fresh clothes they wore. Therefore, the murderer started the fire as a distraction, waited until everyone was outside and then hid the body, before finally disposing of the guard costume in the blaze.

And yet Mervyn was seen in the alley, wearing his Buttons outfit, at the time when he should have been disposing of Hutson. It was all very confusing.

Park-Coombs was jumping to conclusions, on that Clara was certain.

"He has been doing that a lot recently."

Had he?

Pressure from above, someone pushing him to make arrests.

Who?

What about Chang's police corruption theory? That Park-Coombs is in the middle of it all?

No, that can't be true.

"Your crumpet is burning."

Clara jerked out of her thoughts at the quiet statement from O'Harris. She snatched the crumpet from the flames just before it was beyond salvation. Fingers burning from the heat of the crumpet, she dropped it onto a plate and accepted the dish of butter O'Harris offered her.

"Something's wrong," O'Harris said as she spread butter onto the crumpet, watching the yellow daubs melt into the holes. "I mean, more wrong than you having a murder to solve. Something has upset you."

Clara wondered when she had become so obvious. When had her feelings become written across her face. Or was O'Harris simply so attuned to her these days he could hardly fail to notice her anxiety.

"Tell me about it," O'Harris continued. "I am always here to listen."

Clara glowered at her crumpet, any appetite she had evaporating. Truth was, she did desperately want to talk to someone about her concerns and fears. This business with Chang felt wrong and was leaving her sleepless at night. And then there was the threat that Jao Leong posed, a threat she hoped would only stalk her, but she knew deep in her heart that if Jao learned of her involvement than no one around her would be safe.

"You have gone so pale. I really want to help," O'Harris persisted, his voice soft with concern.

Clara tilted her head towards the fire. Shut her eyes to enjoy the warmth on her skin. Before she had even fully made up her mind the words were spilling from her lips.

"I have been told that there is corruption within the

police concerning this gang business in Brighton."

Having her eyes shut meant she could not see O'Harris' reaction. She quickly opened her eyes and looked at him. He was sombre.

"How reliable do you think the information?" He asked.

That was a good question.

"Honestly? I am not sure," Clara sighed. "Let's put it this way, the person who told me received the information from someone else. Even as I say that, I realise how dubious it sounds. I have no idea if their source if reliable, or how they came by the information. Nor do I know if the person who told me was being truthful. I think they believed the information, at least."

O'Harris frowned, taking in the complexity of the situation.

"That would explain how this gang has been operating right under the noses of the Brighton constabulary," he said, a thought that Clara had considered more than once.

It was odd that the gang had been operating apparently for months with no one in the police noticing. The only other option was to assume the police were ignorant because they were so busy, or perhaps incompetent. Not a great solution.

"Clara, as much as I hate seeing this gang running amok in Brighton, I think the only thing you can do is step back and wait. Sometimes you have to let things be someone else's problem."

Clara wanted to remind him that not so long ago the situation had been very much their problem when Private Peterson was the one in trouble with the gang, but she understood why he was saying such a thing. This gang business was scary, a monster lurking just out of sight and it did seem too big for them to deal with.

"There is something else," Clara said, feeling the need to defend why she was so upset. Why she could not leave this alone. "The person who informed me about police corruption, also implied that Inspector Park-Coombs was involved."

Captain O'Harris' eyes went wide in surprise, but he was prevented from immediately replying by the arrival of the cook and the hot water bottle. Only after she was gone could he speak, and that gave him a moment to think.

"I won't deny I have never entirely liked the inspector. I have always felt he was watching this place, waiting for one of my guests to suddenly turn into a murderous monster. I think he sees the worst in people and is cynical beyond belief. But even I would not think of accusing him of corruption," O'Harris spoke at last. "This is very serious Clara."

"I know," Clara smiled weakly. "I have lain awake worrying about it. Park-Coombs is a friend and I don't want to believe this, yet there is something about the suggestion that makes sense. He asked me to keep away from the gang business."

"Because it was dangerous," O'Harris pointed out.

"Yes, that is the obvious assumption. It also keeps an outsider, someone not under his authority, from poking their nose into his business."

O'Harris pondered the information.

"He was quick to condemn Peterson," he remarked.

"Pressure from above, he said, pressure to resolve the case. Was that true?" Clara frowned. "Now your crumpet is burning."

O'Harris snatched the toasting fork from the fire, but his crumpet was beyond rescue. He sighed as he dumped the charred bread onto a plate.

"What can you do about it?" He asked.

Clara shrugged.

"I don't know. Maybe there is nothing I can do," she offered him her untouched crumpet.

O'Harris accepted gladly.

"I think you need to hang back and see what happens. Keep your ears open, of course, but otherwise carry on as normal. If this is true, then more evidence will come to light."

"Maybe," Clara was tired of being glum, and she had not come to see O'Harris to tell him her woes. This was meant to be their time together. She purposefully speared a new crumpet on her toasting fork and placed it into the fire. "I am going to forget about it for a bit. I have this pantomime affair to solve, anyway. Let's talk about something else, what have you been up to?"

The change of subject was refreshing and as O'Harris started to talk Clara relaxed a little. Whether there was police corruption or not, simply sitting around worrying about it was not going to achieve anything.

Chapter Seventeen

There was one other person who might have insight into the relationship between Mervyn Baldry and Stanley Hutson, and Clara decided to speak to them before visiting the police station, to see if there was any truth in the suggestion Mervyn held a grudge against his former acting partner.

It was close to the start of the evening performance when Clara found Donald in his father's dressing room, putting the finishing touches to his make-up. For a brief moment, as she entered the room, it was like seeing a ghost. Donald perfectly mirrored his father, the only giveaway being the lack of belly fat. But imagine Stanley Hutson had been on a mild diet and you could easily assume he was the man sat at the dressing room mirror, applying bright red paint to his cheeks in vivid circles. Donald turned to her and it was a strange sight. Few people ever saw the dame up close; she was a vibrant figure on a stage, her make-up garish so that even the back row would be amused and startled by her gaudy look. Up close it was like a child had thrown a tin of paints at a life-size doll. Aside from the bright rouge on his cheeks, Donald wore shocking blue eyeshadow, heavy kohl around his eyes, a jazzy pink streak highlighted each eyebrow and his lips were a pulsing apple red, shiny and glossy. All of this was laid upon a thick cream white foundation layer, making the colours even more stark and electric.

There was nothing subtle about the make-up and with Donald's own hair slicked back and held in place by a hairnet, ready for a wig to be placed on top, he looked somewhat absurd. But, then again, that was the point of the dame – she was ridiculous.

"Sorry to disturb you so soon before a performance," Clara said, closing the dressing room door behind her.

She noted that the make-up made Donald look sour rather than jovial as it was meant to. She wondered if that was accidental, or whether he was really rather displeased by her arrival.

"No matter, Miss Fitzgerald, I assume this relates to my father's murder and that is much more important than a pantomime," the lipstick had been applied to make it seem that Donald was permanently pouting, but Clara thought she detected a change in his expression, nonetheless, and his tone was sincere. "Take a seat, you don't mind if I continue to get ready?"

"Go ahead," Clara wondered how much more he had to do, he seemed already painted to excess. "I hope not to take too much of your time. I just wanted to ask your thoughts on the arrest of Mervyn Baldry."

Donald was flicking face powder onto his features, his eyes shut as a cloud of dusty particles engulfed him.

"I was surprised," he said.

Clara could taste the face powder in her mouth and smell its slight perfume in her nose. She wanted to sneeze.

"Why was that?"

"My father and Mervyn were good friends. In their day they were the best Buttons and Dame double-act on the circuit. My father would often say he had never found a man to replace Mervyn. He played opposite a different Buttons every year, but was never satisfied. That was why he went out of his way to encourage Mervyn to return to the stage," Donald replied. He had picked up a pair of long glass earrings. "You have probably heard from Maddock the story of their falling out?"

"I have."

"Most people assume Mervyn would be angry with my father because that outburst cost him his role. Of course, my father was not really to blame. Though some have hinted he broke Mervyn's morphine bottle on purpose. He didn't, of that I am certain. My father was a professional, Miss Fitzgerald, and he knew Mervyn needed the morphine to perform. He would not have deliberately sabotaged the pantomime, even if he was worried about Mervyn's addiction," Donald slipped the loops of the earrings through pierced ears. "People called him cold-hearted and cynical because he ignored Mervyn's problems as long as the man acted well on stage, but no one appreciated that my father was also gripped by his demons. It would have been hypocritical for him to condemn Mervyn's drug use, while he carried on with his drinking. Not that he did not care for his friend and begged him to get help, but they were men who both understood their own weaknesses and accepted them."

"Then there was no lasting animosity between them?"

"No," Donald was amused by the suggestion. "My father refused to press charges and did all in his power to ensure the police did not pursue the matter themselves. He would have seen Mervyn back on the stage, but the theatre director refused and insisted Mervyn be released from his contract. My father never worked for that director again.

"Afterwards, Mervyn felt he needed a break from the stage, to get himself clean. He sought professional help and my father was always there assisting him, visiting him when he was in a special hospital for addicts. It was a long journey, but Mervyn made it. My father offered him the chance to resume their double act, but Mervyn needed more time. He moved into radio for a while, where there was not the same pressure of an audience before you."

"And there was no resentment that Mervyn chose not

to resume his role as Buttons?"

Donald smiled softly, it was a gentle, teasing look.

"Miss Fitzgerald, my father and Mervyn were close friends. Mervyn was often at our house in London, he spent every Christmas with us and during the panto season would spend hours backstage to support my father. I told you, they understood each other," Donald's smile disappeared. "Mervyn is the last person I would imagine killing my father."

He rose from his seat and picked up a towering pink wig that was waiting for him on a side table. Turning back to the mirror, Donald carefully placed it on his head and adjusted it until he was satisfied. The transformation was complete; Donald Hutson was now every inch his father.

"Thank you for speaking to me," Clara rose from her own seat. "I know it must be hard stepping into your father's shoes."

Donald pulled that soft, sad smile again.

"My father would have wanted this. In a way, I am keeping him alive. The audience think I am him. It is… consoling."

Clara was not sure about that, it didn't seem entirely healthy for a man to imitate his father to make it seem as if he was still alive, but who was she to judge? If hearing people mistake him for his father brought Donald some comfort, then she was not going to say anything.

She left Donald preparing himself mentally for his entrance onto the stage and headed in the direction of the police station. She was not totally convinced Mervyn did not hold a grudge against Stanley Hutson, after all the man appeared to have badgered him into returning to the stage – maybe Mervyn had resented that? But she was also not convinced that Mervyn was a killer. And she wanted to know who the mystery witness was and how they came to be aware that Stanley Hutson was dead before anyone else.

~~~*~~~
~~~

Inspector Park-Coombs was working late, as had become his habit recently. With everything that was going on in Brighton, he was spending less and less time at home, and had even had a camp bed moved into his office, so he could catch some sleep when the opportunity arose. Clara thought he looked tired and a little haggard, as if he had just recovered from a bad case of flu. Seeing him, she at once felt terrible for even considering that he might be accepting money from Jao Leong. Park-Coombs was a good honest man and Clara was certain of that. She smiled as she spotted him leaning on the desk-sergeant's counter, signing a form.

"You look like you could do with some of Annie's best treacle tart," she said.

Park-Coombs glanced up and a slight smile graced his lips.

"Sounds nice. Anything to cheer me up with that weather outside," he tilted his head towards the dark, rainy night beyond the police station doors. "My only consolation is that I am no longer required to walk the beat."

"Certainly it is not the day to discover your umbrella has sprung a leak," Clara waggled the offending article, which was folded up and dripping water onto the floor. "Have you got a moment?"

"It will be about Mervyn Baldry?" Park-Coombs could not hide his groan.

"Yes," Clara admitted. "He is facing some very serious charges."

"He seems not to appreciate that," the inspector shrugged. "He is denying everything, naturally."

Park-Coombs finished with the form he was signing and pushed it towards the desk-sergeant.

"Best you come to my office."

The inspector seemed weary as he climbed the stairs to the office. His head drooped in a way Clara had never seen before, and he appeared to have aged by several decades. Clara felt her concern for him increasing.

"Are you all right, Inspector?" She asked as soon as they were in his office.

"I am tired," Park-Coombs replied. "And I am wondering whether I am as competent a police officer as I once thought. But it will pass, I am sure."

Clara could not quite shake her worry for him as he indicated she should sit down and then took his own seat behind his desk.

"So, why don't you think Mervyn the killer?" He jumped straight to the point.

"It is more a case that Donald Hutson thinks it unlikely. Mervyn and Stanley were friends. They had put the assault eight years ago behind them and it was Stanley who encouraged Mervyn to appear in this pantomime."

"And yet we have evidence to suggest they were not the greatest of friends," Park-Coombs countered.

"You mean the button in Stanley's hand? We don't know how that got there."

"But we have a witness who says Mervyn followed the dead man after they came off the stage."

"That is something I want to discuss," Clara leaned forward in her seat. "The only person who knew Stanley was dead, outside of the killer, and who was connected to the pantomime was Mr Maddock. None of the cast knew that Stanley was deceased until early this afternoon, when Maddock told them. Most of the stagehands still do not know he is dead. Maddock is keeping it a secret so as not to disrupt the panto."

The inspector was silent, staring at his hands as they rested on his desk. Clara knew he was taking in this information and reaching the logical conclusion.

"An innocent witness to Mervyn following Stanley could not have known the man was dead until this afternoon," Park-Coombs laid out the idea carefully.

"More to the point, Maddock has not told anyone Mr Hutson was murdered. You understand?"

"I do," Park-Coombs gave a tired groan and pressed a hand to his forehead. "This witness has insider knowledge that Stanley Hutson was killed."

"Yes," Clara was pleased she would not have to labour her point.

"That means there was someone else at the theatre who saw Hutson dead, and they happened to have also seen Mervyn following him," Park-Coombs continued.

Clara wanted to groan. That was not what she had meant at all.

"Surely, if someone innocent came across Mr Hutson's corpse they would have raised an alarm?" She pointed out.

"Mr Maddock didn't, or at least not at once. These show folk are funny souls. Nothing matters to them as much as the show carrying on. I reckon the witness saw the body, realised they could do nothing about it and that the pantomime would be interrupted and so kept quiet."

"That would require a very cold person," Clara said.

"Maddock thought that way."

"That's different. Maddock did not ignore the body completely. He found me and asked for help. He reported the situation to the police as soon as he was able."

"As did this witness," Park-Coombs continued doggedly.

"Supposing this witness is really the killer?" Clara countered. "Wanting to throw you off their scent? What better way to do so than offer you another suspect?"

"Who conveniently happened to have lost a button found in the dead man's closed fist?" Park-Coombs replied solemnly. "No, Clara, for once I think you are trying too hard to see complications that are not really there. The witness saw the body, was in such shock they could not at once act. Instead they slept on it, realised they knew something that could help catch the killer and thus came to me."

Clara didn't like the logic of that argument. How many people could see a body and not react at once? Maddock had clearly been shaken and distressed by the incident. He had not calmly carried on, but had fetched Clara as soon as he could.

"I would like to know who this witness is," Clara said. "I would like to speak with them."

Park-Coombs twitched his moustache.

"I promised them anonymity. They were very upset and scared. They were fearful about telling the truth."

Clara was not happy about that at all. If she did not know who the witness was, she could not figure out if they were honest, or if they really were the killer.

"That is quite a predicament," Clara kept her tone level despite her annoyance. "Why is this person so fearful?"

"Didn't want to lose their role in the pantomime," Park-Coombs answered. "I told you, these actors think more of that damn show than they do about a murder. You don't go talking about one star murdering another without some trepidation that you might be in trouble for doing so."

"You are aware that several witnesses saw Mervyn outside in the alleyway, wearing his Buttons costume?"

"Your point?"

"The timings! Mervyn would have had to have changed into the royal guard costume, murdered Stanley, started the fire, hidden the body, changed costume again and then appeared outside," Clara was amazed he refused to appreciate what she was saying. "It was all so tight."

"Witnesses can be unreliable," Park-Coombs said. "Maybe Mervyn only was in the alleyway at the last few moments of the fire."

"And maybe your witness is mistaken and he did not follow Stanley Hutson," Clara used his own statement to indicate the flaws in his argument.

The inspector was unmoved.

"As far as I can see, my case is water-tight. Sorry Clara, but this time, you are the one who is wrong."

Chapter Eighteen

Captain O'Harris had been troubled by Clara mentioning the possibility that Inspector Park-Coombs had fallen to the temptation of corruption. Clara might have shrugged off the suggestion, wanting to believe the man utterly honest, but O'Harris was rather more cynical. Recent experiences had left him with a rather jaded opinion of the police force. Perhaps it was wrong, perhaps he had taken the events concerning Private Peterson's near arrest for murder rather more personally than he should have done, but the fact remained that he had developed a deep distrust when it came to the reliability and the judgement of the police.

That was why, after Clara had left, he found himself running over the idea that someone within the police (namely Inspector Park-Coombs) was taking bribes from this new gang on their doorstep. Though he tried to shrug off the notion and ignore it, telling himself that he was best to rely on Clara's better judgement when it came to the situation, he could not let the thought be.

Maybe, he admitted to himself, though only in the vaguest way, it was because he had a grudge against Park-Coombs for the trouble he had caused the captain and his convalescence home, that made him so keen to believe the worst of the man. O'Harris did not like to imagine he was the sort to hold a grudge, and so he brushed off the suggestion almost the moment it sprang to mind. No, he was worried because he cared about Clara, and she was clearly worried. She did not know what to do with the information she had been given and that was obviously a problem. He wanted to help, and there seemed only one way to do that.

After all, if Park-Coombs was corrupt, then Clara could be in danger when she worked with him. Supposing her next case caused her to discover information about someone he was taking bribes from? How far would the inspector go to protect himself?

O'Harris was so caught up in his own prejudices that he had completely forgotten that the inspector could be entirely innocent and that someone else might be the real bad egg in the force. Instead, he began to mull over how he could get to the truth, how he could really help Clara. He eventually came to the conclusion that the only option was to watch Park-Coombs and catch him in the act of working with the enemy. That could take a long time, of course, but O'Harris was prepared to do whatever it took to discover the man's guilt.

With all that in mind, O'Harris slipped from the home once it was dark and headed for the police station. He might be too late to catch the inspector tonight but, then again, he might have picked just the right moment. He chose a spot opposite the police station, where a deep shop doorway offered him shadows to hide in. He could watch the station doors and see who came and went. He was too late to see Clara arrive at the station, so he was unaware that she was inside.

The time ticked by. O'Harris was cold and he wished he had put on a thicker coat, at least he had remembered to wear gloves. A distant church clock rang out the half hour and he realised it was seven-thirty already. Perhaps he had missed the inspector.

O'Harris started to contemplate what he was doing. He felt as though he was looking at himself through the eyes of another person and trying to explain to them why he was hanging around in a doorway on a freezing night. The logical arguments that had brought him to this place now started to sound rather silly. What would Clara say if she knew? He thought she might laugh, or maybe even be cross.

By now he was feeling rather a fool and the biting November wind was making him seriously regret his earlier decision. These things seemed all well and good when you were sat beside a nice cosy fire, all warm and snug, but outside in the bitter chill things took on a different perspective.

"I should go home," O'Harris muttered to himself, his voice seeming very loud in the near empty street.

Even though some shops were still open, few people were around. Everyone who had the opportunity was tucked up in their homes, the dark, winter's night safely shut out behind doors and curtains. Only those who had no choice were wandering the roads.

What was he doing?

O'Harris stamped his feet and told himself he was being damn stupid. Park-Coombs had probably gone home hours ago and was enjoying an evening by his own fire. Blowing on his freezing hands, O'Harris started to move out of the doorway, finding that the icy weather had left him feeling stiff and sluggish.

It was at that same moment that the inspector walked out of the police station. There was a large light over the police station doors, and its vivid glow illuminated the face of Park-Coombs making it easy for O'Harris to see who had emerged. The inspector glanced about, rubbed his hands together and then set off up the road.

O'Harris had frozen in place and for a horrible instant he seemed unable to summon the strength to move, it was as if the surprise of Park-Coombs suddenly appearing had knocked his senses about. Slowly he roused himself and then he was gripped by indecision. His earlier resolve had deserted him and now he was wondering what sort of craziness it was to suppose the inspector was corrupt and that by trailing him he could prove it. He seemed stuck in place by his dilemma; then his earlier suspicions returned, and he decided, for better or worse, that he had to follow Park-Coombs.

Spinning on his heel, he at first could not see where the inspector had gone. He thought he had lost him, until a moving shadow beneath a streetlight marked the policeman's progress. O'Harris took a deep breath, then he started to pursue him.

O'Harris had done surveillance work during the war, but always from the seat of an aeroplane. Flying over enemy territory with a photographer taking pictures of trenches and gun emplacements had not exactly been secretive. You could not hide a plane, if people did not immediately see it, they certainly heard its engines. The trick had always been to get the job done quickly and get away before the Germans started to fire on you.

Tracking a person was a different game, but O'Harris surmised that with a little common sense it should not be hard. He kept several paces behind Park-Coombs and was always on the opposite side of the street to him. He avoided the streetlights if he could, skirting their pools of light, and when the inspector turned corners he always walked on a little ways before doing the same. That way he could see the inspector walking away down the turning, while appearing to be heading in a different direction.

O'Harris fully anticipated that Park-Coombs was heading for home. His ideas of subterfuge and bribery had been frozen out of him by the brisk night. He was rather hoping the inspector would turn into a house soon, so that he could head for home as well. All the time he was walking, a voice inside O'Harris' head scolded him with derisive comments, reminding him that he was being an idiot, that he had read too many novels, that he was being ridiculous. It was hard not to believe the voice, especially as the inspector looked so casual as he walked, like a man with no troubles on his shoulders. Surely, if he was accepting bribes, he would act with a bit more cunning?

O'Harris was so caught up with his internal dialogue of self-doubt, that he did not immediately realise that they had walked in the direction of the infamous alley – the one where Peterson had been stabbed, and which acted as a rat-way for this newest gang's nefarious drug smuggling. The inspector did not turn into the alley but walked the road that ran adjacent to it and finally came to a halt close to the picture house that stood in the centre of the row, looking a touch out of place between the shops and houses. A gated side alley ran down behind the picture house and Park-Coombs entered this without hesitation.

O'Harris walked past the alley on the opposite side of the road and made no indication that he had noticed anyone enter it. He did, however, take note that the gate remained slightly open. After walking several paces, O'Harris turned around and walked back, crossing the road at an angle and keeping his head down. There did not appear to be anyone around to notice him, but just in case he wanted to seem like a person caught out in the cold, trying to keep warm and avoid the harsh wind sweeping into their face.

The picture house was not open that night and its foyer remained curtained in darkness. There was a sense of isolation and loneliness about the street that gave O'Harris pause for thought. It suddenly occurred to him that it was on a night like this, in a nearby alley that had been equally deserted, that Peterson had found himself in trouble. Hardly a helpful realisation under the circumstances.

O'Harris drew level with the gate to the side alley and paused. He pulled a cigarette pack from his pocket and went through the process of removing a cigarette and lighting it as a means of explaining to anyone who happened to be watching why he had suddenly stopped. He wanted to appear to be a casual passer-by who was using the slight shelter afforded by the alley, with its setback gate, as an opportunity to light a fag without the wind blowing it out. He was also cautious that the light of his match could not be seen through the open gateway.

He stood just beyond the opening, out of sight and listened. There was no sound in the alley and O'Harris started to wonder if he was making a mistake. Supposing Park-Coombs was the first to arrive to this place, which was clearly a meeting spot (O'Harris was pretty certain the side alley only led to the yard of the picture house, therefore the inspector could not have used it as a cut-through) and someone else was due to arrive? What would they do if they found O'Harris by the gate?

Coming to a quick decision, O'Harris began to walk on again, huddled up over the warmth of his cigarette and he was glad he did, for he was only a few paces up the street when he was passed by a pair of burly men, who banged him with their shoulder.

"Hey!" O'Harris said without thinking, turning to the men.

One glowered at him and O'Harris made the pretence that he was hurrying along. In fact, he only went a short way before glancing back again. Both men turned into the side alley and slammed the gate behind them.

O'Harris took a moment to regroup. Oddly, now his suspicions had been confirmed he felt an element of astonishment, as if he never really believed his doubts concerning the inspector. Catching his breath, O'Harris headed quietly back to the gate and stood outside to try to listen to the conversation beyond.

"You're late," that was the distinctive voice of Inspector Park-Coombs. "I don't like freezing my nose off hanging around for you."

"Yeah, well, I don't like consorting with coppers, but we have to do what we have to do," another, deeper voice rumbled back.

"You know what's good for you Huggins," the inspector said, his voice hinting at a growl. "Now, have you brought it?"

"Yeah," hissed the man named Huggins. "Look, I don't

like meeting here, someone might notice."

"Good point," Park-Coombs conceded. "We can choose a different spot next time. We don't want anyone suspecting what we are doing."

"We would all be in trouble if that happens," Huggins replied. "Is it enough?"

There was a rustling noise that sounded like paper being flicked through.

"Plenty. For the moment," Park-Coombs replied.

"Then we are off."

O'Harris heard footsteps heading in his direction and barely had time to dash across the road and hide in a doorway before the two mean looking thugs, one rather ironically named Huggins, emerged from the gateway. They both looked up and down, as if checking the coast was clear and then departed the way they had come. The darkness swallowed them up and O'Harris lost sight of them.

Trembling in the shadows, only partially from the cold, O'Harris watched as Park-Coombs emerged from the gateway. He was pushing what appeared to be a brown envelope into his coat pocket and also took a moment to survey the area before heading in the direction away from the thugs' route.

O'Harris was breathing hard, like he had run a race. His heart was pounding, and all his senses seemed to have heightened inordinately. What had he just seen?

Obviously, he had witnessed the very thing he had expected, the thing Clara most feared, on his first night of trying. While a part of him was revelling in his luck, another part was reeling from discovering he was correct. Inspector Park-Coombs was meeting with the enemy and accepting bribes, it was plain as day. But how on earth was he going to convince Clara of that? She trusted Park-Coombs and would not willingly accept his treachery, even if she had considered it herself.

O'Harris felt in a daze, but there was no point hanging around in a doorway and freezing to death. Pushing himself into action, he started home. He had all night to think over what he had heard and how best to explain it to Clara.

He felt a little sick at discovering he had been right all along, that his suspicions, if enhanced by his personal dislike of Park-Coombs, were not without foundation. This was going to rock the Brighton constabulary; corruption at such a high level was truly painful and would disintegrate what faith the public had in the police force. Why had the inspector done it? Just for the money, or because he had some other agenda? Whatever the case, it was a terrible situation and O'Harris felt truly bleak as he walked home.

Clara would be devastated by this news. She believed the inspector her friend, had placed so much trust in him, now she would discover he had been working to his own whims. O'Harris could not even begin to imagine how she would react, though he was fairly certain she would be furious.

As much as he was glad, even satisfied, to have discovered the truth, O'Harris could not help but wonder if it would have been better if he had remained at home by his fireside that night.

Chapter Nineteen

While the inspector may have refused to give Clara the name of the witness who had seen Mervyn Baldry follow the deceased Stanley Hutson, he was prepared to grant her permission to speak with the accused. He had informed her that he doubted she would get anything of use from the man and then explained that he was headed home for his supper. Clara was left to her own devices.

Mervyn was being held in a cell at the back of the police station. Clara was shown to him by the desk-sergeant, before he went back to his duty. Mervyn and Clara were alone, the other cells being empty. Clara looked at the sad former Buttons, sitting in his shirt sleeves and trousers. His costume had been taken from him so his understudy, Erikson, could take his place. Mervyn looked as if he had been stripped of everything that made him who he was. He seemed to have shrunk in on himself. Clara coughed politely to gain his attention.

"I know," Mervyn muttered. "You are the private detective Maddock has hired."

"I thought you might want to talk to me?" Clara said. "I am trying to find who killed Mr Hutson, after all."

"Haven't you heard?" Mervyn scowled at her. "They say

I did it."

Clara waited a heartbeat, then she asked;

"Did you?"

Mervyn clutched the edge of the bed he sat on in his cell and glowered at the concrete floor. He gave a hard laugh.

"Of course I didn't, but no one is going to believe that."

"Why not?"

"Because of the witness, and the button, and because of what happened so many years ago. I guess you know about that?"

"About the assault on Stanley? Yes, Mr Baldry, I do," Clara kept her tone neutral, wanting no hint of her own feelings to appear, not yet, anyway. "However, what has happened in the past need not have any bearing on the present. If you would talk to me for a bit, we might be able to understand this mystery better."

"I don't know who killed Stanley, if I did, I would have brought them to the police myself," Mervyn said bleakly.

"Then, maybe talking will help me to understand you better, Mr Baldry, and by understanding you, I might be able to see what really went on the other night in the theatre."

Mervyn shook his head.

"I don't see how I can be any use to you."

"I only want to talk," Clara persisted. "You seem to have accepted this situation too readily."

"I am a realist," Mervyn shrugged his shoulders with a sigh. "I see the way the police mind is working. Too many black marks against my name."

"That does not mean you should give up and allow Stanley's real killer to escape justice," Clara pointed out. "Even if you have lost hope for yourself, surely you owe it to Stanley to help find out who did this?"

Mervyn was silent. He stared at the floor of his cell, shuffled his feet, looked like a man who has simply accepted the woes life has thrown at him. His depression was alarming and Clara was not sure how to combat it.

"Stanley persuaded you to come back to the stage, didn't

he, Mervyn?" Clara had dropped formalities in an attempt to connect with the man before her.

Mervyn scraped at a dark spot on the concrete floor with his toe.

"He did, does that make things worse or better?"

"I can't say," Clara admitted. "Did you want to come back to the stage?"

"Not so much want," Mervyn lifted his chin a little, thoughtful. "I needed to come back, needed to prove to myself I was still a real actor. Stanley called it fighting my demons, I called it proving a point to myself. I wanted to remind myself that I was not a washed-up has-been."

"And Stanley had missed you. He had never met a performer who matched him as well as you did."

Mervyn nodded, though the movement was so subtle it could have been a twitch.

"We worked well as a double-act. Stanley never hid the fact he missed performing with me. You know, even after what I did, he was always there for me," Mervyn's mouth twisted with sorrow. "You don't get many friends like Stanley Hutson. I'm not sure I even deserved his forgiveness, but that was Stanley for you. He never gave up on me. I'm nothing without him."

Mervyn's voice wobbled and Clara saw that his depression and despondency was as much a product of grief for a lost friend, as it was a result of his current situation. Mervyn had given up because he could not face life anymore, not without the one person who had supported him and given him strength through the darkness.

"I am very sorry Mervyn," Clara said softly. "You have lost a good friend."

Mervyn smiled sadly.

"No one is going to believe that though, everyone is just going to see the distorted truth the police will present and they will say I killed him. That I lost my head. What else could you expect from a drug fiend?"

"But you are not a drug fiend now, are you?" Clara leaned against the bars of the cell, as close as she could get to Mervyn to watch his face.

"No, not since that night..." Mervyn tailed off. "Was hell getting clean. Stanley saw me through it."

"Tell me again about the last time you saw him," Clara continued.

Mervyn's eyes took on a distant look.

"We had finished the final scene before the interval. Stanley was shaky because of that earlier nonsense of being booed. He could suffer terrible nerves on stage and it did not take much to knock his confidence. People don't realise that, they don't realise how difficult it can be to act," Mervyn sniffed. "That's why I was away from the stage so long. I lost my nerve. Couldn't face an audience, not without the drugs. I was running away, while hating myself for doing it."

"What did Stanley do as he left the stage?" Clara asked.

Mervyn had slipped away again into his own self-pity, he slowly roused himself.

"He turned away from me. I mean, our dressing rooms were next to each other, so he should have walked with me to them, but he turned the opposite direction. I didn't think about it at the time as I was lost in my thoughts. I had been having a little trouble with my lines and I wanted to go to my dressing room and run through the script for the second-half."

"You didn't follow him?"

"No. I went straight to my dressing room," Mervyn insisted, at last a little spark of fight returning to his eyes. "I was there when Mr Maddock told us we all had to get out of the theatre because of the fire."

"He saw you?"

"No, he was in a rush. He just banged on the door, told me to get out," Mervyn shrugged again. "It was all a big panic. Everyone was scurrying around. You could smell the smoke."

"You went straight to the alleyway?"

Mervyn's face fell, as he considered his response.

"No, actually," he hesitated, a look of concern drifting

over his face. "I was more concerned with rehearsing my lines. I glanced out of my dressing room, decided there was no urgent danger and then continued revising my lines for a while. Then the smoke started to become stronger and I thought I better leave."

Clara did not need to tell him that that complicated matters. It meant the police could argue that Mervyn was unaccounted for during the vital time when Hutson was killed.

"What was Stanley's relationship like with the rest of the cast?" Clara changed the subject. "Were there any problems?"

"Not that I saw," Mervyn replied. "I don't think Stanley had worked with many of them before. Maybe Eustace Drake, the one playing the vizier, but I can't think of any difficulty between them. Stanley, as actors went, was fairly easy going and got along with most folk."

"Someone had a serious dislike for him," Clara observed.

Mervyn pulled his morose face again.

"I told you, I don't know anything and thus I am useless to you."

Clara was beginning to agree with him. Mervyn had offered her nothing to explain the scraps of evidence that were pointing at his guilt, nor any means to prove him innocent.

"Had you ever heard anyone call Stanley a thief?" She asked.

Mervyn, for the first time, looked puzzled rather than depressed.

"Thief? That's an odd thing to call a man."

"Not if someone believed Stanley had stolen something from them," Clara explained. "Has anyone ever accused Stanley of doing that?"

Mervyn seemed genuinely confused. He shook his head after a moment.

"I really don't know. I've never heard that said."

Clara endeavoured not to sigh. Mervyn was the most hopeless case she had come across. Most men, or women, were only too keen to protest their innocence and offer as much information as they could think of to help her discover the true culprit in a case. In contrast, Mervyn seemed utterly resigned to his fate. She was beginning to think he would almost willingly be convicted of the crime, as if he somehow deserved the punishment for living a worthless life. Without Stanley's friendship, he appeared to be quietly happy to contemplate a short drop through a trapdoor. Could it be that he didn't even care to live anymore?

"Mervyn, I need you to think over this long and hard. If you come up with anything, anything at all about that night that you think is relevant, please, let me know," Clara took a card from her handbag and offered it through the bars to Mervyn.

He didn't take it.

"Mervyn," Clara was starting to lose patience, "have you forgotten that someone murdered your friend and you owe it to him to discover the truth."

"What does it matter anymore?" Mervyn said weakly. "Stanley is gone, he doesn't know what I do or don't do anymore. Maybe he is better off anyway. This world is cruel and lonely. It's no fun to grow old, to see the spotlight shine on someone else, someone younger."

"The spotlight was shining on you last night," Clara reminded him. "It would still be shining on you had someone not told lies about you. If you only would wake up from this melancholy and realise that you are allowing someone to get away with murder."

Clara would have liked to have given him a shake, but the bars prevented her. She was still holding out the card towards him, but he made no move to take it.

"Listen, you never followed Stanley last night, not even for a moment?"

"I told you," Mervyn grumbled. "He went the wrong way. I don't know why he went that way. I shall never know why. There was nothing down that corridor that could have interested him."

"Someone suggested he might have gone for a drink," Clara was badgering him now, seeing that getting him worked up was a means of making him talk. "What about you?"

"Me? I don't drink. At least, not in the sort of way you mean. I might have a pint at the pub from time to time, but alcohol was never my crutch," Mervyn shot her a hard look. "All this is getting us nowhere, why don't you leave me alone?"

"All right, Mr Baldry," Clara had returned to formal. "I'll leave you alone, just after you answer this last question. Why would anyone wish to see you hang for a crime you did not commit?"

"What?" Mervyn frowned.

"Someone is attempting to frame you. Why would they want to do that?"

"I don't know," Mervyn snapped.

"So, it was just coincidence that the killer chose to lay the blame on you? Just convenient? Not because they have a grudge against both you and Stanley Hutson and by murdering Stanley and framing you for it, they would do away with two birds with one stone?"

Mervyn looked astonished by the suggestion, but the talk had stirred his mind at last. He was thinking finally.

"Someone hated us both? Plotted for me to be accused?"

"Maybe," Clara said casually. "After all, you two were a double-act for many years. Supposing something happened that involved you both and left someone wanting revenge?"

Mervyn was considering this possibility and a spark was returning to him. He turned to Clara with wide eyes.

"Revenge," he hissed. "That's a nasty word."

"And it all too often leads to murder," Clara remarked. "Think about all this Mervyn, think about someone who might have a bone to pick with you and Stanley. When you come up with a name, let me know."

She wagged the card at him. At last Mervyn took it

from her fingers.

"You're talking about someone on the cast hating us both?" He said carefully.

"I am. Though it is also possible it was someone among the stagehands. Whoever it was, they could move around backstage unnoticed."

Mervyn turned the card over in his fingers, like a magician preparing for a conjuring act.

"Tell me, before you go," he said, for the first time being the one to push along the conversation. "How did Stanley die?"

"The police haven't said?"

"They seem to assume I know," Mervyn narrowed his eyes. "For obvious reasons."

Clara nodded, of course.

"Stanley Hutson had his throat cut with a shard of glass. The killer then used Stanley's blood to daub the word 'thief' upon the apron of his dame costume and then hid the body. There is no doubt this was a savage and violent murder, but it was not impulsive, of that I am sure. I think the killer planned this very carefully, including how they might throw suspicion off themselves."

Mervyn had gone pale as she described how his friend had died.

"That's…" he swallowed hard. "Nasty, just nasty. Stanley did not deserve that. What could he have done to make someone that angry?"

"I was really hoping you would tell me," Clara sighed. "No matter, I shall find out. In the meantime, you must keep hopeful Mr Baldry. There is a future out there for you, if you would only stop moping and embrace it. Stanley didn't encourage you back onto the stage just for you to end up wishing yourself dead."

Mervyn seemed too dazed to reply. Clara left him with her card turning in his fingers. Maybe he would remember something, maybe he wouldn't. That would not stop Clara from finding the real killer.

Chapter Twenty

Feeling at an impasse in the Hutson case, Clara rose the next morning to say goodbye to Tommy, hopeful he would find some clue to the mystery in London.

"What are you going to do?" He asked Clara before he left.

"Visit Dr Deáth and see if he can tell me anything else about Hutson's murder, other than that, I am not sure quite where to look next."

Tommy gazed at her as if he guessed there was more on her mind than just the Hutson case, then he nodded.

"I'll do my best to find the solution for all this in London," he said. "Take care, avoid the rain."

He tilted his head to the window, outside where huge black clouds loomed. Clara sighed, it looked like she would need to go out and buy a new umbrella urgently.

She was in the high street as the shops were opening, feeling the threatening early spots of a heavy rainstorm just waiting its moment to drench the unlucky. There was a hint of thunder in the air, just to improve things. Clara darted into the nearest shop that sold umbrellas and found she was not alone in trying to purchase a brolly; the rain had placed the notion in a lot of people's heads and they were all jammed around the umbrella display. Clara sighed again; it was the day for deep sighs. She did not have the energy or inclination to try to push through the throng, so she waited her turn, only to discover the brollies had all been sold by the time she reached the stand.

Amused rather than disheartened by her ironic bad luck, she stepped back outside and discovered the heavens had opened. The temptation was to loiter in the shop doorway until the foul weather had passed, but by the looks of the grey clouds, she suspected the rain had set in for the day. Bracing herself for the inevitable, she stepped out onto the pavement, head down and hoping to make a dash for the next shop that sold umbrellas. She had not gone far when someone stepped out of a side street, directly in front of her. She stopped sharply, nearly running into the person, which was when she realised there was now a large umbrella over her head.

"Might I be of assistance, Miss Fitzgerald?"

Clara stared into the face of a pretty Chinese woman. Since Brighton was not renowned for its Chinese residents, and since the woman knew her name, Clara could make a reasonable guess who she was. But she remembered herself sufficiently to recall that she should not know who the woman was, and so played dumb.

"Thank you," she said. "That is most kind. My umbrella has a leak."

"Most unfortunate, where are you headed?"

The woman had only the faintest trace of an accent, though some of her words sounded a little odd when she spoke, as if she placed the emphasis in the wrong place.

"The nearest shop that sells an umbrella," Clara shrugged with a laugh. "I don't want to inconvenience you."

"No inconvenience," the Chinese woman smiled. There was something cruel about that smile. "I believe the shop just here sells them."

They crossed the road together.

"I'm afraid I don't know your name," Clara said

carefully. "Have we met before?"

"No, Miss Fitzgerald, I am aware of you by your reputation. You can call me Miss Leong."

Clara made no indication that her suspicions had been confirmed.

"Well, I appreciate this kindness Miss Leong, it is never fun to get wet," they had reached the door of the shop and Clara was moving away, she was not sure what Jao Leong wanted, but she was not going to make it easy for her. If she intended to threaten Clara, she could do it among other people.

"Before we part," Leong paused her, "I would like to ask for your assistance."

Clara hesitated; this was an unexpected turn of events. She managed to keep the frown of confusion from her face. She was a detective, after all, people asked for her help all the time, showing worry or bafflement might tip Leong off that she knew more than she was letting on.

"Of course, you have a case for me?" She said.

Leong's smile broadened, like she had just heard a trap snap shut around her prey.

"I do, might we go somewhere quiet to discuss it? There is nothing worse than trying to explain personal matters in the street."

Clara had no intention of going anywhere alone with Leong, fortunately she saw a solution just across the road.

"Why don't we go into the Lyons teashop? It will be quiet at this time of day, and warm."

She feared Leong would protest, even though she had made the suggestion as casually as she could. Leong, however, simply nodded.

"I think a cup of tea might be welcome to take off the chill of the day, yes?"

Clara agreed that would be pleasant and they crossed the road.

Inside the teashop, Clara pointed out a table by the window, away from the only other customer present and removed from the service counter, yet also within view of everyone. Leong made no protest at the choice and they sat down. It was not long before a Lyons tea maid came over and took their request for a pot of tea. Seated, Clara noticed what she had failed to take in before, that she was considerably taller than Leong. The woman was remarkably petite and could have passed for a girl of fourteen, had Clara not known she was older.

Leong carefully propped her umbrella against the window and turned to Clara.

"English weather."

"It's what makes the grass green," Clara replied. "Though rain is much more endurable when you are tucked up at home by the fire."

"Yes," Leong chuckled to herself. "I had not planned to venture out today, but urgent business called, which was fortuitous, as it meant I spotted you and I had hoped to speak to you at some point."

Clara was not sure if Leong was lying. She might have been following Clara for a while, the odds of this being a chance meeting seemed slim, but she made no hint of her concerns.

"Well, I hope I can be of assistance to you. I would not like to think you got wet on my behalf for no reason."

Leong had that disturbing smile on her face again. It was at once self-satisfied and malevolent. Clara felt a chill run down her spine, and doubted it was a product of the rain alone.

"No doubt my situation is one you hear of a lot," Leong began. "A family matter. You must have had much experience in situations involving estranged family members?"

"Most of my cases involve a disagreement between relatives," Clara nodded. "If I was of a maudlin nature, I might reflect on how depressing it is that so many families find themselves wrenched apart by petty arguments and feuds."

"But you are not maudlin," Leong twitched the edges of

her lips.

"It is not who I am. I prefer to see the good in everyone and everything."

"That must be a challenge," Leong raised her eyebrows. "Especially in your line of work."

"Not really," Clara said. "I deal in hope, Miss Leong, as strange as that might seem. I deal in the hope of bringing resolution to people, maybe to bring justice. Though there are sad elements to every case, overall I believe that I make the world a little bit better with each mystery solved."

"A very noble attitude," Leong did not appear to be being sarcastic. "Perhaps then you can solve my mystery."

"I shall try my best," Clara assured her, though she really did not mean that. She could not think what Leong wanted from her and if it was to turn a blind eye to her illegal activities, she was certainly not going to do that. But, for the moment, she was trying to keep the woman on her side and not tip her off that she knew who she really was. "What is your problem?"

Leong did not immediately speak as just then their tea arrived. Once they were again alone, she leaned forward and spoke softly.

"My brother has gone missing."

"Oh," Clara said, not really sure how to respond. "I am sorry to hear that."

Leong waved her hand as if to imply this was not a matter of great sadness for her.

"I think you know my brother, Miss Fitzgerald, he has been in Brighton before. His name is Brilliant Chang."

"Oh," Clara said again, trying to feign surprise and not sure she succeeded. "You have different names."

"Same mother, different fathers," Leong shrugged. "You know all about my brother I assume?"

"Brilliant Chang is a criminal, one who moves in quite exalted circles. We have crossed paths a couple of times, but nothing I could have him arrested for."

"Though you would like to," Leong grinned.

"He ran down a policeman," Clara pointed out. "He

interfered in a theft case I was working on. Whenever he appears in Brighton, there is usually trouble. Fortunately for me, he tends to confine himself to London."

"Until recently."

"What has happened recently?" Clara asked innocently.

"I already said, he has vanished. Disappeared. Evaporated into the night," Leong clenched then unfurled her hand in the air to symbolise something disappearing in a flash. "No one knows where he went."

"That must be inconvenient for his criminal organisation," Clara remarked. "Lost, with no leadership."

"Exactly," Leong purred. "However, my interest is not for his illegal activities, my interest is to know what has become of my brother. We may not be close, but it would be remiss of me not to discover where he is and if he is well. Our mother is distressed."

Clara hid that she knew Leong and Chang were orphans, let the woman play her game as long as it meant she had no idea Clara was already working for her brother.

"I imagine you are going to ask me to locate him?" Clara said. "But why me? Why here in Brighton? Surely there is a detective in London better placed to find him?"

"From the little I have learned, I believe my brother is in this town," Leong explained. "Brighton has always held an appeal to him, it is the place he likes to retreat to. If he has gone anywhere to lay low for a while, it will be here."

Clara frowned, and this was not feigned, there were holes in Leong's story that even had she not known what the woman was up to would have concerned her.

"Do you know why Chang vanished?"

"No. It was very abrupt," Leong said with no hint she was lying. "You see why I am concerned?"

"Perhaps your brother is trying to hide from something? Perhaps it would be safer, considering his occupation, to let him remain hidden?"

"I am not the enemy, I am his sister," Leong said, her sweet tone not able to mask her insincerity. "No harm would come from me finding him. I just need to know he is well and safe, for the sake of our mother. She worries so."

Clara was becoming annoyed by Leong's glib lies. She shoved down the emotion, taking a sip of her tea as she composed herself.

"I have no qualms taking on your case, Miss Leong, but if your brother is determined to remain hidden, I fear that I shall not be able to find him. I know a little of Chang and he is a cunning, careful man. As much as I believe in my abilities, I also believe he is capable of proving my match."

"You put yourself down, Miss Fitzgerald, unfairly I should say," Leong managed to force a bit of warmth into her eyes. "My brother is good, but you have cornered him more than once. While you might not have ensured the police snared him, I know you foiled his schemes. I think if anyone can find him, it is you."

"And if he is not in Brighton?"

"Then you shall tell me that and I shall pay you all the same," Leong made it all sound so easy. "Will you take the case, Miss Fitzgerald?"

Clara knew she could not refuse. Whatever game Leong was playing – whether this was her testing Clara because she suspected her of working with Chang, or because she genuinely thought she could use Clara to get to her brother – she had to go along with it.

"You just want me to find him?" Clara asked.

"Yes. I only want to know he is well and safe. Miss Fitzgerald, my brother is a criminal, I have no illusions about that, but he is still my brother and I would not see harm come to him. I don't know what trouble he is in or why he is running, but I will do all I can to help him. That is why I ask for your help. Do you see?"

"I do," Clara said. "I shall do what I can, Miss Leong, if he is in Brighton I shall find him."

Leong's grin moved into Cheshire Cat territory.

"I shall be forever grateful to you for this," she bowed her head to Clara. "When you learn anything, you can reach me here."

She handed Clara a card from one of the smarter hotels

in Brighton. Clara knew how much that place charged a night and she must have shown some of her astonishment in her face.

"You see you need not have concerns about me paying my bill," Leong was amused as she stood up. "I hope to hear from you soon, Miss Fitzgerald."

Leong took her umbrella and left the teashop. Clara sat alone, feeling utterly bemused by this turn of events. What was Leong doing? Was she hoping that Clara would locate her brother and betray him to her? If she did not suspect Clara was already working with Chang than that seemed the likeliest scenario. Leong guessed her brother was in Brighton, but could not find him herself, so she was hoping an outsider could.

It was all too confusing, but the one thing Clara knew for certain was it was too dangerous to seek out Chang and warn him. No, she would have to wait for another time when he came to her. Until then, she would make the pretence of looking for him in case Leong's thugs were watching her.

Clara had to be careful. Very, very careful.

Chapter Twenty-One

How remarkable that a morgue could feel safe and comforting after a confrontation with Jao Leong. Clara walked down the steps at the entrance, heading below ground. The walls were tiled in white and situating the morgue as deep as was possible meant it was cool all year round. In winter it was positively freezing, and Clara had seen icicles forming on the ceiling before now. Like some icehouse for the dead, the perpetually cold morgue enabled Dr Deáth, the police coroner, to keep the dearly departed suitably chilled.

Dr Deáth was not the sort of person you would imagine in a morgue, though his name did seem to dispose him to working with the deceased. Many of his family members were doctors to the living, which seemed mildly disturbing considering their appellation. More appropriately (or not depending on your viewpoint) his cousin worked as a funeral director. Dr Deáth was always cheerful, often found humming to himself as he worked. He did not become depressed over the bodies that found their way to him, instead he treated them with thoughtfulness and respect, but not with a grimace on his face. He had once explained to Clara that just because you were dead didn't mean you wanted to see everyone around you looking morbid.

Clara could hear the good doctor humming as she entered the main room of the morgue. He was stood at a table, working on the body of an elderly man, wearing his thick rubber apron that protected his clothes from the inevitable splatter. Fortunately, he had not yet begun cutting into the corpse when Clara appeared.

"Dear Clara!" He said brightly. "Excuse poor Mr Wiesz, he suffered a fall down the stairs of a certain hotel and there are some questions about how it came about. I don't suppose I can answer them, seeing as how a shove to the back or even tripping by foot is not something likely to leave a mark on the body. Still, we do our best."

Clara had become somewhat immured to dead bodies since her early days as a detective. She cast her eyes on Mr Wiesz without any real sense of horror or fear, the commonest reactions people felt to a body. She was not even shocked at the sight of a corpse these days, which perhaps said a little too much about her daily activities.

"That would explain that nasty lump on Mr Wiesz's forehead."

"Ah, you would assume so. However, I have been informed that most likely happened when he fell out of bed a short time before his, erm, plummet," Dr Deáth had a peculiar look on his face.

Clara took the bait, aware he wanted her to ply him for further information.

"Old men fall out of their beds from time to time," she said.

"Usually, however, they are either alone or with their wives. Mr Wiesz was with a scantily clad young lady."

"Oh," Clara saw the picture he was attempting to paint, "and in a certain hotel too. Might Mr Wiesz have died in a brothel?"

"I couldn't possibly say," Dr Deáth grinned. "Though it has occurred to me that that is quite an exciting way to go when one has passed a certain age. A lot better than dying in a hospital bed."

"I wonder if Mr Wiesz would agree," Clara smiled, her eyes twinkling with hidden amusement.

"If only we could ask," Dr Deáth chuckled to himself. "Now, how may I help you? Ah, it will be about the Hutson case?"

Dr Deáth walked towards a wall lined with what might look like metal cupboards. They glinted beneath the illuminated lightbulbs. Deáth opened one in the middle, revealing a deep, narrow chute, within which rested a corpse. The large proportions of the body, which only just squeezed into the tight space, confirmed the man was Stanley Hutson.

He emerged from the chute feet first.

"Had I been Mr Hutson's doctor when he was alive, I might have had a conversation with him about his lifestyle," Dr Deáth noted as he pulled the drawer tray out to its full extent so Clara could see his bloodless face once again. Hutson looked relaxed in death, as if he was sleeping. "The liver showed signs of cirrhosis, a result of drinking too much. I would say the man had been an alcoholic in the past, thought I didn't notice any signs of recent alcohol consumption. All his organs were surrounded by fat and I noticed the arteries of the heart were clogged and hardened. I should say he was perilously close to having a heart attack, if he had not already had a minor one or two. The lungs were also very black and shrunken, I would say he was a heavy smoker.

"There was water retention in the legs that was not a product of death, but something he suffered from in life, and there were one or two signs that made me suspect he was in the early stages of diabetes. Quite frankly, he was not a healthy man and I would have given him a year or two, at the most, if he did not make some serious effort to improve his health."

Clara looked at the former dame, who had made his career from being larger than life, in all ways. Sad to think that beneath the bright wigs and gaudy costume, here was a man living perilously on the cusp of serious illness and death.

"His murderer clearly did not know this," Clara observed. "Or else was impatient."

"Yes, that person's actions certainly scuppered Mother Nature's plans," Dr Deáth pointed to a thin line around the corpse's neck. He had done a good job of cleaning the wound and positioning the head in such a way that the line was virtually invisible. "I'll sew it up before he goes to the undertakers. Until then, I have to leave it for the police to inspect. Not that I imagine Park-Coombs will want to take another look."

"Can you tell me about the killing stroke?"

"There were three, actually," Dr Deáth gently moved Hutson's head back a fraction, revealing the bloody gash in his throat. "The first was relatively short, a slightly tentative stroke, perhaps. Either that or the killer was not as near as they would have liked to be. In any case, the first cut though not long, was sufficient in depth to begin a fatal process of bleeding.

"The second stroke I daresay was dealt quickly afterwards, before Hutson had much chance to react. This one was longer and went up along the jawline, nearly striking the earlobe. The stroke was deeper too, and would have cut through the windpipe, effectively preventing Hutson from calling out.

"Now, there was a bump to the back of Hutson's head that indicates he fell back hard to the floor. The bruise occurred when he was alive, and I suggest, though I cannot be certain, that it was after the second blow was struck that he fell back. The third slice is significant, because the angle is different. The first two indicated the killer cutting at an upward angle, the tip of the weapon piercing beneath the jaw, with the slice marks indicating the knife was held at an angle of around 45 degrees."

Dr Deáth held his finger to his throat to indicate how the thrust was performed.

"Now, this implies the killer was holding the weapon in the hand rather like you might hold a fire poker, or certainly the way you thrust with a knife. However, the last stroke was different," Dr Deáth changed the position of his hand, now he was pointing his finger parallel to his throat. "The last blow, I would say occurred when the killer was on top of Hutson. He was thrusting down, rather than upwards, the cut clearly different to the first two, with the point of the weapon going horizontally into the neck, rather than piercing upwards. That is why I think Hutson had fallen at that point, banged his head and the killer was crouching over him.

"That last blow was wholly unnecessary. Hutson was doomed by the second stroke. The third cut was savage enough to penetrate to the spine and scrape the bones of the vertebrae. It nearly severed the head. I would imagine Hutson died very rapidly after that.

"Oh, and there is a defensive wound on his hand that probably occurred on the second slice. The index finger is cut to the bone."

"Nasty," Clara sighed, thinking of the brutality of the killer. "What does this tell us about the murderer?"

Dr Deáth became thoughtful.

"The angle of the first two strokes suggest someone smaller than our victim, so they had to cut upwards. I doubt they were the same height as Hutson."

Clara quickly ran through her mind the relative heights of Hutson and Mervyn Baldry. Having seen them on stage together, she was fairly certain they were of a similar stature. Hutson wore high heels when he was dressed as the dame, which would have made him slightly taller than Mervyn. Without those on, he must have been close in height to his comedy partner.

"Was Hutson wearing shoes when he was removed from the laundry basket?" Clara asked.

"No," Dr Deáth replied. "His feet were bare."

Since no shoes had been found at the murder scene, the likeliest supposition was that Hutson had taken them off the moment he left the stage and had walked down the corridor barefoot. She doubted the shoes were terribly comfortably, especially for a man of Hutson's girth. He would slip them off the second he could, but she could check that to be sure.

In any case, the angle of the strokes, and the lack of shoes, seemed to indicate Mervyn was out of the picture as the killer. He would have been too tall to cut Stanley in such a way.

"How much shorter would you say the killer must have been?" Clara asked.

Dr Deáth gave this a considerable amount of thought, then he held up a hand before himself, as if judging his own height.

"As we are both aware, I am not a tall man," Deáth grinned. "My feeling is that the killer must have been of a similar height to me or smaller. Hutson was a good six foot in bare feet, his murderer could not have been much more than five feet."

Clara was surprised by this, such a small killer also would rule out the implicated Erikson, who was as tall, if not a fraction taller, than Mervyn Baldry. She racked her memory for who among the performers might fit such a height deficit.

"You know, this suggests one of the women members of the cast. I can think of none of the men so small as you mention."

"Nothing is set in stone," Dr Deáth hastily pointed out. "There might be another reason the killer cut at such an angle, but my instinct would say it was due to the person being smaller than Hutson."

Clara studied the body again.

"How many of your men did it take to remove Hutson from that laundry basket?"

"Two," Dr Deáth said automatically. "And they were strong lads. He was a heavy fellow in life, and nothing like being dead to make you even heavier."

"You see what I am thinking?" Clara said. "Supposing the killer to be a woman, no more than five foot in height, how could she drag Hutson to the laundry room and stuff him in a basket?"

Dr Deáth nodded along.

"She couldn't and, quite frankly, dragging this corpse along the floor would have left a blood smear. No, Hutson had to have been carried to that laundry basket after he had bled to death. Still would have been a risk of blood drops, but those could be missed. He may have been carried in a blanket, anyway."

"Killers," Clara mulled over this possibility. "Or one killer and her accomplice. Still, even with help a woman would have struggled to carry Hutson. It almost makes me think there was a third person present to dispose of the body. Those laundry baskets are tall, not easy to heft a heavy man into, especially when you are short."

"That is a fair assumption," Dr Deáth agreed. "But how does that help you?"

"I'm not sure it does, as such. If three people were involved, well, they could easily give each other an alibi for the time of the murder, say they were all out in the alley together. That means I can no longer rely on those alibis. It also means that people I previously thought could not have been involved, are back in the frame."

In her head, Clara reminded herself that among those back in the picture was Mervyn Baldry. He might not have killed Hutson, but he could have been responsible for hiding his corpse. Clara felt all her previous assumptions coming crashing down around her ears. She was suddenly back to where she had begun – except for one thing.

"A female killer," she muttered. "The height thing, it points to a woman plainly, and there are not that many on the cast. There are the dressers of course, but most of the stage crew are male. No, I have only a handful of women to consider."

"I'm sorry I was not more helpful," Dr Deáth said with genuine disappointment. "I fear I have made things more complicated for you."

"No, you have been helpful," Clara promised him. "I just have to consider how this new information fits into what I already knew."

Dr Deáth pushed Hutson's corpse back into his narrow, metal tomb and closed the door. For the time being he could tell them nothing else.

"You know, I watched Mr Hutson perform many years ago," Dr Deáth said with a wistful look in his eye. "I thought him rather good, not that I had much experience of pantomimes to compare his performance with."

"From what I have heard, every pantomime wanted him as their dame," Clara agreed.

"Well, that is something I suppose. I mean, we all seek a certain immortality from our time on earth, and Mr Hutson has his. The country's greatest dame that ever performed, not a bad epitaph."

Clara thought it could be better, if he had not been slaughtered so brutally. That was going to be the thing most remembered now.

"I best let you get on," Clara said to Deáth. "Thank you for your assistance. I am sure Mr Wiesz is getting impatient now."

Dr Deáth smiled at her, a glimmer in his eye.

"The dead are never impatient, Clara, that is the preserve of the living and, I must say, it is what draws me to working with the deceased."

Clara was not quite sure how to take that, but she smiled to the curious doctor and said a final goodbye, deciding it was time to head back to the theatre.

Chapter Twenty-Two

Rupert Maddock found Clara backstage, staring into the redundant space where the ropes of the disused pulley system hung. She was staring at the distinctive, dark brown stain on the floor. If she half closed her eyes, she could almost make the ominous spread look like the shape of a man, rather than a deformed puddle.

"Miss Fitzgerald," Maddock distracted her. "Any news about Mervyn?"

Clara drew back from the rope room and blinked her eyes as the bright light of the corridor replaced the darkness of the tiny space.

"The evidence of the coroner indicates the killer was considerably shorter than Mr Hutson. That rules out Mervyn as the killer."

Maddock let out a sigh of relief.

"At last, some good news! When will the police release him?"

"I cannot say for sure, but this new evidence is pretty conclusive. There is one problem, however."

Maddock's expression of delight descended to

dejection.

"Oh?"

"The coroner is also certain it would have required at least two people, possibly three, to carry Hutson from this place to where he was found in the laundry basket, and that means everyone is back to being a possible suspect."

Maddock flopped against the nearest wall, looking deeply distressed.

"What now?" He asked weakly.

"I want to see all the costumes," Clara said. "I am guessing the killer wore Erikson's royal guard costume, since it was covered with blood. But the accomplices would likely have blood on their clothing too. Not so much, maybe only spots if they were careful and carried Hutson in a blanket, but I am hopeful they did not get away without some trace of blood being left on them."

"What if the costumes have been washed," Maddock pointed out.

"Blood is very durable. I have to try, at least."

Maddock showed her to the costume racks backstage. The dressers were not present, and Clara had her leisure to work through all the clothing. She was disappointed to realise that many of the outfits were red, black or dark brown, which could easily hide a drop of blood. She concentrated on the lighter coloured costumes, but it seemed the killer and their accomplices had been clever enough to don outfits that would hide the spatter. It made sense, considering the killer had borrowed Erikson's royal guard uniform for the purpose. There had been some careful planning involved in this crime.

Failing to find what she was hoping for, Clara stood back from the racks and stared out onto the empty stage. Supposing the accomplices were not from the cast, but from the stage crew? For that matter, supposing the killer was one of the dressers, both of a suitably small height? They would have taken their clothes away and washed them thoroughly. Clara sighed. It was a dead end.

"Nothing?" Maddock asked with despair in his tone.

"No," Clara replied quietly. "Mr Maddock, I believe this killer may have been a woman, and there are only a handful of them among your cast and working backstage."

Maddock nodded slowly, taking in this information.

"A woman?" His eyes widened. "That is quite horrible, to think a woman could do such a thing."

"Actually, women are typically as bloodthirsty as men," Clara answered him. "If a woman is driven by anger or some other passion, she can do terrible things. How many women are in this production?"

Maddock seemed to be trying to rally his thoughts back into order. The revelation had stunned him.

"Erm… there are six women in the cast. Miss Burns and Miss Allen, of course, and then four girls in the chorus."

"What about backstage?"

"Working you mean? Oh, there are the two dressers, that's it. The heavier work is all done by men. We keep the pantomime on quite a tight budget, so there is no one helping the cast with their hair or make-up, and backstage crew are kept to a minimum. In fact, most of the stagehands are employees of this theatre and I do not personally pay them."

"What of the dressers?"

"Maud and Dolores work for the company. I need reliable dressers; they have to know their job inside and out."

"My point, Mr Maddock, is this crime though designed to look like a sudden act of violence, really appears to have been carefully planned out. I don't think this was done in the heat of the moment, rather someone had concocted this scheme prior to the night it occurred and had been thoughtful about how to go about killing Hutson while diverting suspicion from themselves," Clara explained. "This indicates the people involved were very familiar with Hutson. They had to have been to have had a motive to want him dead. They were not people who barely knew him."

"I see," Maddock was solemn. "Then, we have to

wonder who among the women here had a reason to want him dead? Maud and Dolores have been with the company for around a decade and have worked with Hutson several times in the past."

"What of your two leading ladies?"

"Audrey is quite new to the scene, very up and coming, as they say," Maddock spoke softly, seeming troubled by the thought someone might overhear him. "She has been in a handful of amateur performances before this panto. She auditioned for me and I was sufficiently impressed to offer her the role of Aladdin. I can see this being a stepping stone to greater things for the young lady."

"Had she worked with Hutson before?"

"She had never done a panto before and Hutson only does pantomimes these days. It's a long season, what with the first rehearsals, then the dress rehearsals and the three months of performances. All told it can be five or six months of rehearsing and performing. Stanley was finding it increasingly exhausting and would take three or four months after panto season to recuperate. Then he would come to me and we would start talking about what the next pantomime should be."

"I didn't realise Hutson was that involved in the panto," Clara said, surprised by the news.

"Oh, Stanley had a huge say. We worked together to pick the pantomime, then we worked together on the script, picking out the songs we wanted and commissioned new ones," Maddock came to a halt as the words slowly hit him. "I am going to really miss him, you know. It shan't be the same, writing a pantomime without his input. He always did the jokes."

Clara smiled at the unfortunate director in sympathy. His loss went beyond being simply a professional problem, he had lost a friend, someone who in many ways he had come to rely on. Only now was Maddock realising what had been snatched from him.

"What about Miss Allen," Clara nudged him a little, to remind him what they were discussing.

Maddock blinked.

"Grace Allen has been on the theatre scene a few years now. Started out in child roles but has made the transition to adult work. That does not always happen, you see. Miss Allen has been somewhat underwhelming as Princess Zara, if I am truly honest," Maddock shrugged. "The charms of childhood mask a myriad of flaws in acting ability. I'm afraid I rather erred in hiring Miss Allen."

"That is quite a harsh assessment," Clara remarked.

"You saw her performance the other night, honestly, what did you think?"

Clara took a moment to remember the other night. It seemed an awfully long time ago that they were sat in the theatre watching the panto and with no knowledge that the dame was about to be murdered.

"I can't say I really remember her performance," Clara admitted.

"Precisely," Maddock nodded. "Though, at least it is better she is forgettable than if she was memorable for being so bad."

"Why did you hire her if she is such a poor actress?" Clara asked.

Maddock almost seemed to start as her question sparked his memory.

"Why, it was because Stanley said we should. He near enough insisted we hire her."

Clara jumped onto this new information.

"Why would Hutson say that? How did he know Miss Allen?"

Maddock was frowning, trying to remember those early discussions about who should play what role.

"I think Miss Allen had performed in pantomimes before, as a child. Stanley must have known her from then and wanted to help her find her feet as an adult actress."

Clara wondered if it was just a simple act of kindness that had brought Grace Allen to this company, or whether there was far more to the story. Could Grace have a grudge against Stanley? Might she consider him a thief for some reason?

"I need to talk to Grace Allen," Clara said firmly.

Maddock gave a small groan, perhaps fearing another of his cast would be disappearing to a police cell, then he glanced at his watch.

"She should be here shortly. Would you like a cup of tea while you wait?"

~~~*~~~

Grace Allen arrived a couple of hours before the matinee was due to begin and went straight to her dressing room. That was where Clara found her. As a leading lady, Grace had the small, cupboard-like room to herself, and that meant Clara could talk with her privately. She knocked on the door and waited to be asked to enter.

"Miss Allen?"

Grace was sat at the narrow dressing table, putting the first stages of make-up on her face. She looked at Clara with clear disdain, then groaned to herself.

"If I had known it was you, I would not have said you could enter."

Clara stepped fully into the room and closed the door behind her. Now she was here, she was not going to give Grace the chance to kick her out.

"I need to talk to you about Stanley Hutson."

"I really don't have time," Grace muttered. "I have so much to do."

"It won't take long if you are cooperative," there was one spare chair in the room and Clara sat on it, making it plain she was not leaving. "Had you worked with Hutson before?"

"Straight to the point, then?" Grace grumbled, thumbing greasepaint from a pot. "Am I a suspect? I thought they arrested Mervyn?"

"Mervyn is not the killer," Clara said firmly. "The coroner's evidence has proven that conclusively. And I have my doubts about the witness who supposedly saw him
~~~

following Hutson."

Grace had frozen in place. Clara was starting to wonder if she had hit on something.

"I don't suppose you know anything about that, do you?"

Grace came to life again, taking greasepaint up on her finger and applying it to her forehead.

"I don't, no."

"I think whoever went to the police and told them Mervyn had followed Stanley Hutson was trying to place the murder upon him. They suspected he was the culprit, but knew there was not enough real evidence to prove it, unless someone saw him go after Hutson," Clara did not add, that another motive for pointing the finger at Mervyn would be to distract attention from the real killer. Let Grace think she was suggesting she was motivated by thoughts of justice, rather than something more sinister.

Grace gave an awkward cough, as if her throat had gone dry, and then applied more greasepaint.

"Well, if Mervyn is not the killer, who is?"

Clara was not thrown by the less-than-subtle, change of subject.

"I'm working on that," she said. "I hear you knew Hutson quite well?"

"We had been in some pantos together before," Grace shrugged. "He was a kind man."

"He persuaded Mr Maddock to cast you as Princess Zara," Clara pointed out.

Grace hesitated again, and though Clara could only see her face via her reflection in the dressing room mirror, she was certain there was a hint of sadness to her expression.

"I didn't know that," she said. "Stanley always took an interest in me. He was very good friends with my mother and father. My father writes songs and music for stage productions, he wrote a number of the tunes in this pantomime. My mother was a great actress, before her sudden death."

"It seems Mr Hutson was watching out for you," Clara

said softly. "You must have been angered by his murder."

Grace had given up on the greasepaint. Her hands rested lightly on the dressing table, her eyes stared off into some distant place.

"He was a friend. It hasn't been easy for me getting work as an adult actress. I've had to use my mother's name more than once to obtain roles. I never realised Stanley had helped me get this part. That was good of him."

"Strikes me he was well liked by most people, which makes it strange he was murdered."

"Yes. Yes, I thought that. He didn't seem the sort of person anyone would want to harm," Grace frowned. "But, you know, there was all that talk about Mervyn Baldry's fight with him years ago, and it seemed logical that maybe he snapped again. People were whispering Mervyn was a little unhinged."

"And is that why you went to the police and told them you had seen Mervyn follow Stanley? Because you wanted Stanley's killer to be brought to justice?"

"He could have done it. It made sense he did it. But the police wouldn't ever notice him if they weren't pointed in the right direction," Grace caught herself. "I never said he killed Stanley. I only made them think."

"Yes, I see that."

"If you think me awful, so be it, but Mervyn seemed a likely killer. He attacked Stanley once before and… and you are right, I didn't want to see this turn into one more unsolved murder. There are too many of those."

Grace dropped her head forward. She did not appear to be crying, but Clara felt her grief and anger over Stanley's murder was genuine. It seemed she was close to ruling out another suspect.

"How did you know Mr Hutson was dead?" Clara asked.

Grace took a heavy breath.

"I saw him slumped in the pulley room. His throat cut," Grace struggled to say the words. "I couldn't say anything because I was not meant to be there, you see? Even though it was horrible."

"Not meant to be there?"

Grace's head drooped even lower.

"I go to the pulley room to smoke. I'm not supposed to smoke because it wrecks my singing voice," Grace mumbled. "Mr Maddock gets very angry about it. I needed a cigarette and it was the only place that is empty, but that's where he was, Stanley. I thought at first he had done himself in, so I hurried away, pretended I had not seen it. Only later did I think that it looked more like he was murdered and then I remembered Mervyn being right behind Stanley and that terrible thing that happened in 1913."

"And you leapt to a conclusion."

Grace shrugged.

"It made sense, who else would have a grudge against Stanley? I don't like Mervyn, anyway, he says odd things about my acting."

"What did you really see that night when you left the stage?" Clara asked.

The woman hefted her shoulders up and down, indicating she had not seen much.

"I left the stage with everyone else and headed for my dressing room. I had to change costume, retouch my make-up and have a cup of tea before the second half. I was also trying to avoid Audrey."

"Aladdin? Why?"

"She isn't very nice, that's all. She likes to critique my performance," Grace snorted. "I saw nothing and that's the truth. Now, could you let me get on with this?"

Grace flicked a hand at the make-up pots before her. Clara decided she had heard enough. For the moment she had no more questions.

She left Grace's dressing room and stood in the corridor, still feeling as far away from an answer as when she began her investigation.

Chapter Twenty-Three

Since Clara had no safe means of getting a message to Brilliant Chang, being uncertain if she was watched or followed, she decided that for the moment she would have to push aside the troubling problem of Jao Leong and hope that Chang contacted her soon. She headed for home to spend some time contemplating the Hutson case and try to find a strand of logic to the whole, sorry situation.

Annie was pleased to see her home; it had been lonely in the house without Tommy and Annie was only truly at her best when she had other people to fuss around. As much as Clara might have liked to nudge Annie into doing a bit more with her life, in reality she was quite content seeing that everyone around her was well fed, warm, wearing clean clothes and altogether happy. As she had told Clara firmly, if everyone was a detective or did important things, the world would come crashing down around their ears, so it was jolly good that some people found delight in caring for others. Clara could not argue with that.

Bramble bounced up at her leg as Clara entered the

kitchen and sat down at the table to join Annie for tea.

"No progress then?" Annie asked sympathetically.

"Is it that obvious?" Clara groaned. "I know that more than likely a woman killed Hutson. I just can't say which woman. My current array of clues has dried up."

"Well, a cup of tea will give you the chance to think things over, and it is best to be out of that filthy weather. Did you get a new umbrella?"

Clara's mind jumped back to her meeting with Jao Leong at the mention of umbrellas and she was surprised she did not reveal to Annie her anxieties, they felt very plain to her, but Annie made no mention of noticing her fears.

"There is a shocking lack of umbrellas for sale in Brighton," Clara answered her, trying to forget that buying a brolly had been completely knocked from her mind by Leong hiring her.

"Oh dear," Annie frowned. "No wonder you look like a drowned rat and you smell like… chemicals?"

"I went to the morgue," Clara explained.

Annie gave a very deliberate shudder.

"I don't know how you can bear it, being around all those corpses."

"I don't find them frightening or disgusting," Clara shrugged. "They are just people who have stopped living. Often they just look like they are asleep."

"Sounds ghoulish to me," Annie repeated the shudder and held her head up as if such antics were beneath her.

"You forget that someone has to take care of us when we are gone in spirit, if not in body. They must be certain we were not encouraged to our ends by foul play and then prepare us for our final departure, either to earth or fire. That is surely a very noble thing?"

Annie shifted uncomfortably.

"Well, there is that," she muttered. "Still I am glad I am not responsible for them."

She wandered off to retrieve warm scones from the oven. Clara smirked to herself, even though Annie had been home alone, with no one to cook for, she could not help herself but continue to bake. And, somehow, she had timed her scones to perfection, so they would be available when Clara walked in.

"You have a touch of the clairvoyant about you, Annie," Clara chuckled.

Annie looked at her baffled.

"You seem to have known when I was coming home and made sure there were warm scones wanting," Clara elaborated.

Annie gave a huff through her teeth.

"This is my third batch," she laughed. "I offered to make scones for the church's winter fair this weekend."

"Oh," Clara said, somewhat disappointed that Annie had not been magically in tune to her arrival home. "How many more have you got to make?"

"I am aiming for one hundred, just to be on the safe side."

Clara could not hide her astonishment at this mammoth task Annie was undertaking.

"Surely the fair will not sell through one hundred scones?" She said.

"They will once people get a taste of mine," Annie said proudly. "And they sell them cheap, so everyone who comes in buys one. Last year they sold seventy-six scones and were having to bake more there and then. That won't happen this year."

Annie smiled with satisfaction at her latest batch of scones, certain that she would be able to over-provide for the winter fair and prove her worth as a cook. For if there was one think that Annie did see as her purpose in life, it was demonstrating to Brighton that she was the finest cook the town had ever seen. A church fair was just one step on the journey.

"Can I try one?" Clara asked.

Annie cast a scowl in her direction.

"You will not touch my scones, Clara Fitzgerald, you will mess up my count."

Clara smiled to herself. It had been worth a try.

While Annie was putting the scones to one side to cool, there was a knock on the front door. Annie pulled a face as she debated whether to abandon her tray of scones or answer the door. Clara resolved the matter for her.

"I'll get it."

She had it at the back of her mind that the person at the door might be someone she would prefer Annie not to meet. Her stomach was in knots as she tried to walk calmly down the hall. Had Leong sent someone to harass her? Or was this a messenger from Chang? How had she become caught between the pair of siblings? Clara was beginning to wish she had never heard the name Brilliant Chang, but you can't change the past.

She braced herself as she opened the door and was infinitely relieved to see that the person on the doorstep was Captain O'Harris.

"This is a nice surprise," Clara smiled, her trepidation evaporating like smoke.

"Sorry to disturb you, I needed to have a word."

"John, I am never sorry to see you and you must feel free to interrupt my day at any time," Clara told him gently.

Captain O'Harris paused for a moment, then a boyish grin appeared on his face.

"You called me John."

"Well I am not going to go around calling you 'captain', that would be insufferable, and O'Harris is much too formal for us these days, would you not say? After all, you call me Clara."

O'Harris was still grinning as he stepped inside, delighted by Clara's informality. The pair of them were still getting used to the idea of being more than just friends. The torturously slow rate they were discovering their feelings for one another was driving Annie and Tommy slightly mad, but nothing was going to rush them. Both needed time to come to terms with the idea of not being independent loners anymore, and both were a little wary of making themselves vulnerable to another person.

"Come into the kitchen, it's warm there. But don't expect a scone, Annie is being fiercely protective of them," Clara declared as she led him to the back of the house.

Annie heard the statement and gave her another scowl, before smiling at O'Harris.

"We'll need more tea," she said. "The scones are for the church winter fair, that's why they are off-limits. You know full well, Captain O'Harris, that you are welcome to my scones any other time."

O'Harris reddened a little, finding the statement somewhat alarming, even though Annie had no notion of what she had said. Clara muffled a snort of laughter.

"Take a seat," she said in a strangled voice and O'Harris joined her at the table.

"I hoped I would catch you in, I needed to talk to you," O'Harris said as he took his chair, his humour was rapidly replaced by a morose expression. "After what you said yesterday, I took this idea into my head that I should follow the inspector and see if there was any truth to the accusations you had been told."

Annie appeared at the table with a teapot, her face fallen.

"What is this?"

Clara had also become sombre.

"Someone has accused Inspector Park-Coombs of taking bribes from this new gang in Brighton," Clara explained to her, seeing no reason Annie should be kept in the dark. "It is obviously a very serious thing."

"I know you were not convinced by the accusation, yet it worried you and I hoped to be helpful," O'Harris continued. "I was not trying to interfere, as such, but thought a fresh pair of eyes on the matter might be useful."

"I fear you are going to tell me something I would rather not hear," Clara said softly.

"Honestly, Clara, once I was out there loitering by the police station, I thought myself the biggest fool there ever was. I really thought I was quite crazy, and I nearly went home, but then Park-Coombs emerged from the police station and I followed him instead."

O'Harris paused for a long time.

"Clara, I saw something that I really think suggests Park-Coombs is working against us in this matter."

Annie thudded the teapot down on the table and Clara suspected she had nearly dropped it.

"No, that can't be!"

"I can only tell you what I saw," O'Harris said, hearing the anger in her tone. "I followed Park-Coombs to the picture house, the one near the alleyway where Peterson was attacked. He went down a side road, a dead-end next to the building and he was joined there by two men I can only describe as thugs. While I did not see what happened, I heard them talking and know they gave Park-Coombs an envelope. I think it contained money. I think they were paying him off."

"I won't believe it!" Annie snapped. "Not of the Inspector. There are constables on the force I would hesitate to trust, for sure, but not Inspector Park-Coombs. You are wrong, O'Harris!"

"All right Annie," Clara calmed her. "John was only doing what he felt was right and trying to help us."

Annie did not look satisfied; she had a deep frown on her face.

"The matter does seem suspicious," Clara said to O'Harris. "I never would have believed it had it come from anyone other than you. You cannot tell me anything more?"

"Not really, only that they agreed to meet in a different place next time and from the sound of it, these were regular meetings. I'm sorry Clara, I don't think I really expected to find the Inspector up to anything untoward," O'Harris gave a deep sigh. "I was angry with him, wanted to get back at him because of the whole affair with Peterson. I was so keen to find out he was a traitor to the force, and yet, once I did, I felt so awful."

"I think you are wrong," Annie said in a quiet but firm

voice. "I think there is an honest explanation for what you saw."

"That would be good, Annie," O'Harris said gently. "I would like that."

Clara was struggling to get what O'Harris had told her into her head. The words were there, but the meaning refused to stick. To think that the inspector, a man she had trusted so much, a man she considered a friend, would meet with thugs and accept money broke her a little inside. She tried to see some other reason for the meeting, but why would they be giving him an envelope of money if it was not a bribe?

Clara felt betrayed and that blossomed into anger. How could he do this? How could he destroy all he had worked for? For the sake of money?

Clara closed her eyes, the implications sitting on her like a lead weight. She felt someone reach out and clasp her hand. Opening her eyes, she saw O'Harris was staring at her with a worried expression.

"I am really sorry," he said.

"This is not your fault. I just..." Clara could not say that she was disappointed that Brilliant Chang had been correct, and that it was him who had first raised her suspicions. "I am angry with the inspector. I feel he has let us all down."

"And I think you are judging him too quickly," Annie said sharply. "Maybe you ought to get his side of the story before jumping to conclusions? Has he not been a good friend to us? He deserves to be able to defend himself at least."

Annie's anger, which was for a wholly different reason to that which Clara was suffering, made her stop and think. Annie was right, the situation was easy to misinterpret, there could be another reason why he was taking money from thugs – couldn't there?

"If it was you Clara, wouldn't you want to be given the chance to explain yourself?" Annie persisted. "Wouldn't you want to be judged on your past actions, rather than on suppositions and an overheard conversation? No offence to you, Captain O'Harris, but it is all too easy to read the wrong thing into a situation, especially if you have a preconceived idea already in your mind. We see what we want to see sometimes."

"Fair point, Annie," O'Harris gave her a placating smile. "I don't take offence for your logical argument. Had there not been this accusation spoken to Clara…"

"And who told Clara that? Is this person someone you would trust above and beyond the inspector, Clara?" Annie demanded.

Clara had a very simple response to that.

"No. I don't trust this person, nor did they tell me who gave them the information in the first place."

"Chinese whispers!" Annie said, casting up her hands as if that solved the problem. She had no idea how close she had come to the truth. "Well, I would have thought the inspector had earned a little more respect than that. Surely he deserves the benefit of the doubt?"

"You are right Annie," Clara said, finally making up her mind. "He does deserve that. I think recent events have muddled all our thoughts and left us feeling… distrustful. The inspector has his flaws, but I have never considered him anything but honest."

Clara turned to O'Harris.

"That does not mean I doubt what you saw, John, just that we must be careful how we interpret it. I am trying to think of an innocent reason, and I am not succeeding, but I agree with Annie that I must not leap to conclusions."

O'Harris nodded.

"That is for the best, I would hate to condemn a man on so little. After all, if these rumours spread, this could end the inspector's career and land him in prison."

That was a sobering thought, one that really caught Clara's attention.

How useful to Chang would it be if the inspector was considered corrupt?

How useful, indeed.

Chapter Twenty-Four

Tommy arrived home late that evening. It had been a long tiring day for him, and he walked through the front door looking shattered. Tommy's war wounds had left him with a slight limp that most of the time was virtually unnoticeable, but when exhausted the defect became more pronounced. Clara could see by the way he was dragging his leg just how weary he was.

"Have you had any supper?" Annie declared the second she saw him, taking his coat and hat from him before he was barely out of them. "Sit down and I shall cook you some bacon and eggs. Food on trains is terrible. You'll need a good strong cup of tea too. Did you eat the sandwiches I sent you with?"

Assailed by this string of questions and statements, Tommy had no idea what to say. He stumbled into the front room and slumped in a chair, grateful to be back in his own home. Annie disappeared, talking about making up a hot water bottle for his stiff leg.

Clara sat down opposite her brother.

"Sorry," she said.

"Sorry?" He opened one tired eye.

"I didn't think about how exhausting this would all be

for you. It was selfish of me to send you."

Tommy made a scoffing noise.

"I might be a little travel sore, but it certainly won't kill me. Anyway, don't you want to know what I turned up?"

"I do," Clara leaned forward in her chair. "Anything that could point to the killer?"

"Possibly. I went to various theatres asking about Stanley Hutson, most people were extremely talkative. On the whole he seems to have been well liked, just a touch of professional jealousy here and there."

"From other dames?" Clara asked.

"You got it," Tommy grinned. "Some felt he was overrated, stated that quite bluntly. Others mentioned his drinking habits, though from what I can tell that was largely in the past."

"Anyone mention the incident with him and Mervyn Baldry?"

"A couple of people, but the general consensus was that the pair had remained friends afterwards. Stanley had forgiven Mervyn and Mervyn was keen to make amends. There was no suggestion of a lasting grudge."

"Not terribly helpful," Clara sighed. "Other than to make it seem less likely Mervyn was the murderer."

"True, but that wasn't the only gossip I came across."

Clara brightened up.

"Do go on, I hope it is good. Something terribly scandalous that will explain all this."

"Well, you shall have to decide that," Tommy flipped over his hands in a gesture of uncertainty. "The rumour I heard came from several sources, but it was a little vaguer than I would like. The gist of it seemed to be that many years ago, back when Stanley was just beginning to make his name, he stole some of his characteristic quirks or performance techniques, whatever you call them, off another actor."

"Stole," Clara took care over the word. "Was that precisely what was said?"

"Yes, the people who offered this information used that

word. You see, I went in with the premise that Stanley was being threatened, that I was working for Mr Maddock to determine the origin of these threats and whether Mr Hutson was in any danger. I told people that the word 'thief' had been used in these threats."

"And this tempted people into gossiping," Clara nodded. "It makes sense. Theatres are rife with rumours and actors are some of the worst gossips going, especially when the matter concerns a rival. I suppose Stanley was condemned by his own success. Jealousy being a great one for sparking hate."

"Something like that," Tommy agreed. "Anyway, once I mentioned the term thief, people seemed to come alive. That was when they remarked on these old rumours, and they are old. I mean, Hutson started performing last century, he has played a dame for, what, thirty years?"

"Around that," Clara concurred. "I wonder where he began? Could it be we have to delve so deeply into his past to find a reason for his death?"

Tommy was about to reply when Annie reappeared with his supper and a pot of tea. She placed a tray of food on his lap and the teapot by the hearth to keep warm. Clara noted the contents of the tray.

"A scone?" She pointed at the baked delight with an accusing finger.

"So there will only be ninety-nine for the church fair," Annie said without a hint of remorse. "Tommy needs the sustenance."

Clara raised an eyebrow at her, pretended to be offended, then started to chuckle.

"What is the joke?" Tommy looked at them perplexed.

"I am sure Annie will explain her epic scone cooking to you at some point, for the moment, I would like to hear more about these rumours concerning Hutson. Sit down and join us Annie, you look tired too."

Clara had noted that Annie seemed to be dead on her feet. So much industrious scone baking had left her unusually worn-out. Clara motioned Annie to sit, even as she began to protest.

"Oh, all right," Annie gave in, though she didn't seem to mind. "What has Tommy discovered?"

"It's not a huge amount to go on," Tommy admitted, feeling a tad under pressure now. "Just some of the people I spoke to said Hutson had stolen his act from someone else. Though, to be fair, there is more to an act than words and gestures. The actor must perform them in a certain way that makes them his own."

"That is a good point," Clara nodded. "And, of course, this could all be jealousy at play. A fellow actor might think Hutson stole their way of giving a line or playing a part, but it is more coincidence than reality… hmm, what would be the word for stealing a person's way of performing? Not plagiarism like in writing, maybe there isn't a word."

"Mr Hutson has been hugely successful," Annie said steadily. "If there was any real truth to these rumours, you would think someone would have spoken up and made a fuss."

"Depends on whether they had a case. I'm not sure it is illegal to steal someone's act," Tommy replied. "Also depends on if the person was inclined to protest. Some people just prefer to leave things alone."

"How compelling were the rumours?" Clara asked him.

Tommy considered for a moment, then said;

"I heard the near exact same story from several different people, and it had clearly been talked about a lot. Seems to me it was a well-established rumour, whether that makes it true or not is another matter."

"Who was the actor Hutson supposedly stole from?" Annie asked, sitting quietly in the chair with her hands folded in her lap. Her eyes were starting to droop as she fought the urge to fall asleep.

"No one could tell me that. One fellow said it was a chap called Olson who had performed once in Sleeping Beauty at the Palladium. Another thought the man named Smith and that he had never appeared in panto but had been an understudy for another actor when Hutson came across him. Most did not know who the person was, but they clearly liked the rumour and believed it."

"Hutson had a lot of rivals, simply because he was so famous and such a proficient performer, all this could be gossip-mongering by those who were envious of his stardom," Clara mused. "Then again, there might be something."

Tommy was shovelling bacon and eggs into his mouth with enthusiasm.

"It was the only thing I was offered that could explain why someone would want him dead. While a number of the people I asked seemed unsurprised by my suggestion Hutson was being threatened, they could not give me any real explanation for it other than the rumours I mentioned. He seemed a decent fellow, but what was unspoken was a sense that he had a ruthless streak when he was younger which saw him thrust his way into the starlight," Tommy paused over a forkful of eggs. "I think he became nicer after his success was assured and he felt settled in his role. I don't know, there was this undercurrent I couldn't quite explain. Most of the people I spoke to were younger than Hutson too, so probably were not in the theatre when this role-theft took place."

"Mervyn might know about it," Clara leaned back in her chair, feeling the fire lulling her to sleep too. "Mervyn is around the same age as Hutson and they began their careers at the same time. The problem I see, is why would someone wait this long to strike? We are talking thirty years and there must have been far better, far less risky opportunities to attack Hutson during that time. What makes this season so different? Is it the show, could there be a symbolism to that? Or something else, something important we are missing."

"Oh, that reminds me," Tommy paused to head to the hall and collect the briefcase he had taken with him to London. "One of the directors was a bit of a Hutson fan and has been collecting newspaper clippings about him for years. Nothing sinister as such, though he seemed desperate to have Hutson perform in his panto at some point. He is going to be terribly disappointed when he learns Hutson is dead.

"Anyway, when I mentioned the threats and trying to find something to explain them, he offered me his scrapbook of cuttings. It isn't just about Hutson, it contains clippings about this director's own shows and about others stars he follows."

"Sounds unpleasantly obsessive," Annie gave a shudder.

"No different to those people who collect clippings about the royal family or cricket players," Tommy shrugged. "I suppose it could lead to unhealthy obsession, but this director seemed grounded. He also had a complete collection of pantomime programmes from every London theatre dating back to 1905. He showed it to me. Shame it didn't go back further, else I might know when Hutson began his career."

"Every programme from every pantomime held in London since 1905?" Clara said in amazement.

"Carefully filed in albums by year. Even had a number of amateur production programmes. Honestly, this man was a panto enthusiast through and through. A walking encyclopaedia of panto knowledge, up to a point, seeing as he could no more elaborate on the thief rumours than anyone else."

Tommy produced the scrapbook and handed it to Clara. She turned to the first page and saw a large grainy newspaper picture of Hutson in full dame regalia receiving a standing ovation. The text beneath the picture indicated this was a special charity performance held before a prestigious audience, including members of the royal family.

Clara flicked through the pages, pausing to scan through articles. There were reviews of Hutson's performances, generally glowing, and several pieces about his charity work. It seemed Hutson regularly appeared at charity events to support worthwhile causes.

There were several pages concerning the split between

him and Baldry. The full details of the matter had been kept from the press, but Mervyn's morphine addiction was a badly kept secret and the newspapers were rife with speculation. Equally, Mervyn's dramatic attack had happened within view of an audience and it was impossible to stop people talking. Clara flicked through these clippings, looking for any hint of something she had not yet heard, but there was nothing new.

As interesting as the scrapbook was for filling in the professional details of Stanley's life, there was not anything that offered an insight into why he might have been killed until she came to a clipping close to the end of the book. At first glance, it seemed an odd thing to be included in the collection, for it was an obituary for another small-time actor. Clara was curious enough about why it had been carefully pasted to the page to read through the entire text, finally coming to a mention of Hutson.

"This is curious," Clara said aloud, noticing as she did that Annie was sound asleep and Tommy dozing off too.

Tommy opened his eyes and gave a drowsy response. "What is?"

"This obituary about a man called Albert Long. According to this, Mr Long began his acting career playing the understudy to a Mr Harper, who was a dame back in the 1880s. Then he started to play dame roles himself and he was partnered by Hutson playing Buttons. It's the original pairing, like Stanley and Mervyn only years before."

"Why is that interesting?" Tommy yawned.

"Well, it might not be, but Long never lived up to the potential expected of him, dropped out of lead roles and ended up in bit parts the rest of his days. It says here, the first year he played a dame, he became indisposed and Hutson took over the role. Stanley was asked about him for this obituary and stated – 'he was a kind and generous man, forever patient with his often ailing health. I learnt everything I know about panto from him, for he was my inspiration. Without him, I should not be here.' Does that not sound curious?"

Tommy was pulling himself from sleep.

"Say again?"

"Hutson is implying that he learned all he knew from Albert Long, but what if someone was to interpret that as he stole Long's act? He replaced Long in his first big role, and Long never played the dame again. The article paints him as a tragic figure who had always hoped for a lead part, but in his one moment of glory his health failed him and Hutson took over," Clara's eyes sparkling. "Can't you see? It could be argued by a jealous mind that Hutson stole Long's role, stole it from under his feet. And that was it for Long, he never achieved anything after that.

"Sorry story really, seems this obituary came from a theatrical paper where someone remembered the fellow and felt he deserved a little bit of the fame he could not find in life, in death."

"You are saying, it is this Long fellow all the rumours were about?"

"Listen to what Huston said, 'I learnt everything I know about panto from him… he was my inspiration… without him I should not be here.' Supposing Hutson meant he learned his dame act from Long? Maybe it was all amicable at first, then as Hutson rose to glory and Long slipped into obscurity, bitterness crept in?"

"Well, it does make a certain logic," Tommy thought about the words. "Especially if taking over from Long was Hutson's big break into dame roles. But there is a problem with your hypothesis that this is motive for Hutson's murder."

Clara looked at her brother.

"I know," she groaned. "I know."

She pressed a hand to her forehead.

"My best suspect is also dead."

Chapter Twenty-Five

Clara arrived at the police station to speak with Mervyn – or at least attempt to – and found the inspector hovering near the front desk. Clara found it hard to look him in the eye as he blithely greeted her.

"Morning Clara. Here to see Mervyn again?"

The inspector did not glance up from the papers he was reading, which enabled Clara to mask her obvious awkwardness around him.

"Yes, I am hoping he feels more talkative today."

"I am releasing him shortly, this is Dr Deáth's report and it clearly states the killer was much smaller than Mervyn. Deáth suggests we are looking for a woman," the inspector finally looked up. "Which rather narrows the list of suspects."

"The killer had accomplices, however," Clara shoved her uncertainties to one side and focused on the inspector's face with a determination that after a moment made him frown and look away.

"Yes, I read that too. Makes it all a little complicated, but find the killer and we'll hopefully find the accomplices."

"I may have the motive for the murder, but it is all rather vague. Hence why I am hoping Mervyn will offer some insight," Clara added. "If I can discover the 'why', then the 'who' should become clear."

"Perhaps," Park-Coombs said, clearing his throat a little self-consciously. "Is something the matter with your eyes Clara? You don't appear to have blinked in quite a while."

Clara remembered herself and shook off her intense stare.

"Sorry, long night," she lied. "Can I go to see Mervyn?"

"Certainly, and if you discover anything pop up to my office afterwards. I have some eye drops the wife bought me which are very soothing on tired pupils. You might like to try it."

Clara gave him a difficult smile and then walked past him, feeling awful that she had been so unable to disguise her feelings. What proof did she have that he was a traitor? None, aside from the confusing conversation Captain O'Harris had overheard and the dangerous words of Brilliant Chang. While she trusted O'Harris, he might have misinterpreted what he heard and Brilliant Chang was likely to have his own agenda. Annie had been right; the inspector deserved the benefit of the doubt. When had Clara become so distrustful of her friends?

Clara was solemn as she arrived by Mervyn's cell and this caused the man to visibly pale.

"They are going to charge me, aren't they?" He said. "I'm going to swing."

Mervyn put his head in his hands and gave out a sob. He seemed to have sobered to his situation since the night before and the impending sense of doom had finally broken his attitude of disregard. Clara felt bad that her expression had been so badly misunderstood, she was really making a pig's ear of things today.

"No, no, Mr Baldry. You are being released. The inspector has evidence you could not be the killer."

Mervyn pulled his head from his hands, his jaw slack with astonished relief.

"Released?"

"Yes. Your innocence has been proved," Clara added.

"However, that does leave us no closer to discovering Mr Hutson's true murderer. I had hoped you might help me."

"I already told you everything I could about that night," Mervyn looked grim. "I don't know what you are hoping for."

"I want to know about an event in Hutson's past," Clara explained. "I think it might be the key to his death."

Mervyn blinked, sudden hope flickering in his eyes. He was more cooperative now the reality of the situation was dawning on him.

"What event?"

"I have heard rumours that Hutson stole his dame act from another actor," Clara said.

"Those rumours have been doing the rounds for years," Mervyn nodded. "Spoken by people jealous of Stanley's success."

"That is what I suspected," Clara agreed. "Yet, there must have been a source for these rumours? I half wondered if it had anything to do with Albert Long?"

Mervyn almost seemed to startle at the sound of the name.

"Albert Long," he muttered to himself. "Now, that is a name I have not heard in a while. One of those all too sad stories of a talent that never lived up to the promise."

"How do you mean?" Clara asked.

"Albert was a dear fellow and he enjoyed comic roles. He played a dame in a small amateur production and was quite the hit, despite his youth. Generally, dame actors are older, it makes the part more amusing to have this old man in a wig and make-up. Albert really made a mark on that role. The next year he was hired to play in a proper panto and his sidekick was a young actor named Stanley Hutson, playing Buttons."

Mervyn smiled to himself.

"Stanley was not a bad Buttons, but the role did not suit him. Amuses me to think about it. He was far too dominant a personality for such a role. Buttons has to be a little subservient, very clumsy and prone to mishaps. Bumbling, that's the word for it. Stanley could never fully lower himself to such a performance."

"From what I understand, he was not required to play Buttons for long?" Clara nudged him.

Mervyn's smile faded.

"Albert Long was never the healthiest of souls. Not sure if it was his heart or his lungs, or maybe something else. Don't suppose the doctors in those days knew either. Anyway, just a week in the role of the dame and he was worn-out and had to stop performing. Stanley slipped into his shoes without hesitation. I think he had been craving that role."

"And he was good as the dame? He mimicked Albert?"

"Well, he had watched him perform, that was natural..." Mervyn tailed off as the realisation struck him. "That could be where those rumours came from, yes, now you mention it. Stanley became 'Albert Long the dame' and maybe some folks whispered he stole the part from him. Not maliciously at first, because we say that in acting, you know, he stole the spotlight and so on. But with time, and with Albert never living up to what he had hoped for, yes, it could have turned into something more sinister."

"Someone might even consider that Stanley was a thief," Clara suggested. "And that he was in part responsible for Albert's failure to become famous."

Mervyn was nodding his head, seeing the way she was thinking and agreeing with it.

"What can you tell me about Albert?" Clara asked.

Mervyn wrinkled his brow as he thought about the question.

"Albert was a few years older than Stanley and was desperate to be on the stage. I saw him perform in something Shakespearian once. Maybe he played Falstaff? Can't really remember. The dame role in that big panto was meant to be the performance that made his name, but having to withdraw so early on scuppered everything. Nothing a director hates more than a sick actor. He might put up with that from a big star, but not a nobody. Word got around that Albert did not have the stamina for lead roles and he never got another chance.

"He played smaller parts, though, and I don't think he was ever out of work. He played supporting parts in some of the pantos myself and Stanley were involved in. He appeared as the old baron in Cinderella, and the king in Jack and the Beanstalk. Roles that did not require great effort and where he was only on stage for a few scenes."

"Did that make him angry?"

"There was a sadness about him," Mervyn said thoughtfully. "Like his life had been a great disappointment. Honestly, we rarely spoke. His death was a surprise."

"Really? With his chronic ill health, I would have thought it would have been expected."

Mervyn looked Clara sadly in the eyes, clearly knowing something she did not.

"You don't know how he died, then?"

"I assumed his illness finally caught up with him," Clara said. "We all know those poor souls who suffer endless sickness and finally are so weak it snatches them away. I imagined pneumonia, or a complication from his existing health problems."

"That is how the papers made it sound," Mervyn concurred. "Have you read his obituary in the London Theatre News?"

Clara tried to recall if the clipping she had read in the scrapbook had been labelled as to its origins.

"I might have," she said. "I read one where Hutson gave a small quote."

"Sounds like the one," Mervyn rubbed his chin. "It was very polite, as far as I can remember, didn't go into details."

"How did Albert die?" Clara asked, feeling a slight hint of dread.

"He hung himself," Mervyn told her bluntly. "He lived all alone in rooms he rented. One evening he came home from playing in a panto. Ironically it was Aladdin and he was playing the sultan. No one had noticed anything amiss with him, the performance had gone smoothly. Mervyn walked up to his lodgings, saying goodnight to his landlady on the way.

"Next morning he did not come down for breakfast. The landlady assumed he was sleeping in. When he didn't appear for lunch, she started to grow concerned. Knowing Albert's health was sometimes precarious she went up to check on him. She received no response from knocking on his door, so let herself in. And there she found him, hanging from a hook he had screwed into a ceiling beam.

"He left a note. Said he was tired of being a failed actor. Tired of being the side part. He was also exhausted by his own ill health and was in a lot of pain. They say that clutched in his hand was the programme from the very first panto he was in, the one where he was meant to play the dame. I guess you could see that as a sort of symbolism."

The story of Albert's passing cast a pall over Clara. She felt slightly numb as she envisioned the poor man hanging from the ceiling, all his hopes and dreams gone, and in his hand the one stark reminder of what could have been. Was it hard to imagine he was bitter? Maybe that he even hated the man who had stepped into his shoes and acquired the fame that should have been his?

"I don't see how this relates to Stanley," Mervyn brought her back to reality. "Albert has been dead several years. He can't have killed him."

"No, but I am thinking that someone who cared about Albert took revenge on his behalf, especially now you have told me the manner in which he died. That would make a person angry in their grief."

"Albert had no wife or children to take revenge for him," Mervyn shrugged. "Though I do see your point. Would make sense of the 'thief' accusation. Someone felt that Stanley had not only stolen Albert's part, but his future."

"Do you remember Albert's act as the dame? Did Stanley permanently take on any of the traits Albert used in the performance?"

Mervyn frowned, trying to rattle the past from his

brain.

"I'm not sure, I can't really remember."

"Alright, what do you know about Albert's friends and family? No one is totally alone in this world."

This was another aspect of the conversation that caused Mervyn to crease his brow in deep thought.

"I think his parents were dead, he might have had a sister? I really don't know. He was a figure in the background, someone who was there but who I rarely noticed. I recall him being friendly with Eustace Drake. That's the actor who is playing the vizier in our Aladdin. Maybe he will know more."

That was something. Clara had a possible motive now, but she could also be barking up the wrong tree. She thanked Mervyn and walked away.

She was about to leave the police station when she recalled that Park-Coombs had asked her to see him when she was done. She toyed with the idea; a part of her not wanting to face the inspector again, then she told herself she was being damn stupid and forced her feet around and back in the direction of the stairs.

The inspector glanced up as she entered his office.

"Anything?" He asked.

"Maybe," Clara loitered by the door. "There is this Albert Long, who killed himself and who some people seem to imply Stanley stole his dame part from. Could be someone was after revenge."

"Is that it?" The inspector asked, looking disappointed.

"Pretty much until I can investigate further," Clara was playing with her fingers nervously. "Anyway, I shall be off…"

"Clara, what is the matter? You are acting as if I make you nervous?" Park-Coombs twitched his moustache, a sure sign he was unhappy.

He looked a little hurt and Clara felt awful. She was acting nervous and treating him like there was something wrong and for what? Vague rumours and possible lies. How would she feel if such a thing was done to her? Pretty horrible. She would not only feel betrayed by her friends, but she would be offended that they had not trusted her enough to speak aloud their concerns. She would have liked to think they knew her better, just as she should know Park-Coombs better.

Clara came to a sudden decision. She made sure the door to the office was shut and came and sat in the chair before the inspector's desk.

"I'm twitchy for a couple of reasons," Clara explained, knowing that once she began the floodgates would be opened. "The first of which is that I have been told you are corrupt."

It was blunt, brutal, but the inspector deserved honesty.

"I do not want to believe this, because you are my friend. But someone witnessed you receiving money from two thugs near the picture house and so now I feel utterly confused."

Park-Coombs had listened in silence, his face reddening with what Clara guessed was anger. She would be pretty angry too if she was accused of being corrupt and working with the enemy.

"I haven't known how to speak about this to you and it has been eating at me. That's why I am acting so awkward. I feel terrible even considering such accusations and I hate that this has been even suggested to me," Clara was speaking fast and had to catch her breath. "It's all this gang business. It has muddled my head. I don't know what to think anymore."

She glanced at the inspector, waiting for an explanation. She thought he was going to explode, he looked fit to. Park-Coombs took a shaky breath.

"Well, that was unexpected," he said and his voice was remarkably calm.

Clara anticipated more, but it did not come. She cleared her throat.

"We have known each other long enough to deserve honesty," she said. "That's why I told you."

"And now you want an explanation?" Park-Coombs

smiled grimly.

"Maybe, if you want to tell me," Clara dropped her eyes to her lap.

"Hmm, explanations are all well and good if you believe them."

Clara lifted her head, fixed her gaze on him and said in a voice that was both calm and serious.

"Try me."

Chapter Twenty-Six

Inspector Park-Coombs sat back his chair and let his hands rest in his lap. The weariness Clara had observed before was now plainly visible – the bags beneath his eyes, the extra lines around his mouth and across his forehead, a hollowness to his cheeks that suggested a loss of weight due to infrequent meals. The toll of recent events was obvious and Clara felt a resurgence of guilt that she had doubted the inspector. He had been pushed to his limits recently and he did not need Clara's suspicions on top of that.

Park-Coombs closed his eyes for just a moment and took a long breath.

"This is not a conversation I ever expected to have with you, Clara," he said, and the hurt in his tone stung.

"No, I suppose not. I spoke in haste," Clara said, feeling she should excuse herself and say he did not need to explain, but just as she was getting up the inspector raised his hand to halt her.

"I want to clear the air, Clara. Obviously you have your reasons for your doubts."

"I am not sure they are good enough reasons," Clara

said unhappily.

"Well, they are reasons, and I don't want this difficulty between us. We need to work together. This is a dangerous time for Brighton, possibly a dangerous time for you."

Clara thought of her association with Chang and Leong.

"Were you angry I told you not to mess about in this gang business?"

Park-Coombs' sudden question distracted Clara from her internal woes. She was surprised by the question.

"No, I mean, I understood it was a task beyond me. If I went poking around, I would likely end up in a lot of trouble for no real reason. I would be putting you to bother keeping me safe. It was different when Peterson was involved, but I have no personal interest in the gang now. Even if I hate the fact it is operating in Brighton."

The inspector nodded thoughtfully.

"That is not one of the reasons you wondered if I was corrupt?"

"No," Clara said firmly, though she recalled that it had crossed her mind. "Look, I think I just got the wrong end of the stick with all this."

"Well, let me attempt to put your mind at ease," the inspector's chair creaked as he rested back in it further. "What this witness of yours saw, I am guessing it was either Tommy or O'Harris? No, you don't have to say who. Anyway, what they saw was me talking with two members of this particular gang. I won't deny that. I have very few ways of getting into this business, and limited resources, some of my superiors are not convinced there even is a problem. You know how they think, if the matter only concerns the working classes and no one with any clout is being bothered, they are inclined to ignore the matter.

"They are more interested in the perennial sheep rustling in Hove. Farmers and landowners have loud voices, you see. So, I have my hands tied. To make matters worse, those who might be witnesses to the trouble are the sort who like to avoid the police. They might have been in trouble with the law themselves, or they might simply view us with suspicion. Basically, this whole affair has become quite a struggle.

"The only solution was to go down a different route. Remember the deaths of Jenny and Callum Little? That upset some folks around here. They were local people and seeing them being dispatched by outsiders, Londoners even, stuck in the throats of a few. I decided to use that to my advantage. I have contacts among the criminally inclined, all good policemen do, and I played on their local pride. I eventually found a couple of local lads who had become involved with this new gang but didn't like the way things were going. They had friends who had been hurt, that sort of thing. They were resentful, but too scared of retribution to do anything drastic. However, they were prepared to supply me with information.

"What your witness saw was me receiving information about the gang. However, they were not entirely wrong in their interpretation. You see, to provide an element of safety for my informants, we have been using the ruse that they are paying me off to look the other way."

Park-Coombs paused and opened a drawer in his desk. He withdrew three envelopes, all of them containing money.

"These are my 'bribes'," he said. "My subterfuge. When this is all done with, I'll donate the money to charity. And, before you ask, my superiors are aware of my shenanigans. I had the sense to run it past them before I started this operation. Since they would not offer me extra manpower or funding to crack this gang head-on, the least they could do is give permission for me to play this game."

Clara found herself staring at the money in the envelopes on the desk before her. There had to be several hundred pounds.

"At least this explains why I was told you were being paid off. As far as the gang leader is concerned, you are a corrupt policeman."

"Exactly," Park-Coombs allowed himself a small smile. "I thought you might have given me the benefit of the doubt, though."

The light rebuke in his voice prodded at Clara's conscience.

"I am a cynic, Inspector. What can I say?"

"You could apologise," Park-Coombs suggested.

"Yes, you are right. Inspector, I am sorry I doubted you, I am sorry I did not come to you at once with my concerns instead of letting them fester in my mind," Clara paused. "I hope you can forgive me?"

"Of course," Park-Coombs said gently. "And I would like to apologise for failing to alert you to what I was up to. I should have known that little escapes your attention."

They both hesitated awkwardly. Park-Coombs' confession had forced Clara to consider her own secrets and how they were plaguing her mind. Her eyes wandered to those envelopes again, thinking about trust and how she was assisting Chang and Leong by keeping quiet. Finally, she decided that she must speak up.

"I have a problem too," she said. "I have been scared to speak about it in case it resulted in something bad happening."

Park-Coombs frowned. He leaned onto his desk, hands clasped together.

"Clara?"

"Brilliant Chang is in Brighton," Clara said. "It's all rather complicated, but it seems he wants to shut down this new gang as much as we do, though his reasons are less community-minded than ours."

"Chang," Park-Coombs muttered the name. "He perceives this gang as a danger to him?"

"If what he has told me is true, he has reason to be concerned. The gang is run by his sister, Jao Leong, and he fears for his own wellbeing. She is ruthless, or so I am told."

The inspector let out an incredulous whistle.

"I didn't know that. The gang leader is a woman?"

"Yes, and Chang is very worried. He wants to use me as a go-between so that he can pass information to the police, to you. He wants his sister arrested and imprisoned before any great harm can befall either him or her."

"Nasty business," Park-Coombs tutted. "Though wouldn't be the first time siblings started a gang war. Has Chang offered you any useful information?"

"Other than his sister is behind the gang, not really. At least nothing that would lead to her arrest, but there is more."

Park-Coombs raised an eyebrow to show he was intrigued but said no more.

"Jao Leong has also approached me. She wants me to trace her brother," Clara found just repeating what had happened somewhat unbelievable.

"She has hired you?"

"She did not exactly give me a choice. Not that she threatened me, rather she just did not give me a chance to turn her down. I confess I was a little dumbstruck by it all too," Clara almost laughed at the bizarre turn of events. "It seems to me that this whole problem is an overinflated argument between two twisted and immoral siblings, with Brighton caught in the middle. I honestly don't know what to do anymore."

Park-Coombs tapped his fingers on the desk, thinking through this new information.

"Clara, you have to keep talking to both siblings."

"I don't really want to, I am worried what might happen if either of them decide I am no longer of use, or worse, learn I have been playing them."

"I know, but you don't really have an option. They have sought you out, and I doubt you will be given the option of backing out. Chang, at least, wants to use the police, or rather me, and that will be helpful. Leong is more complicated, but if she wants you to find her brother, I suggest you at least appear to be doing so."

That was not what Clara wanted to hear.

"Surely, now you know her name, you could just arrest Leong?"

"You know as well as I do that without evidence I can do nothing. I have the word of a criminal mastermind that his sister is leading a gang. It's not going to stand-up in court, especially as few people would consider a woman capable of such a thing."

"More fool them," Clara muttered, but she knew he was right. "Then what do I do?"

"Sadly, Clara, you have become involved in this messy business much like myself. You will have to play a tricky double-game. Tell Chang that Leong has hired you to find him, for a start, see what he makes of that."

"I am not supposed to get in touch with Chang," Clara muttered. "He insisted on that for security, and I don't really fancy taking a chance, even though I know where he is hiding out. When he wants me, he summons me."

"That really does not sound like your kettle of fish," Park-Coombs looked sad. "Since when did Clara Fitzgerald take orders from anyone?"

Yes, since when? Clara disliked the question because it offended her, but it was also accurate.

"I suggest you find a way to contact Chang sooner rather than later," Park-Coombs had become very serious. "Leong will likely have limited patience for you to find her brother, so you need to arrange something with Chang. I think it would be best for your safety."

"I'm not sure I want to be a detective anymore," Clara grumbled. "I have this dread in the pit of my stomach all the time."

"I understand," the inspector offered her what sympathy he could. "With any luck I shall have this whole matter resolved soon and there will be no more Leong to worry about. Until then, you must do everything in your power to stay safe. Any concerns, you must come to me day or night. I could send a constable to watch your back."

"That would be too obvious," Clara replied. "I shall have to manage this myself. No one, apart from you, knows about this. I thought that for the best."

"O'Harris and Tommy might get a little over-protective?"

"O'Harris is already sensitive about this gang trouble.

He wants revenge for Peterson, though he has not admitted that to himself. Tommy isn't much better. They would act rashly and potentially get themselves hurt."

Clara did not vocalise her fears of something much worse happening, she preferred to keep such thoughts secret, even to herself.

"At least I know now," Park-Coombs said calmly. "You ever need help Clara, you just call me."

"I feel terrible, Inspector. I came here and accused you of accepting bribes and you still want to help me."

"You did not accuse me," the inspector smiled. "Besides, I already told you that I had made a good job of making it look like I was corrupt. I actually feel quite pleased I fooled you. Hopefully that means I have fooled Leong too. Anyway, we are friends."

Clara still felt guilty, but his words were comforting.

"I hate all this," she said. "I hate that I am being used, or at least that is how it feels."

"You are not being used," Park-Coombs told her firmly. "You are using them. I have every faith you are cunning enough to play Leong and Chang off each other. Between us, we shall find a way to resolve this mess and make Brighton safe again."

"I hope you are right. Well, in the meantime I need to find the killer of Stanley Hutson."

Park-Coombs pulled a face.

"Killer and accomplices. Dr Deáth said it might have taken three people to move that body," Park-Coombs winced at the thought. "And if Mervyn is ruled out, we are somewhat stumped."

"I am certain the solution lies with this Albert Long and the rumours that Hutson stole his part," Clara said. "I just need to figure out who might be taking revenge for a dead man."

Clara glanced out of the window at the rain. Would it ever be dry again? Her fingers felt chilled and she was not looking forward to the long walk to the theatre.

"Does it sound odd that dealing with an ordinary

murder, one not tied up with conspiracy and criminals is rather a relief. I think this case may be keeping me sane."

"I think I understand," Park-Coombs chortled. "Give me a bog-standard case of sheep rustling, any day. Which reminds me, I need to go over to White Farm and see if the constable I left out there has any news. Would you like a lift home?"

"No, thank you, I think it would be best if we maintain our distance for the duration," Clara sighed, thinking a drive in a car would have been nice. "Anyway, I am going back to the theatre."

"If you see Mr Maddock, tell him his Buttons will be released by noon."

"I am certain that will delight him," Clara smiled.

"I hope so, he has been moping around the station with a face like thunder since the arrest. I don't think he fully appreciates that a man has been murdered and that takes precedent over his little pantomime."

"I imagine he would see things completely opposite," Clara remarked. "The show must go on, and all that."

Park-Coombs twitched his moustache at the adage, clearly not impressed.

"Damn the show, I deal with justice and finding a killer no matter what it takes."

"Some would argue that the needs of the living are greater than the needs of the dead," Clara suggested.

The dirty look Park-Coombs gave her in return summed up his feelings on that particular statement.

Chapter Twenty-Seven

Clara returned to the theatre with Tommy. She had a short list of possible suspects, now that nearly all the men had been ruled out. She was hoping that Eustace Drake might shed some light on who could be responsible for the crime, who might be keen to avenge Albert Long.

They approached the theatre by the back alley, as the main doors would be locked at this time of day. They found Erikson there, sitting on the step before the door and smoking a cigarette. He looked miserable.

"Morning," Clara called out.

Erikson lifted his head and stared at her with a look of dazed sombreness.

"Who is around?" Clara added when Erikson failed to respond.

"Mostly everyone," Erikson took a drag of his cigarette.

"You look down in the dumps," Tommy observed. "What's troubling you?"

Erikson shrugged.

"Ah, women problems," Tommy said at once. "Never knew anything else that can cause a man such heartache as a woman."

Erikson flicked what remained of his cigarette away.

"Yeah, well, too good to be true, I suppose," he muttered. "Been thrown over, not any use to her now, I guess. I've been a bloody fool."

A sudden flash of memory jolted Clara.

"That would be Audrey Burns who plays Aladdin?"

Erikson was taken aback that she knew so much about him.

"Yes. How did you know?"

"It was mentioned you were stood out here with her during the fire," Clara replied. "I believe she also was quick to speak up for you being out here with her when I was asking people about where everyone was the night Stanley Hutson died."

Erikson shivered at the mention of Hutson's name.

"I've been trying not to think about him," he said. "Anyway, Audrey told me to sling my hook this morning. You can't trust women, you know."

Erikson did not seem to realise the irony of his statement, spoken as it was to Clara.

"You can trust me," Clara said. "Besides, a girl like that is not deserving of your sorrow. If she is so cutthroat, you are better off without her."

Erikson grimaced.

"Yeah, probably," he mumbled, then he rose and headed into the backstage of the theatre as quickly as he could.

"Young love," Tommy said in a mocking tone.

Clara elbowed him.

"Don't be mean, Erikson was clearly enamoured."

"These theatre romances never last, name me an actor who has remained married to the same woman all his days?"

"I'll think about it," Clara said, certain there must be at least one who had broken the mould. "But you know what it is, people always assume they shall be different."

"Erikson was the chorus boy and Audrey was the lead, that was never going to end well."

"You are such a pessimist."

"I prefer the term pragmatist. Men don't cope well

when the women in their lives are more successful than them. Simply the way things are."

Clara shook her head, not wanting to believe that statement as she entered the theatre. It did not take them long to stumble across Maddock.

"Good news, Mervyn should be released in time for the evening performance, if not the matinee," Clara told him.

Maddock's shoulders sagged with relief.

"One piece of luck at last," he groaned. "Wait, does that mean the police have identified the real killer?"

"Not yet," Clara said. "But I am getting closer."

Maddock nodded, still looking fraught.

"I would beg you to hurry, Miss Fitzgerald, the company is in turmoil wondering who did this terrible thing."

Clara knew there was simply no way to hurry an investigation, it dictated its own pace, but she did not say that.

"Can you point me in the direction of Eustace Drake?" She asked.

Maddock suddenly went pale.

"You don't suspect him? He is a stalwart of the stage!"

"No, no, that's not it," Clara told him swiftly. "I simply want to ask him about Hutson's past. Specifically about a fellow actor named Albert Long."

Maddock looked puzzled.

"Albert Long has been dead nearly four years," he said. "Poor man could not face the fact he had wasted his talent. It was a terrible tragedy. Stanley spoke at his funeral."

"I have heard rumours that suggest Hutson stole aspects of his dame performance from Long, being Buttons to his dame in their first pantomime and then taking over the role when Long became ill."

Maddock shook his head.

"Jealousy, that was all that was," he said. "Actors are catty creatures and there are plenty who are envious of Stanley's success. I wouldn't pay any heed."

"Yet, if someone else did take those rumours seriously,

and had reason to be deeply upset by Long's suicide, then they might consider taking revenge, whether the stories were true or not. That is a motive and a reason for writing 'thief' on Hutson's clothing."

Maddock seemed to reel back from this revelation. He was more than a little shocked by the news.

"Those rumours have been doing the circuit so long, no one really listened to them," he said, mostly to himself. "Stanley never, ever caused Albert any harm. He felt sorry for him, tried to always make sure he had a part in the productions Stanley was involved with. That was who he was. He wanted to help. Stanley was always helping."

"As he helped Miss Allen to get her part in this panto?" Clara asked.

Maddock gave a slight groan.

"Yes, he insisted, said she deserved a chance. He was too kind, you know? Sometimes he failed to see the reality of a situation. Miss Allen is a has-been, a child actress who is unremarkable as an adult performer. She just has to accept that. But you could never explain these things to Stanley. If I was not careful, I would end up with every role in the panto being filled by Stanley's charity cases."

Maddock was distracted by a stagehand appearing and calling his name. There was an issue with one of the backdrops that had snagged the evening before and torn. Maddock excused himself to deal with this minor emergency, pointing as he left to Eustace Drake's dressing room.

"Sometimes I think if anyone was going to get murdered it would be Maddock," Tommy whispered to Clara. "He says some harsh things about his cast. I didn't think Grace a bad actress."

"Were you possibly distracted by the skimpy costume and exotic dancing she did?" Clara teased him. "If I recall, she had extremely limited lines and did a lot of sitting around looking pretty."

"That's slightly harsh."

"I was merely observing that her performance was

rather uninspiring."

Clara knocked on Eustace Drake's dressing room door and a male voice asked her to enter.

"I think that somewhat mean, there was the cave scene," Tommy continued their conversation without interruption.

"If I recall that involved her screaming and swooning," Clara raised an eyebrow as she opened the door. "If that is acting, the theatre has truly gone downhill since last I was here."

Clara appeared in Eustace's dressing room with a smile on her face. The older man was sat on a sofa eating a hearty sandwich and reading the newspaper. His vizier costume remained on a hanger, waiting for him to don it.

Eustace Drake had turned sixty-four just a few days earlier and out of his make-up he rather looked his age. He was stout with a jowly face and a lot of wrinkles. His hair was grey verging on white and cut short for the purposes of wearing his vizier head dress. In his day he had been well known for his roles in Shakespeare and other sophisticated plays, now he tended to only appear in pantomimes, spending the rest of his year at his country estate where he happily enjoyed his semi-retirement. Unlike many in the company who either seemed bitter or despondent about their careers, Eustace was perfectly content. He liked his roles, he liked his life. He had settled into a routine that suited him and if some might argue he wanted for ambition these days, he would soon remind them that it was a worthy ambition to be happy and to enjoy life.

He smiled pleasantly at Clara.

"Hello, Miss Fitzgerald, isn't it?"

"That's right," Clara said. "I wondered if you had a moment to talk?"

Eustace grinned.

"Certainly. I don't have to start getting ready for ages as yet," Eustace motioned to a pair of chairs by his dressing table and Clara and Tommy sat down. "I imagine this is about dear Stanley? That hit me like a brick. To think he was murdered."

"Actually, I hoped you could help me in regards to another actor. Mr Albert Long?" Clara asked.

Eustace wrinkled his brow, his face becoming a map of tiny lines.

"Long has been dead for a while now."

"I know, I just wondered if it was possible someone blamed Hutson for his death. You see, someone wrote the word thief on Hutson's clothes, and that had to be for a reason. I then discovered rumours that Hutson had stolen his dame performance off someone and wondered if that someone was Long."

Eustace seemed troubled by the suggestion.

"Albert played a dame once, yes, but he took ill and was replaced."

"By Hutson," Clara pointed out.

Eustace thought about this for a while.

"Albert was unlucky, I think that was the way of it. His health was suspect and he never could make a breakthrough to bigger roles. That first dame part should have been his ticket to a brighter future, but to suggest Stanley stole it from him is to misunderstand the circumstances."

"People don't always see things correctly," Clara explained. "Especially when they are unhappy with their lives. They blame others. It is a form of jealousy."

Eustace still seemed confused. He contemplated his sandwich for a bit, then placed it back down on a plate.

"Albert's dead, you know?"

"Yes, but I wonder if there is someone looking for revenge on his behalf?" Clara said. "Someone who did not take his death well and places blame for it wrongly upon Hutson's shoulders."

Eustace tilted his head to one side.

"Albert had friends, but none I could imagine doing this."

"It may help you to know that I suspect the killer of Hutson is a woman."

Eustace's eyes widened. He was silent a while, his eyes straying to his costume. What he was thinking was a mystery, maybe he was contemplating his journey through the theatre and the jealousies and spite that had followed him. He had found a peaceful place to exist now, but he might well remember earlier days when securing a role meant pushing someone else out of the way.

"Albert was a complicated soul. He didn't really have many women friends, not… not like that," Eustace was not meeting Clara's eyes. "He preferred male company. In all ways."

"You are suggesting Mr Long was inclined towards men romantically?" Clara said cautiously.

"Happens a lot in the theatre," Eustace said nonchalantly. "You rather take it as the norm. Not that I am that way inclined, but I know plenty who are. They even once said that Albert and Stanley were something more than friends during that first panto season, but that was a lie. Stanley liked women. My point is that I can't think of any woman friend of Albert's who could have done this. He didn't have that many and none are on this cast."

"What about his family?"

"Parents are dead," Eustace said. "He had a sister. She lives in Gloucester, I think. She has nothing to do with the theatre. Married an accountant, which is about as far away as you can get from an actor."

Eustace chuckled.

"What was her name?"

"Lizzie," Eustace said. "Which I suppose was short for Elizabeth. I remember her coming to the theatre where Albert was performing a few times in the early years, then she drifted away. I saw her at Albert's funeral. She clasped my hand tight after it was all over and said she remembered us all so well, from those happier times."

"Were Albert and his sister close?" Tommy asked.

"Once, before she married," Eustace replied. "Sadly, the husband disliked Albert. I think he was one of those prudes who get sensitive about a man who likes men rather than women. It is all nonsense, nothing wrong with that sort. I've worked with so many over the years and some of them are really big names, men everyone thinks of as being womanisers. Anyway, Albert and Lizzie lost touch and I think we all rather felt that contributed to his death."

"What happened to Albert?" Clara asked. "I mean, why did he do it?"

"No one really knows," Eustace sighed sadly. "He had a part and for once it looked like things were going well for him. I think he was a little lonely, but we all get like that from time to time. I'm not married, you see, which is why I like the pantomime season. Christmas can be a time when you notice being alone more than ever. I guess Albert just couldn't cope with it anymore."

Clara felt terribly sad for this man she had never met, even if his death had been the possible catalyst for a murder.

"Do you know the name of the man Lizzie married?" Clara asked.

"Nope. He never came around the theatre and I was certainly not invited to their wedding. Albert went, of course," Eustace looked apologetic. "Sorry, that isn't helpful is it?"

"Not your fault," Clara smiled at him. "I don't suppose you have seen Lizzie recently?"

"Not since the funeral," Eustace shrugged. "There would be no reason."

"No, no there would not," Clara decided they had learned all they could. She rose, thanked Mr Drake and departed the dressing room.

Outside, she paused with Tommy.

"Another dead end?" Tommy spoke.

"I don't know," Clara admitted. "I don't want to let go of this just yet. It is the only lead we have got and the only motive we know about."

"Then we try to find out more about Lizzie Long?"

"Yes, I think so. Else it is back to the drawing board."

Tommy pulled a face that mimicked Clara's thoughts

about that. This was proving a tricky problem, with no obvious motive for murder and all the suspects seemingly accounted for.

"You see, if Albert had a niece, she could be in the cast," Clara mulled. "Might have followed in her uncle's footsteps."

"And avenged his death?" Tommy looked grim. "All right, that's our next step. Trace a niece and hope for the best."

"Or try to find someone else with a motive."

Clara was looking down the corridor at Grace Allen, who had just entered her dressing room.

"Either way, it's time we solved this."

Chapter Twenty-Eight

On the way home from the theatre, Clara excused herself to go into a shop and buy an umbrella. She had spotted a nice dark red one for sale in the window. Tommy said he would meet her at home and carried on his way. Inside the shop, Clara discovered the umbrella was not of the quality she had anticipated from viewing it in the window and was somewhat disappointed. She was debating whether or not to purchase it, the price tag being slightly extravagant for what she was getting, when a male voice spoke behind her.

"Might I be of assistance?"

She turned, expecting the shopkeeper or at least one of his staff and instead found Brilliant Chang. He was muffled up with a scarf and wore an old hat on his head that would not have looked out of place on a scarecrow. The judicious application of make-up had taken the usual light chestnut sheen of his skin down to a pasty and rather sickly looking grey. He was wearing round glasses, which did a clever job of masking his obviously oriental eyes. Despite this disguise Clara recognised him at once.

"You are taking a chance," Clara observed.

"A worthwhile chance," Chang said quietly. "We need

to talk."

"I should say," Clara sighed. "Look, I have been wanting to speak to you for a while, but I stuck to our arrangement not to contact you unless you first summoned me."

"I appreciate that," Chang said. "Which is why I am here. I've been trying to catch you alone for ages, but you will keep going into that damn police station."

"I am on a case," Clara said touchily. "Besides, if you were to work with the police, perhaps this matter would sort itself out sooner."

Chang snorted.

"Let's not talk nonsense. Look, the library is across the road, no one will be looking for me there. Let's go across and discuss what has been happening."

Clara simply nodded. She returned the umbrella to the display stand and allowed Chang to have a head start to the library. After fifteen minutes had passed, she followed, trying to look nonchalant while at the same time having her eyes peeled for signs of trouble.

She found Chang in the reading room, which happened to be empty at that time of day and allowed them a private place to talk. Chang had dropped the scarf from his chin and was fanning his face with his hat.

"I am boiling," he grumbled.

Clara had no reply to that and she wanted to get down to business before they were disturbed.

"Your sister approached me," she said bluntly.

Chang gave a start, which troubled Clara. She had hoped he had a suitable network of informants about the town keeping him up-to-date with things.

"You did not know?"

"No," Chang admitted, looking displeased. "What did she want?"

"She hired me to find you for her. Obviously she did not say that she was involved in criminal activities in the town, just that she was concerned for your safety."

"Huh? Yes, because she is the reason my safety might be in question," Chang stalked back and forth across the room. "This is unsettling."

"I should say, I feel like a piggy in the middle between you two and I am not terribly happy about it. Jao is going to want results and I don't want to think what will occur if she discovers I am working for you."

"Don't let her discover it," Chang shrugged at Clara as if this was obvious.

Clara had not expected sympathy but had hoped he might show some understanding.

"Between the pair of you, you have put me in a dreadful position," Clara told him sharply. "I can barely sleep at night for worry."

"You are a detective, that's part of the job," Chang brushed aside her concerns. "Eventually this was going to happen, or did you think you could exist without someone taking a grudge at some point?"

"I was hoping you might offer some reassurance," Clara folded her arms and glared at him. "Right now, I think I might be safest to just tell your sister where to find you and get her off my back."

"You can't do that!" Chang snapped.

"Why not?" Clara demanded. "I've got to look out for myself, and you are not offering me any sort of protection from Jao's wrath, should it fall upon me. I owe you nothing Chang, you are part of the reason this whole affair has occurred in the first place."

"This is not my fault!" Chang snapped, then he realised how loud his voice was and cringed.

They both waited to see if the librarian might appear and reprimand them for being noisy, but no one came. Chang sagged a little with relief.

"This was not meant to happen. I never expected Jao to do this."

"And yet she has," Clara said. "Chang, you are hiding out in an old house in the countryside while your sister runs roughshod over this town. It looks to me as if your empire is falling down around your ears. You have a handful of loyal men, the rest you don't trust and the longer you hide away, the more they will imagine you are scared and will turn from you. You are a general hiding from his army. Sooner or later you are going to end up with a major desertion problem."

"Don't you think I know that?" Chang retorted. "I am playing a dangerous game keeping in isolation, but I have to do it."

Clara looked at him sadly.

"From an outside perspective, it looks to me as if you are finished."

"Never!" Chang growled. "This is a strategic withdrawal."

Chang clutched his head in his hands and slowly it dawned on him that he was acting like a man with a target on his back. He had come into Brighton dressed like a working-class nobody for fear of his sister and he would only be there for as long as it took to speak to Clara before running back to his house and hiding away. Every way you looked at it, he was acting not as the powerful criminal gang leader he was, but as a hunted man terrified of everyone.

Clara saw the reality creep over him and with it came a hardening of his resolve. She felt a faint glimmer of hope. Chang was a criminal, the enemy in many regards, but right at this moment she felt he was her only chance of stopping this gang business and ensuring that she and the residents of Brighton were safe from Jao Leong.

"Supposing you are right," Chang said. "I still have to move cautiously. Jao has a lot of support in town."

"Maybe not as much as she thinks," Clara replied. "Some of those working for her have been angered by her reaction to a pair of Brighton citizens. She murdered a man and woman well known in the criminal world because she decided the man was a traitor. This has left a bitter taste in the mouths of local lowlifes. They don't like the fact that an outsider killed one of their own. I think a reaction is swelling up and if you could encourage it, then it might just be the key to ousting Jao."

Chang's eyes glittered as he absorbed this information.

"Jao never did understand the diplomacy involved in this life. If she is stirring up resentment, that is good, and completely as I expected from her. But she has power and influence, which will stay the hand of those wishing her harm."

"True," Clara said. "But you are forgetting something."

Chang fixed his attention on her.

"Jao has one disadvantage that I can fully appreciate and which she can do nothing about," Clara continued. "She is a woman, and many men find it hard to work for a woman. They might at first accept the situation, but gradually it festers within them. I know how that is, since I spend most of my days being confronted by surly men who do not like the fact that a woman is asking them questions. I can only imagine how much tougher it must be if that woman happens to be running a criminal organisation."

"That is a good point," Chang said, stroking his chin in thought. "And Jao will do little to help overcome that prejudice. She has never been, shall we say, a woman of subtlety. She will bludgeon her way to power, that is all."

"She poisoned one of her employees who failed her," Clara added. "He died before my eyes. He had been loyal to her up until that point. He had refused to say a word, then he realised she had turned on him and you could see how that cut to his heart.

"How many of her employees are now nervous that they could be next? That sort of reactionary punishment is prone to backfiring, and leads to people questioning their loyalties."

"Yes. Yes, you are a very good observer of human nature," Chang grinned at her. "Jao always said I was too lenient on my men. That I gave too many second chances, but there was a reason for that. Everyone fails from time-to-time, showing a touch of mercy instils respect and even a little gratitude. It seems to me Jao has forgotten this."

"And you can use that?"

Chang paced again, but this time it was not due to anxiety, rather it was because he was thoughtful.

"You have given me an idea, Clara, a way of dealing with this affair. But I must tread carefully," Chang paused before her. "My sister will want results from you and she lacks patience. You want protection from me, then I shall give it. Tell my sister of the house where you met with me when she next contacts you. I shall not be there when she comes calling, but it will at least seem as if you are doing your part."

"I need a way to contact you Chang. I can't go on just waiting for you to find me. I may need to let you know something urgently."

Chang nodded.

"I shall arrange a go-between. Someone you can deliver a message to and they will pass it to me. Will that suffice?"

"I want to be able to speak directly to you," Clara persisted. "Not just pass along messages."

"Of course, if you need to speak to me, then the go-between can arrange it," Chang was looking happier, his old confidence returning. "What of the police? Did you follow up the information I gave you about a possible traitor among them?"

"I am working on it," Clara lied. "Look, Chang, whatever you plan to do, it must not put any more people in danger, do you understand? I don't want to see full scale gang warfare breaking out on the streets of Brighton."

"Give me some credit," Chang looked hurt. "I am far more discreet than that."

"But you are also very angry, oh, you are masking it well, but it is there bubbling away beneath the surface," Clara caught his eye and held his gaze. "This is personal, Chang, and don't deny it. And I know how nasty personal disagreements can become."

Chang was silent a while, his enthusiasm dimming slightly. He turned to look out of the window of the reading room. Clara could only see the reflection of his face in the glass pane, but it seemed he had grown solemn.

"There is nothing crueller than betrayal by a family member," Chang said softly. "Jao's actions have cut me deep."

"From where I am standing, it looks as though her actions have nearly destroyed you," Clara said gently. "It takes a strong man to rise up from such a crisis and recover himself. This difficulty will either make you stronger than before, or it will be the spark of your destruction."

"You are such a cheerful soul," Chang threw at her sarcastically.

"This is hardly a cheerful time," Clara pointed out. "People have died unnecessarily already. I don't want to see worse occurring."

Chang was quiet for some time, then he spoke in a soft voice.

"Why are you helping me? You hate me."

"Yes," Clara agreed. "Or rather, I hate what you do, I am not sure I have developed enough feeling for you to hate you personally. The reason I am helping you is quite simple. I think you are the only way we are going to rid Brighton of this trouble. As much as I respect the police, I don't think they have the manpower and resources to crack down on Jao."

Clara did not say that Park-Coombs had already told her that sheep-rustling was of more interest to his superiors than a gang running around and causing trouble for the lower classes. It would only be when Jao's activities started to interfere with the lives of the middle and upper class residents, or impacted on Brighton's legitimate businesses that the police chiefs would pay heed. By then, Jao's network would run so deep it would be nightmarish to untangle it.

"You know what I like about you Clara? Your honesty. You are blunt and brutal, but that appeals to me. You don't pander to me and you certainly don't lie," Chang's reflection in the window glass bore a smile now. "I suppose that is why I am drawn to you. Well, if we are to be unconventional allies for the time-being we ought to get on with things. No more hiding away, no more chasing shadows. I have to stand up and face my sister."

Chang turned around and started to arrange the scarf over his chin once more.

"I shall let you know about the go-between as soon as I have arranged it. Stay safe Clara."

Clara had hoped for a little more from him, something that would actually provide her with physical protection, but Chang was not going to offer her more than he already had. He pulled his hat down around his ears and disappeared from the reading room. Clara was in no rush to follow. It would be safer to keep as much distance between her and the disguised Chang as possible.

To waste time, Clara went to the reference section of the library and pulled out the Who's Who for 1917, the year Albert Long passed away. She was not entirely surprised to discover he did not have an entry. She then headed to the non-fiction shelves and browsed for books on the theatre. It was within a thick volume on the history of the pantomime that she found something that caught her attention and made her pause. Clara went to the front desk and checked out the book at once, she had to show Tommy what she had found out.

It was now an hour since Chang had left and Clara felt confident she was safe to leave. Book in hand, she headed for home, finally with an idea of who might have killed Stanley Hutson.

Chapter Twenty-Nine

Clara laid the book out on the table before Tommy and pointed to a black and white photograph. The picture was of an older gentleman, a head shot that looked to have been taken for a publicity still. The man looked off to one side, not meeting the eyes of the viewer. He did not smile, but had a serious, perhaps thoughtful expression. The caption beneath the photo indicated that the sitter was the late Albert Long, who had been worthy of a small section in the book due to it being his misfortunes that thrust Stanley Hutson into his lifetime role of the dame.

The author of the book appeared sympathetic to the plight of poor Albert and had written a bittersweet paragraph or two about a talent that never had the chance to shine. Though Albert had failed to fulfil his early promise, he had been a consistent supporting actor in the festive theatrical circuit. He was known for his dastardly villains and bumbling kings or sultans. While he never got quite the spotlight Hutson or Baldry achieved, he had a small following of dedicated individuals who valued his performances. It seemed the author of the book was one of these and had made the time to pay tribute to this unlucky performer.

The author skimmed over Albert's suicide with a bland statement about the actor being tragically snatched from life too soon. The book, which had been published the year before, contained a wealth of pictures of famous pantomime actors, sourced from various places, but it was the picture of Albert that had caught Clara's eye.

"Interesting and all, but how does this help?" Tommy asked her after he had read through the brief biography of Long.

"You are failing to read the small print, remember the motto of the good researcher? Always check the sources and footnotes," Clara pressed her finger carefully to the page, marking the line of text beneath Long's Photograph. "It states the source of this photograph. 'Courtesy of Mrs Elizabeth Burns.' Now, we know that Albert's sister was called Lizzie and she would seem a likely source for a photograph of her brother. She would have taken possession of all his belongings after his death, including all his publicity shots."

Tommy stared at the caption, slowly absorbing this information.

"Lizzie Burns, wife of an accountant. Wait, Audrey Burns!"

"Exactly!" Clara retrieved the programme from the pantomime performance and flicked to the page that contained a few lines about Miss Burns.

"'Miss Burns is new to the pantomime scene and shall be undertaking the prestigious role of Aladdin for the first time. Miss Burns was educated in Oxford and has performed in amateur productions since the age of ten. Her passion for the theatre was inspired by her late uncle and encouraged by her mother. She is delighted to be part of this year's production'," Clara read the slightly dull text. Clearly there had been limited things to say about Audrey and some filling had been required. "It doesn't say who her uncle was, but if we begin to make loose connections then we might suppose it was Albert Long."

"It is a possibility, but there could be a completely unrelated Elizabeth Burns who supplied this picture and she may not have a daughter called Audrey Burns," Tommy replied.

"Coincidences, Tommy," Clara said. "That is three coincidences. One, that a woman with the first name of Albert's sister supplied that photograph of him after his death. Two, that Audrey has the same surname as that said woman. And three, that Audrey is stated to have been inspired by her uncle to take to the stage. Surely that number of coincidences suggests something."

"And your theory is that Audrey Burns killed Hutson in revenge for her uncle's suicide? What, she felt he had been thrust from the limelight by Hutson and that had eventually been the trigger for his suicide?"

"Maybe," Clara had to admit to herself that there were a lot of holes in her theory, a lot of leaps and assumptions, but what else was there to go on? A woman had killed Hutson and labelled him a thief, so far the only one who might have a motive (if she was related to Albert Long) was Audrey Burns. "We need to go to the theatre and run this by Maddock, maybe he can help unravel this."

"He is going to be damn annoyed if his Aladdin is a killer," Tommy remarked. "That will be the third one of his lead actors he shall have lost."

"Mervyn is back, he hasn't lost him," Clara brushed off the concern. "Anyway, we can't let a killer go free. Come on."

With that Clara was heading back out the door. Annie gave her a startled look as she departed up the hallway.

"I was just bringing in tea," she protested.

"Sorry Annie, back soon," Tommy called over his shoulder as he hastened to follow Clara.

Clara was out the front door before Annie could unleash her annoyance upon them.

They arrived back at the theatre in the middle of the matinee. Maddock was easy to find backstage, but he was not keen to be distracted from the production. He followed each line, each move, each song with a hawk-like gaze and did not want to be disturbed. It took Clara all her powers of persuasion to convince him to leave the wings and head for the laundry room where they could talk in peace.

"I don't like leaving a performance," Maddock puttered. "It feels like bad luck."

"You were watching every step when Hutson died," Clara pointed out. "Seems to be bad luck doesn't much care for what you are doing."

Sobered by this statement, Maddock said no more and allowed Clara to explain.

"I think Audrey Burns is the niece of the late Albert Long," Clara began.

Maddock blinked at this statement.

"Audrey?" He thought for a moment. "I know Long had a niece."

Clara gave a relieved sigh, for until that point she had not been certain of even that key fact. She had been fumbling about in the dark, hoping her conclusions were not just puffs of hot air.

"What can you tell me about Audrey?" She asked.

Maddock frowned.

"She auditioned for Aladdin back in June. I could see she had talent, but she had done absolutely no acting in professional productions, only in amateur shows. I was reluctant to cast her in the lead and offered her a part in the chorus to begin with."

"Something made you change your mind," Clara said.

"Well, yes," Maddock flushed a deep red and looked uneasy. "You see, Audrey approached me and begged for the part of Aladdin, said it would be the making of her career. It is hard for actresses to get started. So many are auditioning for the roles and, quite frankly, a lot of producers go for looks rather than ability. Audrey is not the prettiest of things, though with the right make-up that can be overcome.

"Anyway, I felt her plight, but I had already given one major role to an actress out of charity, namely Grace Allen.

I was reluctant to do the same with another role, especially if I could place a familiar face in the part. Pantomimes sell so much on who is performing the key roles.

"That was when Audrey made me an offer. She said if I let her take the role of Aladdin, she would ask for no payment in return. Effectively I should have her performing for free. I was not entirely convinced, but she wanted the role so badly, certain it would make her name and I confess that any way of saving money is a bonus for me. Putting on a production of this scale is never cheap and the last few seasons ticket sales have been down."

"Long story short, you have Audrey playing the part for free," Tommy interjected.

Maddock put out his arms and hefted his shoulders in a 'what can I say' gesture. It was obvious he was not really ashamed of his antics.

"What else can you tell me about Audrey, about her family and personal life?" Clara said, not particularly interested in Maddock's financial dealings. "Audrey must have money, if she can afford to work for free."

"She said her mother would support her," Maddock said. "Has never much mentioned her father. Honestly, we have not spoken a great deal about her personal life. But, if what you are saying is true, I am surprised she did not mention it. Most actors would have used such a personal connection to secure a role. No shame in it."

"The thing is, if Audrey had an ulterior reason for joining the pantomime, such as murdering Stanley Hutson, then she might have felt it prudent to keep her family connections secret."

Maddock looked stunned.

"No, surely not!"

"Well, we know that a woman most likely killed Hutson, and we know it happened during the interval with the fire as a distraction. There was a clear message written on Hutson's costume, and that message makes no sense unless we take into account the rumours that Hutson had stolen his famed role from someone. That brings us back to Albert, who lost his first dame role to Hutson and never recovered. Now he is dead, but supposing someone felt bitterly about his suicide, someone such as the niece who adored him and aspired to go on the stage like him. Audrey states that her uncle inspired her. I know it is all supposition, but it could be correct."

"Audrey was in the alley during the fire," Maddock said, looking confused by everything. "She was witnessed there."

"We now know that Audrey had accomplices for hiding the body. Those accomplices would be very keen to provide her with an alibi, as a result providing themselves with one. That means…" Clara came to a halt, a sudden realisation coming to her. "Oh, how stupid I have been, why did I not see that before?"

"What now?" Maddock looked alarmed.

"Mr Maddock, I need to talk to Erikson, urgently."

"No, Miss Fitzgerald, please, the pantomime must continue. I cannot afford another interrupted performance. Allow us to finish the second half before you attack my cast further."

Maddock looked pathetic and Clara relented.

"All right, I shall wait. But Erikson must be brought to me as soon as the curtain drops, understood?"

Maddock nodded, still looking close to despair.

"Understood. You can wait in my office, if you like."

Maddock shuffled them out of sight and had instructions sent out that Clara and Tommy should be provided with tea and sandwiches, a small attempt to keep them occupied and out of his way.

"You scare Maddock to death," Tommy observed to Clara once they were settled in the office.

"I only scare his bank account," Clara retorted.

They passed the time as best they could, discussing nothing in particular, until a very loud round of applause signalled the pantomime was concluding.

"Why are we interviewing Erikson? I thought it was proved he was ill during the murder and could not have been the killer?" Tommy asked.

"We only proved that he was not wearing the guard uniform. He didn't murder Hutson, but I think he knows more than he has said."

They waited a little longer and then a tentative knock came at the office door. Clara called the person to enter and Maddock appeared with Erikson. Erikson looked deathly pale and Clara felt even more sure of the suspicion that had formed in her mind.

"Mr Erikson," Clara said lightly. "Are you fully recovered from your illness?"

"Yes," Erikson answered. "I don't want to repeat it though."

"Naturally, look, I am not going to beat around the bush. I know that Audrey borrowed your guard costume and murdered Hutson while wearing it," the bluntness of the statement had the result Clara had hoped for. What little colour was left in Erikson's face drained away. "She planned on giving you an alibi by supplying you with something that would make you sick and prevent you from going on stage. That might appear an act of kindness, but I think it was more because she liked the idea of casting suspicion on the one other person who would fit your costume perfectly, Mervyn Baldry.

"I am guessing, Mr Erikson, that Audrey convinced you to help her because she said she loved you, and you would do anything for her. She did not make you a murderer, she wanted that part for herself, but she did have you help her move the body. Maybe you also set the fire that distracted everyone and was meant to destroy the guard outfit.

"Lastly, you were able to provide her with an alibi, saying you were with her in the alley. You did all this for her, put your own life at risk for her, because you loved her. Then, the moment it was all done, she cast you aside. You told me yourself, you were no longer of use to her.

"What an odd statement to say, unless you were meaning that Audrey was only with you because she could gain something from your company. And what might that be? You could not help her get a part in this production, so what use did she have for you? Why did you feel she had taken what she needed from you and then ditched you?

"I didn't think at the time that the phrase was peculiar, I was too busy with other thoughts. Now I think I see what you meant. Audrey used you to help her commit murder. You served her because you adored her and thought she adored you back. Instead, she has abandoned you. How am I doing?"

Erikson had his head down, his eye shut. He seemed defeated, but Clara doubted it was because of her words. He had been defeated since Audrey left him.

"She has taken up with Donald," Erikson said bitterly. "I should have seen that coming."

"And, am I right? Did she use you as an accomplice?"

Erikson was silent.

"You know, if you confess and give evidence against Audrey you will likely get a lighter sentence. If you do not, then it will take me longer to get what I need, but I will do it and then you will be cast as an accomplice, in fact, I would suspect Audrey will place most of the blame on you," Clara hoped Erikson had a good sense of self-preservation. "I think you now need to decide if you really want to remain loyal to her, or if it is time to think of yourself."

Erikson took a deep sigh, his head nodded forward. After a long while he sniffed.

"You are right, Miss Fitzgerald, she did use me," Erikson's eyes were wet and he looked scared. "I don't want to hang!"

"Then tell me everything," Clara persisted. "A confession will go a long way."

"All right," Erikson wiped his nose on his sleeve. "All right, I am going to make a clean breast of it. I'll tell you the truth."

Chapter Thirty

Erikson followed his statement that he would make a confession with silence and it seemed he regretted his abrupt declaration. Maddock looked uncomfortable, shuffled his feet and cast Clara a worried look. Clara remained patient; she guessed that Erikson was beginning to see the enormity of what had happened and what was about to tumble down on him, that required a few moments to consider.

Erikson cleared his throat twice, then he seemed to come to a decision.

"I want you to know that I was not involved in the murder. I didn't even know what was going to happen, until after."

"Except Audrey borrowed your costume and gave you something to make you sick," Clara pointed out.

Erikson chewed on his lip, contemplating this clear flaw in his statement.

"I didn't know she borrowed my costume until afterwards and I swear I had no idea about the drug, I just thought I had eaten something bad. Audrey explained it to me later, how she had done it to make sure I could not be implicated in the crime. She had to borrow a costume to cover up her own and stop it getting covered in blood…" Erikson tailed off as his own words rang in his ears. "I didn't want to be involved in a murder, but when she found me she was covered in blood and wearing my costume. She said if I didn't help her she would refuse to say I had been with her in the alley and everyone would think it was me who did it, I just had to help."

Erikson was attempting to play the victim, implying he had been forced over a barrel, however, Clara was not so certain he had been quite so innocently used. She let him continue without questioning his statement, nonetheless.

"It all happened in a flash. I had been in the toilet. I came back to my dressing room and there was Audrey. She had stripped off the guard costume and it was lying on the floor covered in blood. I asked her what had happened and she said she had argued with Stanley, there had been a scuffle and in a panic she had killed him," Erikson looked miserable. "I'm not saying I believed that, but Audrey was hysterical, said we had to hide the body, said if we could just cast a few red herrings about, the police would never realise and it would be all right.

"I didn't have the strength to argue. The fire had already been started, everyone was outside. We had to use a blanket to carry him to the laundry room and it was an ordeal to get him in that hamper. I've never seen that much blood. I felt so sick looking at the mess."

"You didn't really believe it was self-defence, did you?" Tommy said when Erikson finished. "I mean, once you saw the body…"

"I had my doubts," Erikson nodded, Clara still had that sense he was trying to put the best spin on his involvement and say what they wanted to hear. "But I was committed then, I couldn't turn away. They would have seen to it that I was accused of the crime, I knew that even then."

"They?" Clara queried.

Erikson shuffled his feet.

"Donald Hutson," he said. "He was there too."

Maddock gave a groan and fell back into a handy chair.

"Donald helped move the body of his father?" Clara made sure she had heard correctly.

"Yes," Erikson said firmly, but he blinked rapidly and Clara recalled that he had been ditched for Donald. She was not sure he was being truthful.

"I know the rest," Clara said. "You placed Stanley in the laundry hamper, was it then that Audrey wrote the word thief on his apron?"

Erikson nodded.

"Then you all headed for the alley to be seen. In the confusion, who would remember you were late? Especially when you would verify for each other that you had been there the whole time."

Erikson gave another pathetic nod.

"One thing, Mr Erikson, did Audrey explain her reasons for killing Stanley Hutson?"

"No," Erikson said, his voice suddenly filled with anger. "She put me in this position and I don't even know why!"

~~~*~~~

The next stage was to confront Audrey, but Clara wanted Park-Coombs present. Tommy agreed to hurry out and fetch him, while Maddock made sure Audrey did not leave the building. He said he would give her some story about needing to go over a few script changes he was contemplating. Erikson remained in the office, in a chair up one corner, looking condemned already. Clara did not have the inclination to talk to him. She felt he was a liar, that he was trying to make himself look good, or at least as good as he could muster under the circumstances. That made her angry.

It took nearly an hour for the inspector to arrive back with Tommy. He looked harassed, but he greeted Clara politely.

"Tommy says you have solved the Hutson murder?"

"I have," Clara said and she recapped the information Erikson had given her, while Tommy went to fetch
~~~

Maddock and Audrey. Erikson listened to the recitation of his own confession with a growing look of despair. He could not meet anyone's eyes and he slumped over in the chair, trying to hide his face in his hands.

By the time Audrey arrived, the inspector had all the facts that Clara could give him. Audrey walked into the office and was startled at the sight of Clara and Park-Coombs. She did not truly react, however, until she realised Erikson was sitting in the corner and his expression was enough to tell her everything. She turned sharply on her heel, trying to leave, but Maddock and Tommy were blocking the way.

"It's over Audrey," Clara told her calmly. "Perhaps you would like to sit down."

"Whatever he has told you is a lie!" Audrey pointed her finger angrily at Erikson.

Clara did not respond. The actress looked around her at the hard faces and gave a scream of frustration.

"What have you done you stupid fool!"

Erikson cringed.

"They said they knew everything."

"And you believed them?"

"You ditched me Audrey!" Erikson found a sudden resolve and glowered at her. "I owed you nothing and I am not going to swing for you!"

His bluntness stunned Audrey into silence. She turned her gaze to Clara, a look full of hate and rage.

"Are you going to arrest me then?" She demanded.

"I am," Park-Coombs said steadily.

"I just have a couple of questions for you Audrey," Clara said. "I would like your side of the story. I have guessed a lot of it."

"Have you now?" Audrey had furious tears spilling from her eyes and her hands were clenched in fists. "Well aren't you clever?"

"You are the niece of Albert Long?" Clara asked.

Audrey tried to make a noise that indicated that was surely obvious, however her emotions made it come out wrong.

"Yes," she said.

"And you killed Stanley in revenge for your uncle's suicide? You felt Hutson had stolen his chance to succeed on the stage?"

This time Audrey laughed.

"No," she said. "You got that bit wrong. Not so clever, are you?"

Clara did not hide her surprise.

"You wrote 'thief' on Hutson's apron," she pointed out.

"To confuse the police," Audrey shrugged. "It was the first word that came to mind."

Clara felt as if the world had shook under her feet. The word had been intended as a red herring, instead, in a round-about fashion that Audrey could not have predicted, it had led straight back to her. A quirk of chance, that was all.

"Then why did you kill him?" Clara asked her.

Audrey tilted her head. Her tears were gone, now she was arrogant.

"Because I wanted Donald and his father disliked me," she said. "Donald and I, we are true loves. But his father said I was spiteful and only out for the prestige I could get through Donald. That was a lie, but Donald was too sweet to stand up to his father. So, I had to make the decision for us both. I got the part in this play and staged things. I meant for it to look like Stanley had committed suicide, that's why I used the broken mirror shard. People would think it was done on impulse because of the man booing him.

"Only, once he was dead I knew that wouldn't work and I needed to buy myself time to think. I needed to put the blame on someone else. That's when I moved him with Erikson to the laundry room, to hide the body for a bit."

"And that was when Donald helped you?" Clara asked.

This time there was a look of genuine surprise on Audrey's face.

"What?" She turned on Erikson again. "What have you

told them?"

Erikson gave her a nasty look.

"Throw me over for another man, will you? I shall show you! I told them Donald helped us dispose of the body."

"But he did not!" Audrey yelled. "Donald doesn't even know! If he did, if he knew what I had done…"

Audrey suddenly grew pale and dropped to her knees.

"Donald will hate me now, this was not meant to be!" She started to sob. "Donald was never meant to know, but I had to do it, I loved him so much and I could not bear to be pushed from him. I tried to pretend, tried to make people think I was with Erikson, but that was all a lie!"

"Then, if Donald did not help you with the body, who did?" Park-Coombs said calmly. "I can't believe you managed to carry that heavy body between you."

Erikson had his mouth firmly shut. He was determined to implicate Donald, which made Clara all the more certain the man was innocent. She had seen the shock on his face when he heard his father was dead, she did not think that was faked.

Audrey gave another muffled scream of frustration.

"Grace Allen!" She declared. "She helped us!"

This revelation forced Clara briefly into silence. While she had wondered about Grace, she had not really considered her an accomplice to murder.

"Grace?" She repeated. "Princess Zara?"

Maddock gave a groan as if he was dying.

"She would do anything for me. She booed Stanley that night, pretending to be a man. It wasn't hard slipping to one of the side doors and pretending the noise came from the audience. I knew it would make Stanley walk off in a bad mood. All I had to do then was lure him to the pulley room with the promise of a bottle of Scotch. Funny how he lost his reservations about me when there was drink involved," Audrey said darkly.

"But why would she do that? Hutson got Grace the part in this panto?" Clara said, confused.

"He was going to help her lose it too," Audrey said with

a sneer. "He was disappointed with her performance, told her if she did not pull her finger out, she would never work on the stage again. Everyone says he was so nice, but there was another side to Stanley. He didn't like being made to look a fool.

"Anyway, Grace was desperate and all it took was for me to convince her I would help her to improve to get her on my side. I am very persuasive."

Clara could see that. Not only had Audrey manipulated Maddock, but she had seduced Erikson and was now working on Donald Hutson, who was no doubt in need of a sympathetic ear.

"You convinced her to help you murder Hutson?" Tommy asked in horror, trying to get his head around Princess Zara as such a bloodthirsty fiend.

"Of course not! I merely persuaded her I was her best friend in the world," Audrey was pleased with herself now, enjoying the attention and proving how clever she was. "I asked her to come to the pulley room. Once she was there and she had seen the body, she was too shocked to think straight. I told her she had to help me, that I had done her a favour killing Stanley and now she owed me. She wanted fame so badly, she missed being adored by the public. It really was not hard."

"You two are despicable," Park-Coombs grunted. "Right, you are both under arrest."

Erikson reacted with resignation to his fate, but Audrey protested and screamed murder, trying to run out of the room again and descending into hysterical sobs once the inspector had hold of her.

"Just one last thing, Inspector," Clara held him up. "Audrey, you planted the button from Mervyn's costume in Stanley's hand?"

"I hoped they would suspect him," she sniffed. "And Grace would be the nail in his coffin, telling the police she saw him follow Stanley."

"And the fact that you killed him while he was performing in Aladdin held no symbolism?"

Audrey shrugged again.

"I wanted people to think he killed himself after a bad performance, so it had to be during the show. Does it matter that it was Aladdin?"

Clara felt slightly disappointed that the intriguing coincidences in this case had proven to be just that – coincidences.

"Would you like a hand getting them to the station?" Tommy asked him.

"That would be good," Park-Coombs said as he still struggled with the writhing actress. "Hold your horses, miss, or I'll put the handcuffs on you!"

Audrey wriggled with less velocity as he removed her from the theatre. Erikson followed under the watchful gaze of Tommy. Those of the cast still present watched the scene with disbelieving eyes. Donald Hutson stepped forward as Audrey was escorted past him.

"I am so sorry Donald!" Audrey called to him. "I did it for us! Forgive me, please!"

Donald looked confused. Once Audrey was out of the backstage door he turned to Clara for an explanation. It was not a moment Clara had been looking forward to.

"Audrey murdered your father," she told him, there was no point dancing around the truth.

A mix of emotions flickered across Donald's face.

"W…why?"

"Because he did not want you to be together," Clara explained. "I understand your father did not like her."

Donald stared at the door by which the inspector and his suspects had left. A frown slowly formed on his brow.

"I guess he was right."

Donald turned and walked away, looking dazed and hurt. Clara wished she could do something for him. How much loss could a man endure and continue to live? She did not like that question, and she certainly did not want to know the answer.

Clara was glad to get out of the theatre and head for home. There had seemed something so pointless about the death of Stanley Hutson. What had Audrey really hoped to achieve? Did she think she could keep the truth from Donald forever?

Not for the first time, Clara found herself thinking that there was a streak of madness to murder, that only the truly insane would resort to cold-blooded killing.

As this thought filtered into her mind, Clara realised someone was following her. She glanced up as Jao Leong appeared beside her. Clara tried not to tense, she wanted to appear unperturbed by the presence of the woman.

"Good afternoon," Clara said politely.

"Just solved a case?" Leong asked.

"Yes," Clara cleared her throat. "I actually have some information for you."

"Hmm?" Leong smiled brightly.

"I know of an address where you brother has been living. I'm not sure if he is still there, but the talk is he was hiding there."

"Oh, marvellous," Leong's eyes became catlike in her delight. "You are a good detective."

"I don't know if he is there now," Clara repeated herself. "Just that he was there."

"It is a start though," Leong grinned. "And here I was thinking I would need to encourage you to strive harder to find out information. I doubted you, Miss Fitzgerald."

Clara did not like to think about what Leong meant by 'encourage'.

"I hope you find your brother," Clara said, and that was truthful enough, the sooner the siblings could be reunited and work out their differences (however unpleasant that might be) the better for everyone.

"I shall let you know if I still need your services," Leong purred, then she crossed the street and headed away.

Clara felt her stomach relax, but there was still a pall of tension hanging over her. How long would she have to endure this situation? How long before Leong's gang could be crushed and she could be free from the clasps of both brother and sister?

As Clara tried to calm her nerves, it slowly occurred to her that for all Park-Coombs' insistence she keep out of this business, she had been dragged into it nonetheless, and by avoiding investigating she was finding herself in just as much danger as if she was poking about where she was not wanted. The more she considered it, the more she came to one conclusion; if she was going to come through this gang trouble unscathed, she had to be actively involved in resolving it. That meant finding out information and finding a way to get the police chiefs to go after Leong.

Clara wanted to protect her friends and family, she knew where Leong's attentions would turn if she seemed to fail her, or if her talk with Chang was discovered. No, she had to do something, there was no longer a choice.

The sun was setting, the autumn night drawing in and Clara had finally come to a decision. She was going to destroy Jao Leong and heaven help anyone who threatened her or her loved ones.

~~~*~~~

Grace Allen sat in the police cell, her hands clasped neatly in her lap. She looked defeated, but also at peace. Maddock and Clara stood before the bars of her cell, trying to understand.

"She is such a good actress," Grace said softly. "She promised to help me, and she was my dearest friend."

"You barely knew her," Clara pointed out.

Grace gently smiled.

"In this world, you barely know anyone. I didn't want to see Stanley dead, but I know she did it for me. I appreciate that. It was wrong, but she did it for the right reasons."

Clara walked out of the police station with Maddock, dazed by what she had heard.

"I think they are all mad."

"They are actors," Maddock said, seeming to think that
~~~

implied insanity was the norm.

"What will you do now?" Clara asked him. "Regarding the pantomime."

"Oh, I have already re-cast," Maddock grinned. "Truthfully, the loss of Grace was a blessing, I have a very promising young actress ready to replace her. It shall be a bit tight until we have her ready, but otherwise all shall be fine."

Clara was somehow not surprised Maddock had managed to find the positive in the situation and was already moving on.

"And Donald?"

"His name went on the posters today," Maddock beamed. "We can never replace Stanley, but Donald shall make the dame role his own. Yes, all has worked out rather well."

"Except your leading man was murdered," Clara reminded him.

Maddock spun and looked at her, his smile not diminishing.

"Oh Miss Fitzgerald, surely by now you understand. Whatever happens, whatever ill-fortune befalls us, there is but one thing to do!"

"The show must go on," Clara sighed, really fed up with that motto.

"Yes, my dear," Maddock grinned. "The show must go on."